# CHASING CLOUD

A TARXIAN NOVEL

# CHASING CLOUD

DAVID M. SMITH

The Book Guild Ltd

First published in Great Britain in 2016 by
The Book Guild Ltd
9 Priory Business Park
Wistow Road, Kibworth
Leicestershire, LE8 0RX
Freephone: 0800 999 2982
www.bookguild.co.uk
Email: info@bookguild.co.uk
Twitter: @bookguild



Typeset in Minion Pro

Printed and bound in the UK by TJ International, Padstow, Cornwall

ISBN 978 1 91132 022 7

British Library Cataloguing in Publication Data.
A catalogue record for this book is available from the British Library.

MIX
Paper from responsible sources
FSC® C013056
FSC www.fsc.org

*To my children and grandchild*
*who may one day remember me as an ancestor*

# CHARACTERS

## PRIESTS AND TEMPLE OFFICIALS

Trebird ab Tarxian – High Priest
Lamaxe – an assistant priest
The Boy at Tarxian, later Nestra – a trainee priest
Springox – Superintendent of the Temple Compound
The Sweeper – a servant
Mountsea ab Ragusa – a Sicilian priest
Boy at Ragusa – a trainee priest

## FARMERS, TRADERS AND THEIR FAMILIES

Lamool ab Headland – textile manufacturer and local chief
Lillith – his concubine
Eve – her sister, also a concubine
Cliffsound ab Headland, known as Cliff – Son of Lamool
Rocksand ab Graman – Winemaker
Redstone ab Graman, known as Red – Son of Rocksand
Oyeh (Oxyellow ab Deepearth) – Lamaxe's brother
Moonlight – Oyeh's wife
Ossay – Oyeh's son
Seacloud – Oyeh's daughter
Starbright – Lamaxe's mother

Ayya ab Featherstone – a farmer
Skycloud, known as Sky – Ayya's wife
Skycloudyoung, known as Cloud – Ayya's daughter
Chitah ab Flintrock – a farmer
Tornbark ab Treefall – a farmer's son
Blackwing ab Stonecrop – a farmer's son
Highsow ab Hinterland – a Sicilian farmer
Bentwood – a slave
ab Speltland – another farmer

CRAFTSMEN AND WOMEN
Pebble – a sculptor/artist
Chisel – a mason
Freestone – a mason
Greensand – another mason
Smith – a craftsman
Smithyoung – another craftsman

SEAMEN AND PIRATES
Captain Crowfish – a ship's captain
Skinny – a murdering bastard
Fatso – another murdering bastard

# PROLOGUE

## MALTA – THE SACRED ILSE

*About 2500 BC*

The young girl burst out of the hut.

'Come back!' called a muffled voice from inside.

She turned back towards the door her face red with anger.

'No!' she screamed. 'I won't wed him. Not for any amount of land.'

'Come here, girl!' the voice inside reiterated. 'I will be obeyed.'

'Never!' She paused for a moment unsure of what to say next.

'He smells,' she added somewhat gratuitously.

With that the young woman shook her head violently and turning saw her mother looking towards her from far across the field.

The older woman raised her hand in greeting.

'Cloud,' she called, though her voice was lost in the distance.

The girl hesitated for just a moment and then turned back towards the doorway.

'I won't have him,' she called to her father.

'You will obey me!' he insisted. 'I must have heirs!'

'Never! I'd rather lie in the place of the dead.' Then she turned and fled.

She kept running until her lungs ached from shortage of breath. Then, clutching her chest, she sat down on the damp grass. She had been running wildly, without direction, so angry that she was simply determined to get away. Now, as her breathing returned to normal, she was able to look around and notice her surroundings. She was on the very edge of her father's land so she felt that she could safely rest for a few moments and think. He had simply gone too far, she thought. She was not going to be tied to that old man. But what was she to do? Where could she go? Certainly not the Hypogeum, the place of the dead, as she had said. Not if she could help it. There was far too much life in her. But where and what?

As her heartbeat began to return to normal, her brain began to work properly again. She had had hopes of the merchant's son. He was young, rich, and exciting. But not any longer! He wasn't interested in her and the other boys of her age were pathetic. Her father was determined to make a good alliance and the widowed farmer was, in his view, the best bet. If she was dragged back home that is what would await her. There must be a better solution? She thought hard. The morning sun beat down and dried the grass all around her. Realising that only where she sat remained damp from the dew she moved and shook her pleated skirt. Gradually, as an idea began to form in her mind, her face relaxed a little and the ghost of a smile flickered across her cheek.

'Why not?' she said loudly, laughing to herself. Clasping

her hand to her mouth she looked around sheepishly but there was no one else to hear.

'Yes, why not?' she said again. 'He isn't so old, he has status, and he needs a wife.'

She laughed freely now and shaking her pleats one more time she skipped away. There was a solution after all. It was obvious. What's more, her father wouldn't be able to object. He wouldn't dare. Looking back just once in the direction of her father's land she set off with determination but with a much lighter heart.

Then she vanished…

# 1

The funeral procession wound its way slowly along the well-beaten path from the Tarxian temples to the Hypogeum. It was dusk. In front came the eldest son, known as Oyeh, accompanied by his brother, Lamaxe, the assistant priest. They carried their father's body wrapped in a shroud. Behind, the family members followed with large baskets of food. They in turn were followed by friends and members of the wider community, for the corpse had been a well respected farmer. At the very end of the line a small boy dragged a sheep on a length of rope.

At the entrance to the Hypogeum the high priest and certain elders were waiting. Lamaxe recognised Trebird, High Priest, with the Boy next to him. Also present was the Local Secular Chief, Lamool ab Headland, and other worthies; leading farmers like Ayya ab Featherstone and Chitah ab Flintrock. Normally Lamaxe, as a junior priest, would have been standing with them to greet the party but this was his father's body and today he had had to help perform the family rituals. He and Oyeh carefully laid the body down. Then, leaving his brother to speak to the elders, Lamaxe went into the cool of the Hypogeum where he quickly changed into his formal priestly robes of long skirt and head dress. Then the whole family, including Lamaxe, were required to make their obeisance to the ancestors. The parcels of food were carefully placed next to the human skulls, animal bones and other offerings.

Trebird led the way down the steps to the second level. The air was tinged with the odour of the bodies of the recently dead. They walked carefully so as not to trip on any skulls stacked on the lower steps. Some of the skulls were still fresh enough to be almost recognisable though fortunately the light was not good. They washed themselves in herbal water from the ritual bowl though this did little to mask the overpowering stench of decay. At the very bottom of the stairs the two brothers gently laid their father on a slab and began carefully cutting his hair in the ritual fashion. When they were satisfied they washed it and covered his head with ochre. Once they had finished with the corpse, all the mourners began to cut and prepare each other's hair in a similar fashion while Trebird intoned prayers and passed the ancestor sticks over the corpse. When all was ready, the body was lifted and carried to be lodged in the family niche where it would be allowed to decay. Trebird distributed the ergot potion and each settled down to experience the visions of the world of the ancestors while the Boy began drumming using two ancient femurs. After a while Trebird called them together and indicated that the brothers should cover their father's body with the scattered, broken ancestral bones.

All then returned to the upper level. While Lamaxe held it fast, Trebird slaughtered the sheep they had brought, carefully cutting it so that the head and lower limbs remained intact in the skin. He placed this reverently in a basket. The cutting was a skilled job and had to be performed absolutely correctly if the departed was to pass easily into the world of the ancestors. Then, to further drumming by the Boy, Trebird carried the basket back to the burial place and laid the sheep's head and skin on top of where the corpse lay.

By this time a large fire had been built outside on which to roast the remains of the sheep and the mourners retired to enjoy the feasting. Lamaxe felt very strange, his head still spinning from the effects of the ergot. As an assistant priest he normally attended funeral services helping Trebird, though once he had had to officiate without the High Priest and so had acquired his own set of ancestor sticks which gave him the powers of a Shaman. Only now did he fully appreciate what it felt like to be a family mourner. As the second son he was not chief mourner and did not have to give an oration for the dead. That role fell to his brother. All Lamaxe was obliged to do was to engage enthusiastically in the feast and try to comfort the others.

While he ate, sitting with his mother, he was unaware that he was being observed. The small group of craftsmen working on the lowest level of the Hypogeum had secreted themselves in a dark corner while the ceremony was taking place. Now, they reappeared, drawn no doubt by the aroma of the cooked food. Working in the place of the dead, they were always grateful for any fresher smell. However, they took no part in the ceremony. As masons they had their own rituals, though Chisel, the youngest of the masons, did slip outside and help himself to some of the roast lamb. The only one who was really interested in the specific proceedings was in fact a woman, a young sculptor. She watched the assistant priest from within the shadows where she could not be seen. It had been many months since she had last seen her priest but he aroused in her the same urgent feelings that he had before. Still, she could not interrupt his solemn sufferings by showing herself just now. That would have to wait a little while longer.

# 2

A few days later Lamaxe stood silently in the courtyard outside the third temple waiting for the ritual to begin. It was hot and his new haircut felt uncomfortable under his cap. Sweat ran down his face and he fidgeted as he watched Trebird chatting to Lamool ab Headland. They sat on the semi-circular stone bench that hugged the temple wall. He could not hear what they were saying but the priest periodically laughed loudly, if rather hollowly, in reaction to something the secular Chief had said so he assumed that Lamool was telling jokes and stories as usual. The noise of laughter embarrassed him slightly, partly because of his father's recent death but also because he was still sufficiently new to his religious status to feel that ritual occasions should be serious and solemn. He hoped that they would soon go inside where it was cooler.

Eventually Trebird and the Chief decided that sufficient numbers had gathered and, signalling to Lamaxe and the Boy, they rose and stood before the temple entrance, Trebird at the front on the left representing the temple and ab Headland to the right, representing earthly authority. Straight away the Boy came hurrying through the courtyard pulling the sacrificial animal on a leash and Lamaxe joined him behind Trebird. The young priest was pleased that the sacrifice today was only a sheep – not too big or too wild to handle. The others formed up behind according to their importance in the community. This led to a certain amount of jostling towards the back. Finally, the women followed.

Trebird led the procession into the temple. Lamaxe watched him bow his head as he stepped through the temple portal, wincing slightly as his feet struck the cold stone of the threshold. In the dimness of the square court inside, Trebird turned to face the huge stone statue of 'Our Lady' and abased himself before her. The Fat Lady Goddess, at least eight feet high, stared impassively over their heads. After a few moments, the High Priest rose and Lamaxe handed him a guttering torch as they proceeded magisterially into the main body of the temple, stopping only when they had reached the archway marking the point of separation between the outer courtyard and the two apses with their domed roofs where he sat and waited on the stone bench. Trebird raised the torch higher in order to light both the sacred area and the main body of the temple behind him. Lamaxe, with the Boy, followed leading the sacrificial beast. Then all three paused for the congregation to catch up.

Slowly, first ab Headland, and then the others followed their example with the men moving to the right hand side of the temple and women to the left. When all were inside and had suitably arranged themselves, the priests discarded their pleated skirts and, wearing only their loin cloths, moved forward into the most sacred area.

Trebird raised his arms and began an ululation as he turned towards the main altar pausing only to light two smaller torches which cast shadows across the timber roof and reflected in the stone apses beyond. Then he took a special wooden bowl from the stone shelf and poured a libation onto the altar, muttering further prayers. Lamaxe and the Boy remained holding the animal while Trebird's voice rose and fell. The noise made the animal restless and Lamaxe tried to soothe it by stroking its neck and whispering soothing sounds in its ear. As usual, he felt hypocritical but it was essential that the animal did not become alarmed. He remembered once as a boy when a calf had panicked, broken away from its handlers and charged through the congregation. Three people had been injured and the harvest that year had been disastrous. It had been clear that Our Lady and the ancestors had been angered by the sacrilege. The assistant priest of the time had been blamed for releasing the creature and was banished from the community. Everyone remembered that precedent and feared it happening again. Lamaxe's family also had personal reasons for remembering it. His uncle had been seriously hurt by the animal's charge and had not lived for long after the incident.

Trebird ceased his wailing and began the more formal incantations. His voice was eerily clear in the acoustics of the temple as he begged the Goddess for sufficient rain and a fertile harvest, calling on the ancestors to support their efforts in the fields. Lamaxe and the Boy held on tightly to the beast. Whilst he hadn't chosen to be a priest – like all the others he had been 'chosen' – he didn't want blame to fall on him for any sacrilege. Trebird's lamentations were now taken up by the rest of the congregation as the High Priest knelt before the altar, leant forward and carefully removed the spherical stone set into its front. Feeling inside the cavity, he found a small but very sharp flint knife carefully wedged on top of a pile of animal horns and bones. This he removed, before returning the round stone to its place.

The torches threw strange patterns on the walls as Lamaxe and the Boy led the animal slowly forward. It was crucial that when the throat was severed the blood gushed onto the altar and was caught by Lamaxe in a special clay bowl. The two handlers lifted up the animal's head and the High Priest, with one deft flick of his wrist, ended the animal's life, slitting the throat with his shiny flint knife. It gave one bleat and collapsed on the floor. The blood spurted across the altar table and well up the wall behind until it began to drip back in a very satisfactory way. At the same time, Lamaxe collected blood in the bowl which he placed at the altar's centre. All three priests sighed in relief. Our Lady was pleased. As always, the people gasped at the magical way in which the animal's throat was apparently severed by the priest's hand – clear evidence that Our Lady had accepted the sacrifice. Then the assistant priest and the Boy turned the animal's corpse over and Trebird kneeled and slit open the beast's stomach. The intestines boiled out onto the floor and he cut either end before laying them, still steaming, before the altar. He could see no blemish. Now the promised bounty was assured, providing of course the community put in the required hard work in the fields.

Lamaxe made a grand gesture with his arms to distract from Trebird hiding the bloody knife in his loin cloth. By now the High Priest's body was splattered in the animal's blood. The other two, slightly less bloodied, dragged the body of the sacrificial beast to the already prepared fire. Trebird began to lead the people in prayers, while the Boy began the mundane job of preparing the carcase for roasting. Lamaxe quietly withdrew, picking up his skirt as he retreated unobtrusively and unseen. He could still clearly hear Trebird's voice echoing through the temple precincts as he slipped out and ran, as fast as he could, behind the first temple and into a narrow passageway. Bending his head under a lintel he entered the Oracle room. This room had been built onto the back of one of the apses in the first temple. He sat down on the stone bench facing the wall in front of him where there was a small aperture carefully hidden on the apse side by a leather covering through which the voice of the Oracle could be heard. Below this, at foot level was another small opening through which objects could be passed. Lamaxe tried to calm his heartbeat, naturally excited by the kill as well as the swift dash ahead of the rest of the congregation. As he sat, he began playing with the small wooden carving that already lay beside him on the bench, while practising lowering the pitch of his voice an octave or two. It was important for the acoustics that it sounded as deep as possible.

He visualised Trebird turning to the great statue of Our Lady in the third temple while the congregation held its breath. Then Trebird would lead the people out of the temple across the complex into the first temple and the Oracle. Lamaxe heard the shuffle of feet as they arrived. Once they were settled he imagined Trebird raising his arms. Then the High Priest said the crucial words:

'Oh Dear Lady speak to us undeserving souls. Let your great Oracle tell us the future and how your humble servants can serve you and ensure a bounteous harvest for us all.'

There was a reverential silence as the congregation waited in anticipation. Lamaxe took a deep breath, gave one last wriggle to get comfortable and spoke. His deep voice rang through the temple complex, bouncing off the walls and the domed ceiling and echoing down the aisle. He spoke the usual sentiments as had been agreed earlier with Trebird: the harvest would be good but needed everyone's hard toil, careful craft, skilled work and long hours of labour. Above all the congregation must respect the sanctity of the temple, its morality and its servants and pay heed to the sensible ideas of the Chief. They must recognise their reliance on the good will of the great Goddess, Our Lady, for any fortune which came their way, and give appropriate tribute both in goods and in labour.

Then Trebird did his bit of theatre. Lamaxe was less comfortable with this. The High Priest raised his arms and called upon them to 'look up' to the roof of the apsidal chamber. As they did so, he shouted loudly: 'Dear Lady, give us a sign!' Lamaxe then took the wooden carving and rolled it through the aperture just as Trebird fell upon his knees. The congregation followed suit as the High Priest groped around, picked up the item and raised it above his head.

'Look!' he called. 'See Our Lady has sent a sign to us for here is an ear of corn.' The congregation gasped with joy, as they always did at such trickery.

'See, Our Lady approves the task. Now be sure that you do your part.'

The ritual ended with Trebird leading the congregation in a final prayer while Lamaxe prepared to slip back into the crowd. Then they all paraded out of the temple unobtrusively joined by Lamaxe. They returned to the courtyard in front of the third temple and took their seats for the community meeting. Spreading out along the semi-circular stone bench built into the temple wall, each male took his appropriate place according to status. Lamaxe sat next to Trebird who was nearest the temple doorway. On the opposite side sat the Chief, Lamool ab Headland, with the leading elders of the community arranged in order of seniority, the most senior being nearest to the door. The women, forbidden to speak at the meeting, placed themselves opposite, facing the temple and their men, thus closing the circle inscribed by the curve of the bench. In this way, the shape of the meeting reflected the wholeness of the community. Of course, symbolism and reality were not always the same thing. Meetings could be controversial.

The sacrificial meat took some considerable time to cook so it had always been convenient to hold the community meetings during this time. As proceedings developed the smell of the cooking carcase gradually seeped out of the temple portal and pervaded the air. The meeting itself was always in two parts with an interval. The first part was the formal community meeting and the second an opportunity for anyone to raise other pressing matters of general concern. The interval provided an opportunity for the Chief to remind them of their history and culture. The island of Malta was divided into chiefdoms but chiefs had no explicit power as such. They were the holders of the community's history, great storytellers who kept that history alive and their authority came from the respect the community held them in. Each chiefdom had a temple and at least one priest. Tarxian being a large complex and a relatively rich chiefdom also had an assistant priest and a Boy. Trebird opened the proceedings and acted as chair. The main focus of discussion was, as usual, the agricultural situation and trade. In this case, given the time of year, it concerned the prospects for the harvest. Lamaxe's mind tended to wander during this part of the meeting though he felt guilty about it afterwards because he was well aware that it was a practical follow-up to his 'Oracle' speech.

Neolithic agriculture was very dependent upon the elements and its farmers had only their stone tools to produce a good living. This meant long hours, especially for the women who tended to do much of the work in the fields. Over the years, they had seen improvements in agricultural production but it was still necessary to supplement it by the men hunting. Although Lamaxe had personally never been very good at this, it did in general allow the men to feel superior and to enjoy themselves at the same time. Some local farmers had developed crucial trading links. However this was not always appreciated by those farmers not so active in trade who tended to feel that the traders had an easier life. The island was reasonably self-sufficient in agriculture in a good year and also had a supply of fish to supplement the diet but it had grown rich on trade with Sicily and beyond. Lamaxe knew from his childhood friendship with Lamool's son Cliffsound that the main source of wealth was the wool trade which was why Lamool, who ran the textile industry, was the chief of the Tarxian area. Since this provided the wealth and luxuries from which the temple benefited Trebird also had a particular interest in it.

The to and fro of the discussion followed an all too familiar pattern with the farmers complaining that their work was too hard and the temple's tithes too harsh and the High Priest demanding that they fulfil their religious obligations to the full. Trebird complained as usual about a certain reluctance of some farmers to provide their produce to the temple on time and to willingly give the labour needed over winter for minor repairs to the temple structure. While the stone walls of the temples were magnificent, the beautiful and impressive wooden roofs frequently required mending. The farmers in turn complained that the harvest was not yet in and even priests should expect to eat from their own gardens at this time of year. As for temple repairs, the priest knew full well that the time for implementing the labour tithe was after the harvest had been collected and that they always obliged eventually.

As always the farmers' side was led by the biggest farmers, Chitah ab Flintrock and Ayya ab Featherstone. Chitah was in his late thirties and a substantial farmer with lands not far away. His wife had died in childbirth as had the baby so it was widely known that he was seeking a new wife, both to work in his fields and to secure the succession for his family lands. His complaints were supported by Ayya ab Featherstone who was very elderly, well into his fifties. In a society in which infant mortality was huge and the average life expectancy was little more than thirty, that was old. He had substantial lands adjoining those of ab Flintrock and not far from the temple site.

'Farming is most important! Why not ask the traders and leave us alone to grow your food?' he said bad-temperedly. 'Without us, there would be no meat for the sacrifice!'

'And without the traders you wouldn't have clothes to wear,' someone shouted.

There were rumbles on both sides as Trebird responded, letting his annoyance with Ayya show.

'We all work. I tend my own gardens. You must recognise your obligations just as the traders do.'

He turned towards the Chief by his side who nodded and responded on behalf of trade. As he stood and addressed the crowd the fine embroidery on his cloak was picked up by the sunshine. He spoke very formally in a deep carefully enunciated voice.

'I hear Chitah's and Ayya's concerns. For my own part, the textile industry is performing well and you farmers who supply me with wool or who weave textiles for me all benefit. We all have labour problems. Mine are no different to yours and we should not fall out but work together and support Our Lady as best we can. That is how it has always been. I depend upon the farmers in part for my wool. They depend upon me for cloth – even the very cloth in which they stand.'

This last remark caused a ripple of amusement, especially amongst the women, for Ayya was robed in a particularly fine purple cloak of which he was obviously inordinately proud. He had been swishing it theatrically as he talked. He now pushed it back on his shoulders and stood still.

'We all contribute in our own way,' Trebird said,

smiling grimly and stretching out his arms to symbolically encompass the whole community. Ayya huffed but said nothing. The meeting droned on and Lamaxe's mind began to drift into realms of fantasy and remembrance. The bright sun shining on his face reminded him of the long hot summers of his childhood when he had helped with harvesting his father's crops. The priesthood was not a full-time profession and Lamaxe, the Boy and even Trebird also worked in their fields. Trebird had his own garden just outside the temple compound but Lamaxe helped in what was now his mother's vegetable garden on the family farm when he was not needed on temple business. He remembered also the occasional fishing trips with his brother; Oyeh: the march to the coast, the repairs to the fish traps, the smell of the sea in the small inlet as it splashed in his face, the flash of the spear and the excitement of catching the fish as they slithered through his hands, desperately trying to escape and the final satisfying 'thunk' as he smashed their heads on a stone. The two brothers had also gone hunting together but Lamaxe had never been very good with a bow.

As a younger son, he supposed that he was lucky to have been selected for the temple. It was a sign of his intelligence as well as of his position in the birth order which meant that, short of another epidemic, he would not inherit his father's lands. Now he had a comfortable life. He ate well – priests always had first selection from the sacrificial meats. Indeed he enjoyed his life, for the most part. What is more, he had prospects. He had begun as merely 'the Boy', doing menial tasks, butchering the sacrificial animals, with little or no direct engagement with the religious rituals themselves. The Boy was allowed into the sacred area of the temple but only to do the more menial tasks like transporting the sacrifices, cleaning the holy vessels and preparing the carcases. Yet now Lamaxe was an assistant priest learning the rituals and the theology which underlay them and recently promoted to being the voice of the Oracle, although he was barely twenty. His elder brother, who had just inherited his father's lands, had been long married to Moonshine, a farmer's daughter, and had had three children, two of whom had so far survived. Even so, Lamaxe didn't envy Oyeh. He was in general happy with his life as a priest.

After a while his mind drifted back to his meeting last spring with the beautiful sculptor and his enjoyment of her company. There were no priestly prohibitions against meeting women, of course, and, being a fertility goddess, sexual activity was in general approved of. Priests were allowed to marry and indeed Trebird, who might seem old to Lamaxe's eyes, was only in his early thirties and had been married until two years previously when his wife had died of a fever. Since then, the High Priest had seemed to live a lonely life and had become progressively more withdrawn and 'difficult'. Lamaxe, working so closely with him, was very conscious of this. Priests retained an interest in their family's lands but little of Trebird's family remained and he was largely isolated now. Although priests had high status within their communities and tended to live well, there was no overarching religious hierarchy so retaining family connections was very important. In any case, worship of Our Lady was tied in with the worship of ancestors so priests naturally kept an interest in their family, its structure and its sources of income. Some priests went on forever, but others retired and returned to the bosom of their family so there were also sound practical reasons for this as well as theological ones.

Lamaxe's reverie was interrupted by Trebird declaring the main meeting over. Now it was ab Headland's turn. Today he told them the story of the creation myth of the forming of the tribe; of the great warrior Spearman who first decided that the people should not just hunt and gather food but also grow their own cereals; of how he had decreed that the women should plant the crops and the men should hunt and work the animals. Lamool was a great storyteller who seamlessly weaved little jokes into his tale. Lamaxe listened intently. The chief spoke of how, in order to mark this change in their way of life, Spearman had decreed that all men should take the form 'ab' and their land's location to show their new found relationship with the soil. So he became Spearman ab Island and was revered forever after. The chief's tales always cheered people up and the atmosphere lightened.

Then Trebird opened up the second part of the meeting to personal business. Lamaxe found this part of the meeting much more interesting with its snippets of gossip and often amusing family disputes. A few minor issues were raised. One farmer had allowed his animals to drift into the garden of another. A footpath had become overgrown. Lamaxe's thoughts began to drift away again as his nostrils picked up the aroma of roasting meat. He licked his lips involuntarily. Then Ayya ab Featherstone once again rose slowly from his bench. He drew himself to his full height and raised his arms to grasp the edges of his fine cloak in what he obviously thought was a noble stance. His crackly voice boomed across the circle.

'I wish to report that my daughter, Skycloudyoung, known to you as Cloud, has disappeared. We are concerned and with good reason. She has been missing for two days.'

Lamaxe heard a sharp intake of breath from the women's section of the crowd, presumably from her family. He looked for her mother's face but she was hidden in the crowd. No one responded to this plea except for Chitah who rose looking genuinely concerned to express his deep anxiety, adding that he was hopeful that she would soon reappear and that the prospective union between her and himself would be able to go ahead, 'uniting our two ancient families', as he put it.

'And uniting their farmland!' thought Lamaxe cynically.

Trebird rose and addressed the crowd.

'Does anyone have news of her? No matter. Cloud has been missing only a short time. Let us not worry unduly.'

There was a murmur of agreement to this but not in that part of the women's section where Cloud's mother had been. Ayya had remained standing. He glowered at Trebird and spoke again. Stepping forward from the bench until he stood some way in front of the line of elders, he turned and raising his right arm, pointed towards the main dignitary seated there.

'Do not make light of this, priest. She has not wandered of her own accord. I believe she has been taken.' Here he made a dramatic pause. 'I accuse…' He paused again for emphasis, looking around the assembled body. 'I accuse the son of Lamool ab Headland of kidnapping my daughter and of spiriting her away from her family.'

A collective sigh of surprise and anxiety ran around the meeting. Elders did not accuse each other's family of such things with impunity. They certainly didn't accuse the son of a chief. Consequences would follow and these were unlikely to be positive either for the antagonists or for the community as a whole.

Lamool rose carefully to his feet. He looked shocked but spoke formally and with great dignity looking deep into the eyes of the accuser.

'My son, Cliffsound, is innocent. He is not here to defend himself. He left for Sicily immediately after ab Deepearth's funeral on business. As you will be aware my export business is largely conducted by Cliff these days. It brings in the wealth to this community. Do not accuse him without reason.'

Trebird, in turn, rose from his seat.

'Indeed,' he said, rather lamely. 'As I have already said, girls do go missing and no harm done. No doubt it is some trivial thing. It is inappropriate to make unfounded accusations in this way. Let us move on.'

Ayya turned puce with anger.

'He has stolen her!' the old man bellowed.

Lamaxe sighed. Ayya was always difficult.

'When will Cliff return, Lamool?' Trebird asked turning towards the Chief.

'A week or two. It depends on the success of the business and on the tides,' came the reply.

'Then we can only wait for Cliff's return,' continued the priest. 'In the meantime, Ayya can watch for the girl.

You can all do so,' he added as an afterthought gesturing vaguely to include the whole community and apparently dismissing the matter. Chitah looked ill.

'No!' cried Ayya. 'I accuse Lamool ab Headland's family of stealing my daughter or at least of colluding with her in order to prevent her forthcoming beneficial union. I will not tolerate her disobedience and I will not tolerate Cliff's wilfulness. Our Lady will punish them if you will not.'

It was becoming serious and Lamaxe waited for Trebird to calm the meeting down. To his complete surprise, Trebird lost his temper, concentrating instead on Ayya's reference to the Goddess.

'Do not take Our Lady's name in vain,' he shouted at the old man. 'Do you think that the great Goddess cares for the petty concerns of your family? Do not accuse others. Control your own daughter! That is a father's duty, not that of the Goddess!'

Ayya was visibly distressed by this accusation. His hand strayed to the stone axe at his belt. Lamaxe could see that things were getting out of hand but Trebird turned his back on the farmer.

Lamaxe had little time for Ayya's posturing but his sympathy for the family mirrored his own sense of loss of his father. Without thinking twice, the young priest intervened.

'Ayya ab Featherstone is naturally distressed at the disappearance of his daughter,' he said using his Oracle voice for greater gravity. 'In the circumstances, he fails to choose his words with care. However, he has a right to call upon us to help seek out his missing daughter and we should do everything we can to assist. I, as a priest, certainly will. In the meantime, Lamool ab Headland has a major business to conduct which will not wait and benefits us all. He is our Chief and is not going to disappear. If she is not found, then, when his son returns, as surely he will, we from the temple can question him and satisfy ourselves as to whether or not he is responsible. If so, then the next community meeting will deal with him. In the meantime, we must all work together for the common good. Is that not correct, Trebird?'

If looks could kill then Lamaxe would have fallen through the floor. Yet despite the angry glare, Trebird nodded assent before he turned away.

Though he had acted spontaneously this was to become an important speech for Lamaxe, for it established for him a new found status within the community. No longer merely an assistant priest, but a person of some authority to whom people listened. Yet it was dangerous also because this was the speech that should have been made by Trebird and Lamaxe had usurped him. He just could not understand why his boss had not taken Ayya more seriously. The old man was an important member of the community. If the girl had gone off with Cliff for a sexual adventure, no one would really care. On the other hand, to deliberately interfere in a possible union between two important families was a serious matter. Trebird seemed at last to pull himself together. Having concurred with his junior, albeit with something of a bad grace, he rapidly brought the meeting to a close. Ayya replaced his axe in his belt though with no great enthusiasm.

# 3

The formal meeting came to an end and while the younger members went off to play the 'stone ball' game, the leading farmers and traders mingled doing deals between themselves. Lamaxe remained sitting for a while considering the enormity of what he had done. Would Trebird forgive him? It wasn't his place to make a key speech, especially without being invited to do so by his superior. But that had been just the problem, Trebird had appeared to play down the girl's disappearance while Ayya was clearly very angry and convinced that she had been taken. Mind you, he thought, whether she had been unwillingly taken was another matter. The more Lamaxe thought about it, the more likely it seemed that Cloud and Cliff had disappeared together. Perhaps Trebird thought the same and that was why he hadn't taken it seriously, but if this was so why on earth would Ayya make a public accusation? Ayya ab Featherstone was a difficult old man. He was now showing his age but he had always had a reputation for being bad tempered. Surely, though, it would have been in his own interest to keep quiet and simply wait till they returned before he continued to pursue the marriage arrangement with Chitah. The community had a relaxed attitude to sex but took marriage very seriously. Marriage created families and so ancestors and it was essential to become an ancestor in the afterlife. Also, if what was said in the meeting was anything to go by, Chitah was mainly interested in the business benefits of the union. If he wanted a young bride, he wasn't going to be too interested in what the girl had been doing beforehand.

The young priest sat there shaking his head as the others moved away. Trebird glowered once at him, but he was too lost in thought to notice. The High Priest then went back into the temple to see if the Boy was ready to distribute the sacrificial meats. No one else came near Lamaxe though a number gave him approving glances. They would keep an eye on him in future. For his own part he thought about the missing girl. He had known her as a child. She had been much younger than he – perhaps five or six years – but he had suspected that she had had a 'crush' on him. She was always following him, watching for him when he played with his friends. Indeed, Cliff had been one of those friends but it had always been Lamaxe that she had sought out and not Cliff. It seemed that every time he made his way home she was waiting by the path. Whenever he was working in his father's garden or his fields, she would make some excuse to call or wave at him from the pathway. At the time the difference in their ages had seemed enormous. Six years was the difference between a young man and a child and he had only ever thought of her as a nuisance. He used to order her to leave and see her little face crumple in anguish before she slowly dragged herself away. In retrospect it seemed a little cruel but then that is what boys are like, he thought.

Of course now they were both older and the difference in their ages didn't seem so great. She must be fourteen or fifteen summers old he calculated and so of marriageable age, and Cliff was about his own age. That made sense for a mutual affection. As a priest he didn't pretend to know much about the local economy, but he knew that the ab Headlands were rich and important and Ayya ab Fetherstone must be one of the bigger farmers in this chiefdom. He also recalled that Cloud, though a very nondescript child, had grown into a very attractive young woman. He had not seen much of her in recent years until the last spring festival. Then, he had noticed her in the dance. Her long hair had blown out as she spun around with the sun glinting on her locks. She had been quite a stunning sight. Not that Lamaxe himself had been very interested in her at the time. His own interest had been concentrated on the young female sculptor working on the temple decorations.

Escaping from his reverie, the assistant priest became aware that the meeting circle had largely emptied so he rose from the bench and turned to the temple to collect his own share of the food. As he did so he heard a gentle cough behind him which, in proper priestly fashion, he ignored. Then he felt a slight tap on his shoulder. He spun around in astonishment – you weren't supposed to touch priests in the temple compound – to find an elderly woman in front of him, her head and face veiled with a scarf.

'Can I assist you, mother,' he asked, in his best superior priestly voice. 'What causes you to place a hand upon a priest?'

The woman shuddered and bowed her head.

'Forgive me, holiness,' she said, using the formal greeting. Then she let the scarf fall from her face. Lamaxe recognised her immediately.

'Skycloud,' he whispered in surprise.

'It is I,' she replied. 'Skycloud, mother of Skycloudyoung, who is missing.'

He remembered her from his childhood; a harassed farmer's wife who nevertheless had always been kind to the children and frequently turned a wry smile at Lamaxe's own efforts to chase away her annoying daughter.

'I see you still remember Cloud,' she said, observing the look on his face. 'I come to plead with you to help us find her.'

He nearly spoke to her as he had done as a child and needed a moment to pull himself together and remember his current status.

'Mother,' he replied, 'the meeting has decided to await Cliffsound's return. Your own husband agreed with this. What more can I do?'

'My daughter has not run away with Cliff of her own will. This I know.' She spoke definitively.

'But your husband...?' he replied.

'My husband and his plans may be in part responsible for driving her away. However, even though she was angry with him and might have run off she would not have disappeared for so long of her own accord without informing me. Please help me. You were once her friend and you offered help at the meeting.'

'I am but a junior priest,' he continued. 'Trebird is the authority.'

'But you are the one with the sense,' she replied. 'And

you publicly promised to help. I heard you. So did the rest of the community. At least listen to my story.'

Lamaxe was in a quandary as to what to do. If Trebird saw him speaking to the woman he was likely to be even more annoyed with him. He decided that the best thing was to get her out of sight as soon as possible.

'Mother,' he said, reverting to formal speech. 'Not here. I will meet you in private in the second temple once the meats have been distributed.'

She looked around, nodded, re-covered her head with her scarf and hurried away to join the other women.

Lamaxe turned to enter the third temple. As he did so, Trebird stormed out of the building. He glanced at his junior with annoyance in his eyes and pushed past him.

'Trebird,' Lamaxe called, wanting to make his peace with the old priest. 'Please wait.'

The old man turned to face him, muttering.

'I am sorry, holiness,' Lamaxe said using the formal mode of address. 'I did not mean to offend you. I only sought to pacify the community.'

Trebird stared hard at him and then seemed to change his mind. His scowl faltered and he shook his head.

'You did what you thought right, I suppose,' he said, shrugging slightly. 'Let us say no more.'

The assistant priest felt some relief at this.

'What of the girl?' he asked.

'What of her?' came the reply, 'a foolish girl who by her actions could upset the whole community?'

'And when she returns?'

'If and when she returns,' said Trebird, 'we will deal with it. I have been trying to calm down Lamool.'

With that the High Priest turned and joined the elders to eat his food.

It was clear to Lamaxe that nothing further was to be gained by pursuing the matter with his leader and mentor. He went through the temple to the central square in order to collect his own portion of sacrificial meat. The Boy had wrapped it in a leaf, for which he was grateful. He was already splattered with blood from the sacrifice and did not wish to add gravy stains as well. Blood ritual and butchery played havoc with a priest's clothing. His mother was always complaining about his having blood on his clothes which she insisted on laundering for him from time to time. He felt too often that he smelled of sacrificial blood, especially in summer when the weather was hot.

He thanked the Boy and commended his cleaning of the area.

'You made a brave speech,' the Boy said.

Lamaxe was surprised. The Boy was only meant to speak when addressed by another priest. It seemed the world was in flux. He stared at him.

'Sorry, holiness,' the Boy continued, his head bowed. 'I know I should not speak but I was very surprised and impressed.'

'Thank you,' he replied, 'but do not follow my example. Respect your elders.'

The Boy bowed his head as respectfully as he could and Lamaxe sat on the stone bench and began to eat the mutton.

Outside the day was proceeding apace. The old men and community leaders chatted on the curved bench whilst eating their food. The older ones always used these events to negotiate business but some of the younger men had taken up the stone balls which lay in the courtyard and begun a game throwing them onto the stone blocks. The clunk of the balls landing on stone punctuated the conversations. There was much laughter and shouting. The women also fell into groups, eating and chatting about the activities of the day. Life was hard for the women who did a disproportionate amount of the work in the fields. They enjoyed their day off, standing in the sunshine. Lamaxe saw his own mother and walked across to her. She was not supposed to show any affection to him in public because of his status as a priest but when he came close she quietly squeezed his hand and whispered in his ear:

'We have not seen you since the funeral. Come and visit. Come for a meal and I will prepare a goat stew.'

Lamaxe smiled.

'Meat twice in a week?' he said teasing her. 'That is a priest's diet!'

'We had a good goat break its leg. Less milk, more meat.'

'I will, mother. I will come tomorrow.'

Then he turned, took some more meat from the Boy and made his way to the second temple, apparently to eat it. Inside he settled himself on a stone bench and waited for Sky to arrive.

After a while, she came stealthily along the passageway towards him.

'Thank you for seeing me, holiness,' she said, 'I cannot stay long. I have slipped away while Ayya is busy.'

'Welcome, mother,' he replied still using the formal form of greeting. Then he regretted the formality.

'We have known one another a long time. Please, while we are in private, call me Lamaxe.'

'Thank you, Lamaxe. I remember when I used to use your childhood name, Lammy. Please call me Sky. I need your help. I am very worried about Cloud's disappearance.'

'But why?' he asked. 'If she has gone with Cliff she will be safe and surely Chitah will not greatly mind. He is lucky to get a young wife. He can hardly expect a virgin.'

She laughed bitterly.

'He is interested in our land not her body,' she said. 'At least, that is his primary interest, I am sure. Of course, he also wants children.'

'Then what is your concern?' he asked.

The old woman looked him in the eye – something that you were not supposed to do to priests.

'You have known me all your life,' she said. 'You would know if I were to tell an untruth. She has not gone with Cliff, willingly or otherwise. Cliff left to go to his father's boat before she disappeared. I saw him leaving for the coast as he passed our lands.'

'But the coast is some way away and he would have had to pass near the temple to reach it. He could easily have waited for her.'

'Cloud was very keen on Cliff, just as she used to be on you.'

Lamaxe looked embarrassed.

'It is true,' she continued, 'yet I do not believe that he had any particular interest in her.'

'Did he not dance with her at the spring festival,' Lamaxe asked.

She shrugged her shoulders.

'So?' she said.

Lamaxe tried another tack.

'You cannot even be sure that he has left for Sicily. He might have waited at the coast for Cloud and be hiding there with her.'

'But why would he?' she asked. 'No, he was going to Sicily to trade for his father. He takes trade very seriously. It is our major source of wealth. And he had arranged to meet his friend Red there, as he usually did.'

'Red?' asked Lamaxe.

'Redstone ab Graman. Do you not know him? His father grows vines on Gozo and he makes wine. You will find that your High Priest will know the father. He likes his wine.'

'I do know him slightly through Cliff. How do you know this lad?' Lamaxe asked, capitalising on his status as a priest to mask his own young age.

Sky, noting the patronising tone, laughed and replied:

'Red has been here several times to visit Cliff. Cloud knew them both.'

Lamaxe shook his head.

'You ask me to investigate her disappearance but I cannot go to Sicily to check if Cliff is there with Cloud, nor can I check his friend in Gozo. I am a temple priest.'

Sky looked him again in the eye but this time pleadingly.

'If you could go to Sicily, it would set my mind at rest, but you cannot. I do not ask it of you. All I ask is that you investigate other possibilities here. I am sure she has not gone with Cliff, even if you do not believe me. I fear she is here somewhere, murdered or kidnapped or worse. For old time's sake, please help me.'

The more Lamaxe heard from Sky, the less he wanted to be involved but he felt strangely guilty not to help her.

'Tell me about her leaving,' he asked.

She hesitated.

'She left our farm in the direction of the temple.'

'She might have gone in any direction if she wished to mislead you or, more to the point, mislead her father.'

A tear appeared in her eye and made its way down her cheek.

'Did she say where she was going?' he asked more gently.

'She left in a fury, having argued with her father.'

'And…?' he prompted.

'And, yes, they had argued about the proposed marriage. She does not like Chitah. She says he is old and he smells.'

Lamaxe laughed and the woman also admitted to a smile.

'Well, he does, a bit' she added. 'though he is not really so old.'

'He cannot help getting old.' He paused and then added, 'as to the smell, I had not myself noticed it, but I am aware of the taint of blood which hangs over priests after sacrifice so perhaps I would not.'

'But, you are right. She stormed out. She could have run in any direction and then doubled back.'

'Yes, to meet Cliff,' Lamaxe added.

Sky shrugged her shoulders again.

'I thought perhaps she might have gone to the temple to pray to Our Lady. Did you see her at the temple that day?' she asked.

Lamaze gave it some thought.

'Two days ago, you say? The day after my father's funeral. I was not there. I was helping the Boy collect another animal for today's sacrifice. It was from a farm some way away, I am afraid, and quite a walk. Indeed, if she had gone inland we might well have seen her. I doubt that anyone was at the temple. Only Trebird and the temple servants could have been there and it would be unusual for Trebird to be so if there were no ritual duties. He would be more likely in his garden.'

'Can you ask? Can you help? Please?' Her voice was pleading again. Lamaxe had no desire to get involved. This was not priestly work. Yet he thought of the kind woman of his childhood. He also thought about the seriousness of Ayya's accusation against the local chief. Yet how could he help? He did not see how he could ask Trebird about the girl after he had already upset him with his speech.

'Please!' she begged again.

Lamaxe shrugged his shoulders.

'Yes, Sky, I will see what I can find out,' he said, reluctantly.

The relief to her of his offer of help, however reluctantly given, was considerable. Tears rolled down her cheeks.

'Thank you. Thank you,' she said, 'I must go. Ayya will be seeking me,' and with that she immediately headed back down the passageway. As she went he heard her continued thanks gradually getting fainter.

'Oh Lady,' he said to himself, looking up to the dome of the apse roof. 'What have I done?'

He leaned back on the cold stone and thought back to the last time he had seen Cloud. He remembered her as young, attractive and lively as she danced around with the young men at the spring festival. He couldn't remember how many young men she had favoured but he rather thought that he had seen her dancing a lot with Cliff. The trouble was that he had just met the beautiful sculptor and she had received his undivided attention. She was known locally as Pebble – an appropriate name, he thought, for someone who worked in stone. When he had first seen her she had been carving spirals on the temple wall, to celebrate the twirling of the dancing figures she had told him. They were exquisite and so, he thought, was she. The dust motes made by her stone tool as it cut into the rock had been caught by the sunlight which had also been reflected in her hair. That was what had first attracted him over to her but when she turned around at his approach, it was her face that impressed him even more. Not the most conventionally beautiful face but a strong and independent one. The face dominated his memories now and he realised how long it had been since he had seen it other than in his dreams. He forced himself to think of Cloud instead. He could only muster a vague impression of her features. With another shrug of his shoulders he turned and headed back to join the throng outside. He would think what to do about Cloud later.

Outside, the food was finished and the party began to break up. The Chief's area of influence was quite large and some of the farms were a fair distance away. Ayya was in the process of leaving accompanied by friends and supporters. It was impossible for Lamaxe to tell which one was Sky. Trebird was still acting as host of the feast and Lamaxe, having made a sort of peace with him, had no wish to spoil it so he went into the third temple and helped the Boy clear up. They carved the remaining meat onto wooden plates and damped down the fire. The Boy wrapped some extra meat in a leaf for Lamaxe to take to his mother the following day. It was peaceful sitting in the temple out of the sunlight even with the smell of smoke in the air. However, Lamaxe could not settle, thinking about Cloud and her whereabouts. It would never have occurred to him in other circumstances ever to ask the opinion of the Boy, but his mind was not on status distinctions today and the atmosphere encouraged friendship.

'What do you think happened to Cloud?' he asked.

The Boy looked startled, as well he might. Never before had anyone ever asked his opinion on anything. However, he took the enquiry seriously.

'I suppose that she must have run away for an adventure with the lad,' he said. 'I saw her at the spring festival, and if she had offered, I would have gone with her.'

Lamaxe laughed. Although he himself had been 'the Boy' not so long ago, it had not occurred to him that the present incumbent would have such strong feelings about such things. One did not attribute feelings to the lowest level of trainee priest.

'I suppose you are right,' he answered, as much to himself as to the Boy. 'Yet her mother is convinced that she has come to harm.'

The light was fading by now and the inside of the temple was becoming very dark. The Boy lit another torch and they made their way outside, bowing to Our Lady as they passed. The others had all gone so they said goodnight and each returned to his own dwelling within the temple compound, to the east of the first temple. Lamaxe plumped the straw of his bed and lay down but he could not sleep. He went outside and watched as the sky darkened further and the Southern Cross appeared in the sky. The five stars of the Southern Cross marked the home of the Goddess and tonight he hoped she was looking down upon him. Perhaps she would offer some advice. He thought again of the silly young girl who had made such a nuisance of herself and his small cruelties towards her. Then he thought of the beautiful young girl who had danced at the spring festival and charmed the young men, even the Boy it seemed. Had she simply gone off on an adventure of her own to spite her father? Lamaxe knew from experience that her father was a nasty, awkward, tyrannical old man. He could hardly blame a young girl for running away from him. But Sky had always been charming and he could not see that Cloud, unless she had changed dramatically from childhood, would run away from her mother without at least warning her first.

Could Cloud be dead, he wondered. He shrugged his shoulders; if so, what of it? Death was hardly rare in this society. Children and babies died from all sorts of unknown diseases. Many young women died in childbirth along with their babies. Men and women died in accidents in the field. In old age, weakness and overwork finished them off. Then there was the occasional epidemic just like the one that had taken Trebird's wife. Those deaths seemed to strike at random. His own family had been untouched by it. Then there was his father's death. Was he more worthy than his father? He didn't think so. His father had been a hard working and successful farmer and a pillar of the local community who had regularly supported the temple and had even volunteered himself and his workers to Lamool to replace one of the domed roofs. Then there was Trebird's wife. He was the High Priest yet his wife was not saved. It simply passed all understanding. So if Cloud was dead, why should it overly concern him? Death was a normal part of life. People died every day. What was so special about this one that he should have to get himself involved? Yet even as he thought this, he knew the reason why. He had publicly promised to try to help. Well, he knew enough theology to know that you had to take responsibility for your decisions. He had promised Sky that he would do his best, so his best he would have to do. How he wished his sculptor was here to discuss it with. She would advise him what to do. Or at least she would help soothe his brow while he worried about it. Dreaming again of her soothing ways, he gradually fell asleep.

Next morning he rose early and quickly completed his obligations in the temple. He wakened the Boy out of his bed and made sure that he had his instructions for the day. Then, a ritual washing of the hands and face, a prayer before Our Lady's statue and he was done. It was another beautiful late summer day and he strolled rather than hurried on his way. When he arrived at his family home his mother was nowhere to be seen so he sat quietly and taking from his skirt the ancestor stick with his father's image he sought his advice. Strangely, his father was as ambivalent about what to do as he was himself. Lamaxe ended up no wiser. Then he went outside again and was greeted by his mother returning from the fields. Starbright was old and getting frail now. She no longer lived up to the image of her personal name. Well into her forties she was worn out by field working and motherhood. Women were expected to do the bulk of the physical work in the fields as well as on the loom, leaving the men to work the animals, hunt and make tools, but her age and the presence of her daughter-in-law and a few lesser family members and servants meant that she no longer had to labour such long hours. She accepted the sacrificial meats with a smile. Some she put on a wooden plate for herself and Lamaxe to eat with the porridge she had prepared for midday. The rest she put together with some flat bread to take out to his brother, his sister-in-law and the others working in the fields.

After she had returned from doing this, they ate their lunch. Once they had eaten Lamaxe presented her with the ancestor stick of his father. He had carved it himself and while it wasn't as well crafted as his other Shaman sticks it embodied all he felt about his father. She was to keep it until the next ceremony when his bones would be exhumed, defleshed and placed with the rest of the ancestors. Only then would he fully become one of the community of ancestors. Then she began to prepare vegetables for the evening meal along with the promised goat meat. Lamaxe appreciated the honour even if it had arisen from the animal's mishap. He went outside, found his sharpened stick and began to hoe in his mother's garden. There was a certain satisfaction in this simple work after the complex politics of the community meeting. He began to relax. When he looked up he could just make out his brother guiding the family oxen in the fields. Maltese oxen had a very distinctive profile characterised by a large shoulder hump, pendulous dewlap and high rump. On the beast's head he could see its very long and slightly curved horns. Lamaxe loved the shape which was very popular in temple carvings. His sculptor had carved one at the spring festival to bring luck in the coming harvest.

Eventually as the sky darkened, Lamaxe's brother and his family came in from the fields leading the ox and wooden plough before them. After the usual greetings they sat down for their evening meal and while they ate he asked them about Ayya and his daughter. Oyeh knew Ayya as a fellow farmer, though a much wealthier one. Lamaxe's mother claimed that her own grandfather used to describe all farming in his childhood as subsistence with very little difference between farms in the quality or quantity of their harvests. In those days, he used to say, all families were equally at threat in the event of a drought or heavy rain in the wrong season. Then agriculture had improved and surpluses, especially through the wool trade, allowed both for the building of temples and for some specialisation within the farming community, like the growing of vines for wine and specialists like masons and Lamaxe's sculptor. It was then that exchange became possible and trading developed.

Lamaxe, as a priest, had sufficient learning to know that this account could not be entirely true. Temples had been built for thousands of years. He had seen for himself some of the oldest which were far older than the time of his great grandfather. He had also heard that trading, especially with Sicily, was quite ancient. There was an old legend that the original peoples of Malta had come from Sicily by boat. If so, then trading must have been going on for many, many generations. Still, he did believe that his great grandfather had been retelling some kind of folk tale which had a grain of truth in it. In order to build the temples, there must have been a surplus of food so as to spare the labour for building. Similarly, with trade: you could only trade a surplus you did not need yourselves. The wool trade had been particularly important, and still was, because it could involve the whole community in achieving a surplus they could all share. It had started with farmers using sheep and goat hair to make wool which was weaved, usually by the women, to make their own clothes. Then families like the ab Headlands had had a brilliant idea. Exploiting the existing trading links with Sicily, they took finished textiles, at that time made mostly by local Maltese farmers, to Sicily. There they exchanged them for raw wool to take home to make into new cloth which they then re-exported to the neighbouring isle. As the business grew, the ab Headlands developed their own specialist textile facilities, preparing, dyeing and making the cloth from the farmers' wool. They even began making some finer clothes for the local farmers in exchange for the wool. This established a lucrative trade and made the ab Headland family the primary family of the Tarxian area.

Even in years of poor harvest, Ayya usually had a surplus, Oyeh told his brother. Chitah was similar. This is why they both had a high degree of business involvement with the traders and was also how they obtained the few luxury goods which they possessed. Ayya, of course, still complained that ab Headland exploited him. Oyeh and his wife Moonlight worked hard to give themselves a good life but still struggled in bad years.

'He is a bad tempered old man,' Lamaxe's mother told them, in answer to the same question. 'His wife is hardworking and kind but he is mean as well as rich. I expect you noticed the fine purple cloak he was wearing at the meeting. Yet his wife is still wearing the same clothes she has had for years.' The assistant priest thought about that. He had not noticed at the time but it had been true that Sky's clothes had been a trifle frayed. He had assumed it was because she had just come from the fields but they had been meticulously clean and surely, he thought, at the meeting she would be wearing her smarter clothes. It was only now that he realised the contrast between her husband's fine purple cloak and her own dowdy dress.

'What about the daughter?' he asked. 'Is he mean to her?'

'Not so much, Lammy,' Oyeh answered, using his brother's diminutive, 'she always dresses well.'

'Only because he wants to marry her off to Chitah,' their mother interrupted.

'It is true,' said Moonlight. 'Only recently has he given her some finer clothes to wear. I am sure it is to further his business interests.'

They all looked at her in amazement. Oyeh's wife rarely spoke at meals and never to give her opinions.

'Do you know them well?' asked Lamaxe.

'No,' she said, 'I see her when we wash clothes together. She is always kind to me.'

'And she was interested in Cliff?' he asked.

'Oh, yes. But not he in her. Not that she was short of admirers!'

'Who in particular?' he asked.

'Farmers' sons,' she said. 'Tornbark and Blackwing were keenest.'

'I know of them,' Lamaxe told her. 'They were playing the stone game yesterday at the temple. But they seem harmless lads.'

Lamaxe had intended to go to see Cliff's father the next day but now wondered if he should first speak to Ayya.

'He will not tell you anything anyway, Lammy,' his brother told him. 'He will shout and curse, as he always does.'

'A popular man!' was all Lamaxe said.

'And he makes my flesh crawl,' whispered his sister-in-law.

The conversation then turned to more mundane things: the crops, the weather; whether or not the two brothers might find time for some hunting. Lamaxe felt that hunting, never his favourite activity, would be out for him if he did not resolve this problem of the missing girl. Later that night, sleeping in the family house, he couldn't decide what to do first in the morning. Should he speak to Ayya or go and see the textile trader?

# 4

Having slept on it, Lamaxe decided that it would be best to visit Ayya. He found the old man sitting outside his house enjoying the sunshine. In the distance, he could see Sky and some others working in the field. They were using the oxen which by rights should have been men's work. Lamaxe knew that Ayya was very old but even so his sense of propriety was offended. Women did heavy work in the fields, as ordained by the Goddess, but they should not be expected to supervise working animals as well. Despite his inner feelings, he greeted Ayya with the upmost respect.

'Respected, sir,' he offered, 'I greet you.'

'Hello, priest,' replied the farmer, 'and what brings you here?'

This was hardly the respectful way in which even a junior priest like Lamaxe should be addressed. Nevertheless, he kept his temper, knowing the personality of the man.

'I come to assist in the search for your daughter, as you requested,' Lamaxe said, emphasising the final phrase.

The man's mood visibly lightened.

'Here,' he said, offering the priest some flatbread. Out of politeness, Lamaxe broke off a small piece.

'Have you any news?' the farmer asked.

'I fear not,' came the reply. 'I had hoped you could tell me more about the last time that you saw her.'

Ayya hesitated, chewing on his bread, and huffed several times as though debating with himself what to do while Lamaxe stood in the hot sun. Then he seemed to come to a decision.

'Very well, priest,' he said and settled himself into a more comfortable position. 'I have arranged a very good union for her with Chitah, whom you know. He has good lands and the combination of his and mine would be beneficial to both families. Cloud is my only surviving child. Chitah has no surviving children and is in need of a wife. Any issue would have a tidy spread with his lands and my own. The world is changing. Farmers no longer farm for subsistence. I supply food and cloth to the clothier and the other traders and receive fine goods from Sicily in exchange. Have you seen the copperware, priest? The metal work is very fine. Ab Headland has an example. Not that I want trinkets! But, just think! If only it could be made into something useful like tools? It could be made much sharper than flint, I hear. The two farms together would produce a great surplus – even greater with better metal tools.'

Lamaxe nodded, since this seemed to be required. The only Sicilian metalworking he had seen was one small figurine. It had certainly been fine but he could not imagine how a metal tool could possibly be sharper than flint.

'How did Cloud feel about this union?' he asked.

'Cloud? It is not for daughters to question their father's decisions.' He almost spat this at Lamaxe, such was his venom.

'I take it then that Cloud did not approve your choice?' the priest asked gently.

'She did not. We had argued about it for some time, but on that day, I told her that I and Chitah had agreed the bargain and that it would now happen. She screamed at me and ran away.'

'Do you know where she ran to?'

'She will have run to her lover, Cliff – ab Headland's son. He has spirited her away to Sicily with him, as I accused him of doing.'

'Did she say that that was where she was going?' the priest persisted.

The old man sighed.

'She said nothing. Nothing that made any sense, and I was too angry to hear.'

To Lamaxe's surprise, a tear appeared in the farmer's eye and rolled gently down his cheek.

'I was ashamed,' he whispered. 'What would the ancestors think? A child – a daughter – disobeying her father?'

'And yet, an alliance with ab Headland's son would be very prestigious, would it not? More prestigious even than that with Chitah.'

The old man shrugged his shoulders.

'It is true that he is the chief. I suppose he must be the wealthiest person around. But he is primarily a trader. I am a farmer. My forefathers have always been farmers. That is what I know. Marrying Chitah would show respect not just for me but for my forefathers.'

There was silence for some moments. This was all rather outside of Lamaxe's experience and he was unsure of what to say. The farmer seemed lost in his own misery.

'There is nothing more that you can tell me?' the priest eventually asked.

The old man shook his head.

'And you have no actual evidence that Cloud intended to meet with Cliff or, if so, that Cliff knew that she was coming?'

'She must have done so,' he replied. 'Where else would she have gone?'

'I do not know, sir,' Lamaxe replied. 'With your permission, I will ask your wife if she knows anything more.'

The old man did not reply at first. He just sat there looking miserable. Then he began muttering to himself. Lamaxe strained his ears. The farmer was saying something about 'the conspiracy of women, seeking to undermine an honest man's decisions.' Then he raised his head and looked the priest straight in the eye.

'Go ask the woman if you must, but find my daughter. The alliance must go ahead or my lineage will cease. I am too old to father more children.'

The assistant priest couldn't help thinking to himself that if Cloud had at least one lover his family line was probably quite safe but he said nothing. He saw for the first time that underneath the old man's temper and bluster was a rather pathetic person unable to cope with his own declining powers. He bowed his head, thanked him and made his way towards the fields.

Sky saw him approaching and left the servants to continue to work with the beast, steering the priest away from them in order to have some privacy.

'Well?' she asked.

'No real news. Your husband has told me of their argument and her storming off. Have you any idea where she might have gone next? We are a small island. She cannot have simply disappeared.'

'I have told you, I do not believe she went with Cliff.'

'Ayya says she shouted things as she left but he did not hear what she said.'

She laughed.

'He chose not to hear,' she said. 'Cloud cursed him and Chitah.'

'What were her actual words?'

'I did not hear myself but one of the servants said she said that she would rather go to the place of the dead!'

'The Hypogeum? That surely is mere youthful bombast,' Lamaxe replied.

The old woman looked at his young face and the ghost of a smile crossed her face.

'She might have gone to the Hypogeum but I think she is more likely to have gone to the temple to seek advice from one of you priests.'

'Had she done so someone would surely have seen her there,' the priest replied

The woman began to sob quietly. Lamaxe, unused to weeping women, was unsure how to react. He went to put his arm around her shoulders but then remembered her husband watching from outside his house. It might be misinterpreted. In the end he resorted to a comforting phrase.

'I will keep looking,' he said.

She smiled weakly.

'Perhaps you could offer a sacrifice to Our Lady?' she said. 'She may help us.'

She led him back towards the house and presented him with a tiny piglet.

'It is only the runt of the litter,' she said. 'Take it to the temple and offer it to Our Lady. Inspect its entrails. It may offer us an omen which will help.'

She wrapped the animal in an old sack to reduce its struggling and Lamaxe tied a tether around it and onto his left wrist.

'I will do so,' he replied, somewhat reluctantly. 'However, in the meantime there is still enough daylight today for me to visit Chitah. I feel that I should hear what he has to say. You never know.'

With that he made a sign.

'Peace be with you.' Then he waved goodbye with his right hand.

Chitah's farm was adjacent to that of Ayya so it did not take long to walk to it carrying the tiny creature in his arms. It bit him occasionally but priests were used to being attacked by sacrificial animals and on the whole it did not delay him. When he got to the boundary ditch of Chitah's enclosure he was greeted by a woman tending animals in a pen. She smiled at him and bowed her head as a sign of respect to a priest.

'Good day,' he said, 'I come to speak to Chitah ab Flintrock.'

'Yes, holiness,' she answered, 'and your pig?'

He looked doubtful, so she pointed to the creature in his arms and giggled.

'Ah, yes. A sacrifice,' he explained.

Without further comment, she led him into the demesne and, taking the piglet, tethered it to a nearby post.

'I will bring it some water shortly,' she said. 'The master is tending his root vegetables. Would your holiness care to wait for him near the house?'

Lamaxe considered.

'I will go to him in the fields,' he said.

She led him a short distance to where the farmer was bending over his crop.

'Good day, sir,' Lamaxe politely greeted him.

'Is it?' came the reply. The farmer looked him up and down.

'Why am I favoured with a visit from the temple? Have you come to bless my vegetables?' He laughed heartily at this. Lamaxe was only a junior priest but had learned to expect his holy status to be respected. He had already had enough disrespect from Ayya. He particularly detested sarcasm directed towards the clergy and could feel the colour rising in his cheeks as he strove to control his irritation. Nevertheless, he replied with considerable constraint:

'Our Lady is happy that I should bless anything to make it more fertile, though that was not the primary purpose of my visit. I came to speak with you about the missing young woman, Cloud. I had thought that you might wish to co-operate. You supported Ayya when he requested the assistance of the temple.'

The farmer looked somewhat embarrassed. She was after all his affianced, however reluctantly. He wiped his hands on his tunic which already showed evidence of several day's work in the fields. Then, to Lamaxe's surprise, he smiled a gap-toothed grin and indicated a direction to the priest.

'Come. Follow me to my house and take some refreshment. We can talk there more comfortably.' With that he led the way.

They sat outside the house on a bench and Chitah sent for refreshment.

'You will try my own brew?' he said, more as a statement than a question. Lamaxe demurred but the farmer insisted and presented him with a bowl and reed as a straw. He sipped the ale, which proved to be refreshing. Ale is normally very weak but this, he feared, was much stronger.

'Cloud?' he asked.

'Ah, yes,' said the farmer, 'very inconvenient. The alliance has been made. The arrangements between Ayya and I are agreed. It is a most auspicious alliance. My lands and his are both productive and they partly adjoin.'

'And yet the lady does not approve the marriage…?' Lamaxe left the question hanging in the air.

'She is young and foolish. She could make a good life here. No working around the clock as my wife, like she does for her father. My house is comfortable; my farm prosperous. I have a number of servants who would also serve her.'

Lamaxe simply raised an eyebrow questioningly.

'I know I am a little older than her,' Chitah continued, 'but girls expect to marry older men. I am already well over thirty so she would not even have to put up with me for too long!' He laughed at his own joke. Then his face took on a serious look.

'This marriage is important to me. My first wife died in childbirth with our first child. Oh yes, as you see, I have concubines, of course.' He waved towards the woman Lamaxe had spoken to earlier. 'But I have no children from them either.'

Lamaxe nodded.

'I am sorry,' he said.

'I must have heirs,' Chitah continued, clenching his fists. 'I am a wealthy farmer; a respected member of the community. I need heirs to worship me as an ancestor, tend my shade and retain memory of me. Cloud is the daughter of another successful farmer. It is the perfect alliance. We could found a dynasty that would last through time and then I would be remembered for always.'

'And if she returns safely?' the priest asked.

Chitah shook his head.

'There are very few young fertile women on this island and even fewer whose fathers have good farms. I crave immortality. In return I can give Cloud a better life than she has now.'

Lamaxe nodded again. Whatever he thought of Chitah as a person, and the farmer's lack of personal hygiene had become very apparent as they sat and talked together, what he said was true. Many young women would have to make do with less attractive offers. Also, it seemed clear that Chitah saw it as very much in his own interests that Cloud return. He had no motive to see her harmed. Indeed, quite the reverse. He changed tack.

'Where do you think that she has gone?' he asked.

'Her father claims she has gone after a young lover.'

'Cliff?'

'He believes so.'

'And you do not believe this?'

‘I don’t know. I know Cliff’s father as a trader and so have met the lad from time to time. He does not strike me as a young man with a particular interest in Cloud or any young woman. His only interest seems to be travel with his friend from Gozo, but I don’t know. I cannot really tell you more but I do hope she is discovered soon. I am not of an age that I can afford to wait too long.’

Lamaxe gave his thanks and left, collecting his sacrificial creature on his way. As he was departing the same young woman he had met on arrival came running after him with a skin vessel.

‘The master offered you this for the temple,’ she said.

‘Wine? he asked.

‘Beer,’ she replied, nodding her head.

‘Please offer him my thanks.’

His head felt thick in the fresh air after the beer and he was grateful for the walk back to clear his thoughts. Chitah’s speech had confirmed Sky’s view of him but had not much advanced the case. It seemed to him that Chitah had no reason whatsoever to wish Cloud to disappear but every reason to conclude the marriage contract as soon as possible. Nor was he likely to have murdered her in a fit of rage if she had refused to take him. He seemed quite genuinely to want her back. The idea of Cloud as a brood cow was not a very attractive one but it gave the farmer a very good reason for wanting her alive. It also now seemed questionable that Cloud had gone with Cliff, though he couldn’t be sure. He would have to speak to Cliff’s father. Even if she had gone with him, it was likely to have been willingly. He couldn’t imagine his childhood friend kidnapping the girl. However, he could not know for certain until Cliff returned other than travelling to Sicily and he had not the time, the budget or the inclination to do that. Yet, he thought, if she did not follow Cliff, where on earth could she have gone? The only other likely places seemed to be the temple or to meet some unknown person, perhaps one of the other young men. He could think of no reason why she should go to the Hypogeum despite what she had said to her father. Unless, of course, she was attacked before she reached the temple. But then, who could have done that? Otherwise she could only have returned to her own father's farm which made no sense. If her father knew where she was, why on earth would he make the accusation against the Chief's son? A very dangerous thing to have done! He confessed to himself that he was confused and the drink he had taken with Chitah was not helping his condition. So he decided to lie down in the sunshine and rest to allow his head to clear.

He awoke when the piglet began to chew his ear. The sun was falling in the sky and he cursed himself for sleeping so long. Night falls quickly in these parts. It must have been the drink. He still had a headache. Standing up he kicked the drinking vessel in frustration so that it rolled a few feet away from him but fortunately did not burst.

'Just as well,' he said to himself, having second thoughts. 'I will be late returning to the temple. At least I can use the beer as an excuse – an offering to the temple as a libation. That might please Trebird.' He hurried home as the sun went down.

So Lamaxe found himself struggling back to the temple complex carrying both the drinking vessel and a live piglet. It was becoming dark and he began to regret his decision to return with both. Still he felt that he could not just dump either one on the way. Both were intended in one way or another for the Goddess so he was obliged to struggle on. He was still some distance from the temple complex when the rain came.

So much for our prayers, he thought. It came as a complete surprise to him. Dressed formally, he was wearing his cap, but the material was quite inadequate to the task and he was soon soaked to the skin. What is more a wind had blown up to accompany the rain and it lashed into his face as he walked, making it difficult to see the path. More than once he wandered off the way but fortunately the ground was so hard baked from the summer sun that it remained firm under his feet and he managed to stumble back onto the path again. Only once did the pig actually escape his grasp but by dropping the flask and throwing himself at the beast he managed to secure a grip on it. It squealed horribly but survived the challenge. He hugged it to his chest to keep it from the worst of the rain and it seemed to accept the shelter and became quieter.

At last, the bulk of the wall of the temple compound loomed up on him out of the lashing rain. He quickened his pace but so did the rain and once again he wandered off the path. The piglet chose this moment to attempt a second escape and as he sought to recapture it in the dark he stumbled into mud and fell. He was surprised to find the earth so soft at this time of year and it took some effort to right himself and retrieve the animal, now even more slippery. His nice skirt was now not only soaked but filthy. He swore.

'Where in the underworld did all this mud come

from?' he said out loud, though his words were lost in the sound of the rain. He must have wandered into someone's garden. Still, he was now outside the outer wall of the temple complex so, with a sigh he dragged himself into the courtyard and to his hut behind the first temple. Then he secured the sacrifice to the wall and carefully placed the drink skin on the floor having wiped the mud away. The rain continued to pour, beating noisily on the roof so he thought he would make best use of 'the Goddess's blessing' and stripping down to his loin cloth he went back out into the rain and washed the mud off his legs and his skirt as best he could. Returning to the hut he used some bedding straw to dry himself before finding a dry loin cloth to put on. He felt he had done more than enough for one day so lay down to sleep.

The next morning he reported to Trebird, managing to be very vague about how he had stumbled across Chitah. Fortunately, Trebird was in a good mood and sufficiently impressed with the beer that his curiosity was not aroused. He was excited and informed Lamaxe that he would be away all day, visiting ab Headland.

'It is one of the things I was speaking to him about at the ritual' he informed his assistant. 'He has been having a new skirt made for me suitable to my status as High Priest.'

Lamaxe congratulated him. Trebird, smiling happily, agreed to prepare a libation of the beer to give to Our Lady that very morning before he left and invited the young priest to join him. Apart from the community rituals, it was the work of the priests to worship the Goddess in various ways, as well as to deal with any visitors seeking divine guidance or in need of a prophecy. Trebird decided that the libation that morning could form part of the priestly private prayers, with the remainder of the beer being used at some more public occasion. The two priests entered the second temple and began the prayers. The High Priest poured some of the liquid into a libation bowl and offered it to the altar. Then, raising it above his head, he offered incantations until, lowering the bowl, he took a swig from the potion. Lamaxe noticed that it was a substantial drink. Then he offered the bowl again to the altar and then to his assistant. Lamaxe took a sip. After his experience yesterday, he had decided that a sip was sufficient. What was more, without a drinking straw he found his mouth full of sediment. Then he returned the bowl to Trebird who took another deep swallow of the liquid before pouring the remaining dribble onto the altar itself with further incantations. Finally, he replaced the bowl on its shelf and they both retreated to the stone benches.

'A good brew,' commented Trebird, wiping his mouth on his arm. 'I will store the remainder safely in my quarters until it is required again. It will be cool there and so keep it fresh.'

'Yes, Trebird,' replied the junior.

'And now,' announced Trebird, 'I will relax before I leave by playing the ball game. Will you join me?'

'Sorry,' mumbled Lamaxe, 'I have promised to make a sacrifice for someone.'

Once Trebird had gone outside, Lamaxe went back to his hut and, releasing the tether on the piglet, he carried it into the first temple. He chose the first temple as he felt he would be undisturbed. However, the Boy was in there and offered to help. Lamaxe would have preferred to be alone but felt it incumbent to involve the Boy once he had been discovered. Holding the piglet firmly in one hand, he knelt before the altar and carefully removed the stone ball from its setting. Feeling inside the hollow altar he found the flint knife and saying a prayer he sliced through the creature's throat with a single blow. Blood gushed onto the altar, as it should and dropping the body he went to replace the knife. Unfortunately, animal sacrifices are unpredictable and his hand that morning must have been unsteady. Still pouring blood and squealing the piglet began to run around the apse. The Boy lunged across the floor, grabbed it by the hind legs and dashed its head against the altar support. Desperately hoping that this was a good sign and not a bad omen, Lamaxe finished the creature off and laid it in front of the altar in order to slit its belly. The innards spilled out. They both inspected the mess according to the ancient codes. What did they show? Lamaxe raised his head and spoke to the Goddess.

'Please, Our Lady, tell me where to seek the missing maiden.'

No reply was forthcoming. He looked at the entrails again. They were perfectly healthy but gave no clue to the girl's whereabouts.

'Please Our Lady – help me,' he pleaded. What on earth should he do next?

At that moment there came a desperate cry from outside. Leaving the mangled body of the piglet the two younger priests rushed to see what had caused the noise. In the courtyard lay Trebird, rolling in agony and clutching his foot.

'What is it?' asked Lamaxe.

'My foot! My foot!' he cried. 'I dropped a stone ball on it.'

Lamaxe quickly gave instructions to the Boy to fetch a bowl of water.

'Make sure it is as cold as possible,' he said, 'and be quick.'

Trebird continued to writhe on the ground. While they waited, Lamaxe grabbed the foot and manipulated each toe in turn, much to Trebird's annoyance.

'The toes appear not to be broken,' he explained.

The Boy returned dragging a large clay pot and Lamaxe insisted on placing the old priest's foot in the cold water.

'What torture is this?' the priest shouted. 'My foot is freezing.'

Lamaxe smiled.

'Do not worry, your holiness,' he continued, 'my mother is well versed in treating such injuries on the farm and she taught me. It will lessen the bruising and ease the pain.'

'I cannot feel my foot,' moaned the patient.

'Then that is a good thing,' replied Lamaxe, 'we will now remove it and hope that it does not swell too much.'

'You might try the same with his head,' whispered the Boy in Lamaxe's ear, but Lamaxe gave him a disapproving look and he went silent.

'Now fetch some cloth and we will bandage it,' he told the Boy, who rushed off immediately.

Trebird moaned.

'Help me up,' he asked, 'I need to put my weight on it.'

Lamaxe did so but it was clear that it was too painful to stand on.

'You will have to see ab Headland another day,' he told the High Priest.

'No, it must be today,' he answered, 'I will have to send the Boy while you attend to the priestly duties.'

Lamaxe helped the priest back into a sitting position and began to think. He hatched a plan.

'Holiness,' he said, 'let me go to see ab Headland on your behalf. He is a person of great stature and may be offended by your sending a mere Boy. I am of a more suitable status.'

The High Priest gave this some consideration despite his pain. He had no wish to offend ab Headland.

'Perhaps you are right. He is an important man. But I cannot undertake religious duties in this condition. No, Lamaxe, you will have to stay.'

Lamaxe smiled and nodded his head to confirm his own idea.

'Of course you can, holiness. You can sit on a stone bench and the Boy will fetch and carry for you. In the meantime, I will ensure that the skirt you receive is of a sufficient quality befitting your status.'

Then he quickly changed the emphasis of the discussion.

'What colour is it?'

'Green, of course,' came the reply. 'Green is the only colour for Our Lady's priest. It is the colour of fertility, a holy colour.'

'Indeed, sir.'

Eventually Trebird was persuaded but he was still wary.

'You have only met ab Headland on public occasions, have you not?' he asked his junior.

'That is correct. He seems a most upright man.'

'Full of his own importance in public, you mean. He is less upright in private. Don't be offended and mess up the arrangements.'

'In what way?' Lamaxe asked.

'You know that the Chief is a great storyteller. Unfortunately, his stories in private are a trifle too robust for some people. Probably you included.'

Lamaxe didn't know what to make of that but at least by the time the Boy returned, Trebird had fully accepted that he would go in his place.

That solves the problem of how I can interview ab Headland, Lamaxe thought, and I have the perfect excuse to go. Trebird complained some more as he was re-bandaged but once it was done he seemed to accept that the extra support reduced the pain. All was explained to the Boy, who was obviously disappointed that he could not spend the day walking the island and secretly enjoying himself on the way, but pleased that he would be doing proper priestly work, even if it was by proxy.

Before he left Lamaxe slipped back to the accommodation huts and sought out the Superintendent of the Temple Compound. Not a priest, it was he who was responsible for the day to day running of the temples and their fabric. He was a harassed middle-aged man known as Springox, quite nondescript to look at, but important to the operation of the temple. Lamaxe explained what had happened to the High Priest and where he himself was going that day.

'The Boy will see to his demands but please will you be sure that he is suitably fed and watered and that he does not stand too much on his bad foot. If he does it will become worse and we will all suffer.'

'I will do so, holiness,' the supervisor replied. 'The kitchen will see that he is provided for.'

‘Thank you,’ said Lamaxe eager now to start his journey. Even so, it occurred to him that he had not properly questioned the staff about the missing girl.

‘Tell me,’ he asked, ‘two days before the ritual. Were you here at the temple?’

‘Let me see,’ he replied, calculating the days on his fingers. ‘Was that the day that you and the Boy went to fetch the sacrificial animal?’

‘It was. I wondered if you had seen the missing girl anywhere near the temple compound?”

‘Skycloudyoung? Ah! On that day I was only here until mid-morning. I went to see the stone mason about new ashlar for the roof of the east apse of the second temple. You know how poorly constructed it is.’

‘Indeed.’

‘I am afraid that I saw no one. The stonemason lives some distance away so I was gone for much of the day. Since the sweeper normally only works in the morning and evening and there was little for the kitchen to do that day, the only person who would be likely to be here in the day time would be the High Priest. Even then, since there were no formal rituals that day, he may have slipped out.’

‘Does he slip out regularly when I am not here?’ Lamaxe asked.

‘Only occasionally. I think he gets restless if there are no rituals to conduct and enjoys working in his garden.’

Lamaxe thanked him and began his journey.

# 5

Pebble leaned back to admire her work.

*'Finished at last,'* she said to herself.

The sunlight fell upon the deep incisions of the sculptured panel and she could see that it was good. She had been working in the south restoring parts of the Mnajdra temples over the summer. It was unwise to refuse an invitation to work. Although there was no overarching hierarchy of priests, they all knew each other and word got around. In any case, it seemed to be a straightforward job. It had been fun bringing part of the old building back into life. She loved her work and the masons were good company to work with most of the time. She knew most of them, at least by sight. As usual she had had quite a few 'offers' but no one had been offended by being turned down. They all knew what an itinerant life style was like and anything more than friendship was asking for trouble. Her motto had always been to try never to offend anyone as you never knew in what circumstances you might meet again. Mind you there had been that brief dalliance with the farmer's son but it hadn't been anything serious, merely a way of reducing the tensions of the job. She loved her work but it could be stressful especially when there were demanding priests around, which there usually were.

She was still quite young but had been working as a sculptor since she was fourteen when her father had died. He had been a mason and had trained her himself after her mother had succumbed to illness. Ever since she was a young child she had travelled with him and she had always played with his flint tools even before she could properly hold a hand hammer. That was how she had acquired her nickname of Pebble; a nickname that had stuck so that everyone now called her that. No one seemed to remember her real name. As she became older her skills improved. However, she found that handling the huge blocks of stone was rather too much for her slight frame, so while her father had done the big stuff she had begun to concentrate on finishing and had gradually acquired a considerable skill at carving decorations. Other masons told her that she had a definite artistic streak and the priests seemed to agree. So she continued to travel between temples, wherever the work was. Being a mason her father hadn't had much in the way of land to farm so his sudden death had meant that she had had to find a way to make a living. Fortunately, knowing other masons and the temple authorities through her father she had found it not too difficult to be accepted into their rather exclusive world.

She was just cleaning her tools and packing them away when a message came. She was invited to the Hypogeum at Tarxian to do some minor repair work to the trilithon and perhaps to help work on the new third level. The trilithon was just finishing work really but they wanted Pebble's skill and it was a great honour to be asked to work on the great underground complex of tombs. The Hypogeum was greater than any other structure in the known world; certainly in her known world. Only the best masons were asked to work there and major construction had just begun on a lower level to be carved into the bedrock. So, of course, she accepted. Her contribution need only take a few days and it would surely add to her reputation. What is more, it was linked to the Tarxian temples where her young priest lived and worked. It was her favourite temple complex and she hadn't been in the Tarxian region since the spring festival. Also, she was surprised to discover how much she had come to miss her young priest. She liked to think of herself as worldly wise but his very naivety had attracted her. He was so young and yet so serious. She would like to see him again soon. However, she must finish the job here first.

She was bending low over her work, concentrating hard on the final details. Indeed, she was concentrating so hard that at first she didn't hear the two masons approach her from behind.

'A fine arse,' Freestone, the younger one said. 'Like the moon arising.'

She heard him chuckle but didn't acknowledge it and continued with her work. His father, Greensand, smiled but tried to lead him away. The younger one shrugged him off, digging his elbow into the other's ribs.

'Tell me,' Freestone asked, in a voice intended to be overheard, 'Did you ever want to reach out and touch the moon?'

The older man put out his arm to restrain him but he brushed him off again and crouched towards her rear, his arm outstretched. Suddenly, properly aware of him, she tensed and spun around, her sharp chisel raised, pointing straight at his nose, while her other hand held her hand hammer ready at her side.

'You spoke, Freestone?' she asked, not moving the flint from the tip of his nose.

He backed away slowly but she followed him so that the flint edge was just touching the end of his snout.

'Now lady,' he said, 'I was merely admiring the beauty… of your work'

She gave him a disdainful look but allowed the flint to retreat slightly.

'… and thinking that you might benefit from my own excellent skills,' he continued in the same cocksure manner now the immediate threat had been withdrawn. 'I'm sure you could find the use of my own tool to your advantage.'

He smirked at his father, intent on sharing the double entendre. She scoffed and lowered the weapon intending to return to her work. At which point he moved towards her again though this time with both arms raised in apparent surrender.

She looked him firmly in the eye. He stopped. Then her eyes moved up and down his body and she sneered.

'I am very particular about the tools I use,' she said. 'Yours looks to be rather small to me and lacks finesse.'

The young man turned bright red. He was uncomfortable, unsure how to react to this. He couldn't think of a smart reply.

'In truth,' she added, with a wink at the older man, 'it looks a little blunt.'

The older mason laughed and the young man looked even more uncomfortable. Her sharp chisel returned to its threatening position just touching his nose and she now raised the hand hammer higher.

'Easy lady,' was all he said.

The older man smiled at her and put his arm carefully about his son's shoulders.

'Come on, lad,' he said. 'I think you've met your match.'

With that he slowly and carefully led his companion away.

'Good luck, Pebble,' he said over his shoulder. 'Your work is first class.'

Pebble waited until they had gone before she lowered her tools. She realised to her surprise that she was shaking.

*'That settles it,'* she said to herself. *'I'm definitely leaving now. I've had enough!'*

*

She had expected the work at the Hypogeum to prove to be interesting and varied but she found that she had been wrong about two things. It had been supposed to be a question of finessing the fine carving yet what they mainly wanted was work on the new third level which was mostly storage rooms. Since it was a prestigious building it was difficult to refuse but in her view this was straightforward mason's work and demanded rather less than her own skills. Also, the smell put her off. The second thing she had been wrong about was that although the Hypogeum came under the same domain as the temples and was no distance from the temple complex, the only priest she met there was Trebird. She had expected to receive an invitation to go and work on the temples as well but all

Trebird had said was that he had an important job for her to do and he would call for her when he was ready. So she had not seen Lamaxe after all, except at his father's funeral and then she could hardly show herself. She wondered why he had not sought her out. Perhaps he was no longer interested. Nevertheless, she had decided that, even without an invitation, sooner or later she would go to the temples.

She discussed it with her young friend Chisel but he was a straightforward mason so saw no problem with work on the third level. It was a major construction so he was delighted to be busy. Even so, she was sufficiently fed up to risk annoying Trebird and arranged for her payment of an allocation of Emmer wheat to be forwarded on to the temples. She then bade farewell for the time being to Chisel and, rather late in the day, took up her parcel and her tools and set off. It had rained heavily the previous night but today was another beautiful day and she found herself whistling as she walked towards the Tarxian temples. The unexpected rain had refreshed everything so that the hard baked earth took on a faint greenish tinge. She was going back to 'her home'. She realised how silly this notion was. Sculptors and masons don't have homes. The very nature of the job requires them to constantly move to keep in work. Yet, when she had last stayed at Tarxian in the spring she had felt at home. The people were friendly, Lamaxe was delightful and even grumpy old Trebird was all right. At least, he had liked her work so much that he had let her carve pretty much what she liked. Of course, she had liked to carve spirals so the temples were full of them.

She did have one moment of doubt. Would her young priest still want her? If she found him attractive no doubt others would as well. Suppose he had taken up seriously with some local woman. He was so simple and so loyal that she would have her work cut out to steal him away from someone else.

Mind you, she thought to herself, I am sure I have the skills.

But no, the last thing he had said was that he would be thinking of her all the time and aching for her return. Hum, she thought with a wry smile. Perhaps she had said the same thing. She wasn't sure. Still there had only been the farmer's son and he didn't really count, did he?

As she walked she admired the harvest ripening in the dying sun. The world was a fertile place. The Goddess must be smiling on them. Before she reached the temples it would be dark, but she knew her way by the positioning of the Southern Cross in the sky.

# 6

It was mid-morning on that same day when Lamaxe finally set off to visit Lamool ab Headland, the textile maker and chief. His best skirt was still damp and splashed with mud from the night before so he sorted out his second best one. It was somewhat frayed around the hem but would have to serve as he couldn't visit such an important person without wearing priestly attire. It was another bright sunny day after the heavy rain and he decided that he would make the most of Trebird's incapacity and spend the whole day away from the temple. He was sure that the Boy would manage the High Priest though he did have a twinge of conscience and decided to try to pay back the lad somehow at a later time. Since ab Headland's place was beyond Ayya's farmstead, he thought it would be useful to trace in reverse the route that Cloud might have taken had she really gone to the temple on the day that she had disappeared.

He walked through the entrance in the temple compound wall and down the path which led to his destination, fastidiously avoiding the muddy area, now largely dry again. The distance seemed much shorter than when he had returned at night in the rain. He saw a few women working in the fields and asked each if she had seen Cloud or spoken to her on that day. Some were very suspicious of a priest asking questions but even those who appeared to want to be helpful were of little use to him. One thought that she might have seen Cloud shortly before the last festival day but couldn't remember when exactly. Nor was she sure in which direction she had been travelling at the time. Lamaxe decided that it was hopeless. He had had visions of meeting a farmer or two on his way, gaining some useful information and being invited as a guest to join them for a midday snack but there were no important farmers to be seen that day and his stomach was beginning to rumble. He pressed on towards the Chief's domain hoping to get there before his midday meal and a possible invitation to feed at a rich man's table.

He had been friendly with ab Headland's son Cliff as a child but had never paid much attention to the work going on in the trader's compound. Now, he stared with amazement at what he saw. The production area spread some way along the coast and was dominated by three large pits, full of liquid. Before he reached the pits themselves, though, he passed a man treading water in a large wooden box which emitted a pungent smell. As he pressed on he came across clay pots full of herbs and others that stank of urine. He stopped a woman carrying another pot with a lid.

'Good day, sister', he said.

She bowed to him gracefully and offered a greeting.

'Good day, holiness, my name is Eve. How can I help?'

'Please tell me what you have there?' he asked.

'Shellfish, your holiness,' she answered. 'Do you wish to see the master? He will be in the big roundhouse.'

She pointed vaguely across the compound so Lamaxe walked over to the house and knocked on the wooden door. Almost immediately another woman opened it. Her resemblance to the first woman was striking. Noticing his puzzled expression, she smiled.

'You have obviously met my sister,' she said. 'I am Lilith.'

She then asked him his business and he explained.

A voice from inside called out. 'What? A priest? Is it Trebird?'

Lilith turned back into the house and answered that it was not Trebird but a young priest.

'I will come out,' the voice said.

The Chief came to the door with his dog at his side. Lamaxe had seen ab Headland before of course but only ever at official occasions when he had been dressed in his best clothes. Now he was dressed in a tunic which even Lamaxe would have been disinclined to wear. Ab Headland was a fairly short man of perhaps fifty with a heavily tanned and very lined face. On official occasions he had seemed quite overpowering but in his own surroundings and quite relaxed, Lamaxe was forced to revise his opinion now that he saw him close up. The creases on his face seemed more likely to be laughter lines than old age. He smiled at the priest and held up his hand in greeting.

'I have seen you at the temple,' he said, smiling and returning the gesture. 'What do they call you?'

Lamaxe, feeling somewhat intimidated, retained a formal form of address.

'My name is Lamaxe ab Tarxian, sir, assistant priest to the temple of Our Lady,' he replied.

The dog growled at him and ab Headland laughed.

'He can smell a priest,' he said.

'I have been sent by Trebird, the High Priest, on an errand to collect his new skirt.'

'Of course,' the Chief replied. 'You and Cliff were friends when children. I remember the name now though I would not have recognised you. You are Oyeh's brother.'

There were stools set out on the worn grass outside the house and his host indicated that he should sit down. The priest did so and ab Headland joined him. The dog curled up on the ground between them.

'So where is he?' he asked.

'Unfortunately, sir, he has met with a minor accident and so has sent me in his place.'

'It's not like Trebird not to come himself. He likes to sample my wine. What has he done then? Stabbed himself with the sacrificial knife?' With that he began to laugh loudly.

'No, sir, he was playing the ball game and dropped a ball upon his foot.'

Lamaxe tried to say this in as dignified a manner as possible but the Chief creased up with uproarious laughter.

'By the Goddess, I'll piss myself,' he said, rocking back and forth.

Lamaxe was embarrassed by such crudity and so said nothing in reply. The textile maker pulled himself together wiping the tears from his eyes.

'Bring bread and cheese for us,' he called out to the women, clapping his hands.

'Do you prefer water or wine?' he asked.

'I would prefer water, sir,' the priest replied.

The older man laughed again.

'You are wise young man, but I am not and so shall have some wine.'

The food came and Lamaxe found it to be very good. The bread was freshly baked and of a finer quality than he was used to. The cheese was excellent. Lamaxe tried hard not to let the curd drip down his chin. They ate in silence until ab Headland, taking a deep quaff of wine, let out an enormous belch. This started him laughing again and the priest was unsure how to respond.

'Do you know anything about textiles?' the chief asked.

'My mother weaves our own wool to make clothes,' he answered. 'The surplus comes to you, I believe. But I do not understand all that you do here.'

'I will show you around,' he said clearly pleased at the prospect. 'Ask what you want.'

They walked towards the man still treading water.

'What is the purpose of this?' Lamaxe asked.

'He is fulling,' he explained. 'It breaks down the fibres in the wool and makes it easier to clean it and for it to take a dye. Probably your mother does something similar but it looks different on an industrial scale.'

Lamaxe nodded.

'The herbs are for the dyes, of course.' He opened one of the wooden boxes.

'You see in here we have lichen. There are several different vegetable dyes for different colours. This one is for green so we will have used this for your High Priest's cloth. I mix the herbs myself, or Cliff does when he is here. That way we can be sure that the quantities are correct. Then they go into the vats to stew.'

'And what please are the shellfish for?' Lamaxe asked.

Ab Headland laughed again.

'Some may be for supper,' he answered chuckling, 'but the Murex shellfish we also use as a dye. That is the most expensive dye. The one we used for the purple of that rogue Ayya's cloak.'

Lamaxe looked suitably impressed so ab Headland led him back to the stools and they sat down.

'It is a much more complex process than I had realised,' Lamaxe told his host.

'It is,' agreed the other. 'Our cloth is becoming so popular in Sicily that we are constantly seeking extra supplies of wool. That is why Cliff is there now. Still we must be careful. Some of the tribes are becoming interested in our methods. We need to guard them carefully.'

'Who are they?' asked Lamaxe.

'Well, priest, I take it you have not travelled beyond this island. There are many different peoples over the sea with many different cultures and religions. You never know where trouble will spring from next.'

Lamaxe tried to nod sagely, though it meant little to him.

'Not everyone believes in Our Lady, you know,' the Chief continued.

Lamaxe looked shocked. Such an idea had never occurred to him.

'Not believe in Our Lady?' he said. 'But she created everything.'

'There are many peoples and many religions, Lamaxe. Some believe in one god or goddess, as we do, others believe in many gods. The image of Our Lady is worshipped in some form or another very widely but by different names. Some know her as 'Ishtar'. Anyway, she is very popular so I shouldn't worry too much.'

He smiled when he said this, but Lamaxe didn't think it a matter for levity.

'There are many peoples along the sea coasts and many have strong ships,' ab Headland continued, 'so are to be taken seriously. We must be wary and use all our cunning to protect ourselves but we also need to trade with them. However, I don't think we need to worry too much in my lifetime. Our future, after all, is in trade. '

'I see,' said Lamaxe, though he didn't really think he did.

'I will tell you a story which is perhaps illustrative,' the Chief continued, settling onto his stool. Lamaxe knew how much he liked to tell stories.

'There were three men on a boat: a Sumarian, an Akkadian and a Maltese.

'Sorry,' asked Lamaxe, 'Who are these other people? Are they like the Sica?'

'Yes, just different peoples. It was how I was told the story.'

'Oh! Very well,' said Lamaxe, trying to be polite. 'Please continue.'

'Anyway, there was a storm and the boat began to ship water,' the textile maker continued. 'It sank lower and lower into the water. The Sumerian was the first to panic and fearing the boat would sink jumped overboard. But the water was cold and slowly he drowned and his body sank. The next day, the boat was even lower in the water and eventually the Akkadian jumped overboard and he too was drowned in just the same way. After three more days the boat was almost below the water altogether and the Maltese was beginning to be a little concerned but he prayed to Our Lady and at that moment the bodies of the Sumerian and the Akkadian, bloated by the water, shot to the surface.'

'How awful!' said Lamaxe. 'Did this really happen to you?'

'No, of course not. It is a joke, a parable, a tale from which you can gather amusement and perhaps learn a lesson.'

'Sorry,' repeated Lamaxe.

'Anyway, the Maltese sailor leaned over the side and lashed the dead bodies together. Then, leaving the boat to disappear under the water, he climbed onto the bodies and drifted to the shore and safety using a plank from the sunken boat to row and to direct himself.' Ab Headland laughed uproariously at this. Lamaxe was rather horrified by the whole thing. Still laughing, ab Headland added:

'Of course, when I was first told that story, it was told about a Canaanite not a Maltese.'

Ab Headland continued laughing at his story while Lamaxe smiled weakly.

'I see,' the priest said eventually trying to find a moral beneath the tale, 'it shows the power of Our Goddess and the resourcefulness of us Maltese compared to other people.'

'Got it!' the old man smiled and poked him in the ribs. 'Now, is there anything else I can help you with?' he asked, for he loved to show off his trade and his knowledge of the world to a willing listener.

Lamaxe hesitated but then decided to press ahead with the real intention behind his visit.

'I would appreciate your help on another matter,' he

answered, hoping to capitalise on the Chief's good mood.

'Go ahead!'

'Cloud, the missing girl?'

'What about her?' the Chief asked cautiously.

'Well, is it really likely that your son, Cliff might have taken her with him to Sicily?'

'Cliff?' answered ab Headland. 'You know him. You used to be friends. I said that it was nonsense at the meeting. Why, it's about as likely as a bride on her wedding night not farting in her bridegroom's lap.'

This brought on further paroxysms of laughter from the chief. Lamaxe's eyes shot open and his mouth fell wide. He had never heard anything so vulgar and especially from the respected chief of his region. Of course, there was humour on Malta. Lamaxe and his friends often laughed at the shortcomings of others and there was nothing more amusing than someone falling over and hurting themselves, as Trebird had done this morning. But this was different. The first story he had thought in bad taste – making fun of a horrible death. But the second joke was simply vulgar and rude. He did not expect this to come from the mouth of such a respected senior member of the community.

'That's a foreign joke as well,' laughed ab Headland. 'I first heard that from a Sumerian.' Then he saw that Lamaxe appeared shocked.

'By the Goddess, you have led a sheltered life, priest,' he continued. 'You must forgive those of us who have travelled and have seen the world. But I bet you that that expression will still be circulating in hundreds of years' time.'

'I am sorry,' replied Lamaxe, though he wasn't too sure what he was sorry for.

'Don't worry, lad. Anyway, the answer to your question is that I can't think of any reason why Cliff should have run off with Ayya's daughter. He's never shown any interest in her. Frankly, he hasn't shown much interest at all in the local women. He's far too busy helping me with the business and making us all wealthy. Mind you, what he gets up to when he is away is another matter. When I used to sail I had a great time.'

This was followed by another elbow-dig into Lamaxe's ribs. The young priest pulled himself together and pressed on.

'What about Red?' he asked.

'Red? The vintner's son? Well, I have heard Cliff and Red laugh about Cloud being sweet on Cliff,' he answered. 'I don't know about Red. After all he lives on Gozo, though he visits here from time to time. But didn't they say that she was once sweet on you?'

Lamaxe nodded and coloured in embarrassment.

'Neither Red nor Cliff was interested in her?'

'I don't really know, lad, to be honest. All young men are inclined to accept an offer if it's given freely, eh!'

With this he elbowed Lamaxe in the ribs yet again and winked at him.

'Even priests, I suspect. But I can't think of any good reason why he should take her to Sicily now. Not when her father's about to announce her betrothal to a powerful farmer. Cliff doesn't look for trouble. He's a hard working lad, as is Red, and I can't see him risking my business interests by offending Ayya and Chitah. They both supply us with wool and buy our products, though you would never guess it from the way Ayya talks.'

'What about Gozo? Might she have travelled to Gozo to seek them out?'

'Who knows? I can't think of any reason why she should.'

'So it isn't likely that she went to meet one of them after she ran away from her father?'

'You'd have to ask the lads that. I suppose it's possible however unlikely it is.'

He shrugged his shoulders.

That seemed to be that. Lamaxe had asked his questions but he didn't seem to have progressed any further to a solution and ab Headland was becoming bored. He enjoyed talking about his business and making old sailors' jokes but he had no real interest in the missing girl except in that Ayya had made a fuss which threatened his comfort and the unity of the community. He raised his hands above his head and clapped loudly. One of the women came running.

'Lilith, bring more water for our guest to drink before he starts his journey back, and then find me the High Priest's new skirt. The one we made the other day'.

'Certainly, at once, master,' came the reply.

'Still, good luck!' he said, turning back to the priest. 'I hope you discover where she is and stop old Ayya complaining.'

It was clear to Lamaxe that the interview was over.

Then ab Headland stared at Lamaxe, critically inspecting his worn skirt and rather shabby appearance.

'Oh!' he called after the woman, 'and see if we have another skirt in green which is in better condition than his own for our friend here.'

She bowed and ran off and shortly after both women returned, one carrying a very fine embroidered skirt in a dark green and the other another formal skirt, plainer but still of good quality and of a similar colour.

'Here, try this,' ab Headland said, smiling and offering the second one to Lamaxe who protested, though secretly admiring it.

'Don't worry,' ab Headland said, 'it is not expensive.'

'Thank you,' he said, trying to persuade himself that it was, after all, for temple business.

'You're welcome,' the old man said. 'As the chief, my status is bound up with that of the temple and its priests so it is in my interests that you look tolerably respectable.' He laughed. 'Oh, and next time you come, try to have broadened your mind a little.' He laughed again and handed over the clothes for Lamaxe to carry home.

The priest thanked him profusely and took his leave. He couldn't but admire the workmanship of Trebird's skirt. The patterning was particularly fine. As he turned to go ab Headland called him back.

'One other thing,' he said. 'Tell Trebird that he should fetch her now and as soon as possible he is to facilitate the exchange as we agreed. I have agreed the arrangement.'

'Arrange the exchange?' repeated Lamaxe posing it as a question.

'Just give him the whole message. Remember: as soon as she returns he is to facilitate the exchange. That is what we agreed and now is the time.'

Lamaxe nodded. He had no idea what it meant. Had it something to do with Cloud's return? However, the question was driven from his mind when, just as he was exiting the compound, one of the women ran after him and presented him with two small parcels.

'Which one are you?' he asked, not meaning to be rude.

The girl laughed.

'I am Eve,' she said.

'And what are these?' he asked.

She bowed her head as she spoke.

'One is flatbread and cheese for your supper while you return. The other is a special present from the master. They are sweet things made especially from our honey.'

Lamaxe thanked her most sincerely. He was still not quite sure what to make of ab Headland but he appreciated the consideration given to him. Priests were revered in theory but rarely were their stomachs or their bodies so well catered for.

Nevertheless, much of what ab Headland had said worried the assistant priest. He had never really thought about the world beyond Malta and Gozo. He had never even visited Gozo. Oh, he knew about Sicily and that things were traded there. He had seen a piece of their beautiful copper artwork and been very impressed but he had never given any serious thought to the existence of other peoples. Now the idea that there were also many different gods and goddesses really upset him. What must Our Lady think? Could there really be other gods? Or were they like the ancestors who helped their own families but had limited power? Or were these peoples' beliefs simply wrong and the other gods did not in fact exist. He had never before thought of the idea of questioning the existence of the Goddess. He sat down and ate his supper before it got dark. He was not at all sure that he liked this new world that he was being introduced to. He chewed quietly on his bread and cheese, admiring the quality of the cheese despite himself. Should he be enjoying his food when suffering consternation about theological matters? Perhaps not! Yet, ab Headland had said that Our Lady was widely worshipped in many other places. This cheered him until it occurred to him that what he had actually said was 'in some form or another.' Did that mean that there existed other forms and perhaps rituals other than the ones that he had so painstakingly learned? What implications did that have for his carefully learned theology? It was all very worrying.

As to the missing girl, he didn't see what more that he could do. He had spoken to most of the witnesses, except for those who were abroad – and the more he learned about 'abroad' the less inclined he was to investigate it. He sincerely wished that he had his beautiful sculptor to talk to seriously about it; someone who would understand his ideas and his concerns. Only the Boy had shown any interest and, good though his support was, he didn't really think that he could help very much. He was far too junior. Then there was ab Headland's strange message for Trebird. So, rather despondently, he wandered back to the temple compound. The first thing he saw on entering was the Boy who was just returning from giving Trebird his supper. The High Priest was still sitting on the stone bench where he had left him.

The Boy greeted Lamaxe with great pleasure.

'It is good to see you, Lamaxe,' he said.

'How is the High Priest?' Lamaxe asked. 'Still suffering?'

The Boy laughed.

'It is I who have suffered,' he said. 'But I do think that he is much better. This morning he just moaned whereas now he shouts and makes demands. I think that is more like his normal self.'

Lamaxe thought it best not to comment. However, it did prod his conscience for leaving the Boy to do so much.

'Here,' he said, offering the remaining package. 'These are sweet things from the kitchen of ab Headland. They are for you.'

The Boy opened the package and took a wary bite.

'They are delicately flavoured,' he cried with pleasure. 'They are delicious and strange. Thank you, Lamaxe.'

'You are welcome.'

Then the Boy looked up.

'Have you tried them yourself? If not I think you should for they taste like the food of the Goddess.'

'Be careful,' said Lamaxe sternly. 'That sounds like blasphemy.'

The Boy looked shocked.

'I only meant that they are worthy of the Goddess, sir. Please try one.'

Lamaxe did, and saw exactly what the Boy meant.

'Truly they are delicious,' he replied, 'but you have the rest. I must go to Trebird. I have been absent all day.'

With that he left the Boy to enjoy his treat and Lamaxe headed for the temple. Trebird sat with his foot raised onto the bench so Lamaxe carefully laid the new skirt behind him.

'Good evening, Trebird,' he said. 'I hope that your foot is improved?'

'It is tolerable,' replied the High Priest rather grudgingly.

'Please let me see.'

With that Lamaxe lifted the leg and began to unwrap

the linen. It was obvious immediately that the foot's swelling had gone down considerably.

'There you see,' said the assistant priest. 'My mother's remedy has worked. They always do.'

The only response from Trebird was a mumbled 'harrumph!' Nevertheless, the old man wriggled his toes and his face showed some sense of relief.

'There,' said Lamaxe, 'you will be walking again in a few days.'

The priest then looked Lamaxe expectantly in the eye.

'Well?' he drawled looking about expectantly.

'And what is more,' said Lamaxe, turning with a flourish, 'I have a fine new skirt for you to wear when you do.'

The old man smiled, despite himself.

'Where is it? It had better not be the one you are wearing!' he said, his voice rising.

'Of course not, holiness,' Lamaxe replied quickly. 'Ab Headland was kind enough to offer me an old skirt because my best one is still dirty, but yours is new and very fine. If I help you to your feet, you can try it on.'

Without a second thought the High Priest dragged himself off the stone bench. Lamaxe was amused at the alacrity with which he was suddenly able to stand but noticed also that he favoured his other leg. The pain was obviously genuine. He draped the garment across his boss's arms and the older man examined in detail the fine patterns embroidered onto it.

'It is indeed fine,' he said, putting it on and licking his lips with satisfaction. The old man visibly blossomed. 'Indeed,' he said. Then as an afterthought he added, 'You have done well, Lamaxe.'

He twirled around once but then winced and returned to his seat.

'I think now I must retire to my hut,' he said. 'I feel the need for sleep.'

Lamaxe called the Boy.

While they waited for the Boy, Lamaxe remembered ab Headland's important message to the High Priest.

'Trebird, I also have a message for you from ab Headland but I am afraid that I do not understand it'.

'Never mind what you can understand,' his superior told him, getting grumpy as his foot began to tire. 'Tell me the message.'

'He said, "Tell Trebird that he should fetch her now and as soon as possible he is to facilitate the exchange as we agreed." He would say no more.'

A shadow of a smile passed over the High Priest's face.

'Excellent,' he said. 'He has finally made the arrangements. We can move forward.'

Lamaxe looked at him quizzically.

'Move forward how?' he asked. 'Is this something to do with Cloud?'

'Don't you worry about it.' The older priest waved his hand dismissively, 'You have completed your task in delivering the message to me. The rest is my business.'

At that point the Boy arrived and together they helped Trebird back to his hut within the compound. Then Lamaxe himself retired early to bed but the ideas with which he had been presented that day gave him a restless night, as did his further confusion over the fate of the missing maiden and what else he could possibly do about it.

# 7

Next morning Lamaxe rose from his bed with no great enthusiasm. He had slept poorly and his head ached. He had no wish to suffer further complaints from Trebird about his injured foot and felt tempted to leave the Boy to help him out of bed. However, one of the consequences of being a priest was that he had a keen conscience. He should show his High Priest suitable respect. So, he roused himself, splashed water on his face and dressed. He headed for Trebird's hut. Trebird was not in a good temper despite his acquisition of the new clothes. He had been woken early by Springox but had delayed rising because his foot was sore. Then when he had tried to get up on his own he found that he couldn't. Straw used as a mattress was not very deep and he had struggled and failed to pull himself up into a sitting position. He had called for assistance but Springox had been busy and the Boy, who had had a hard day the day before, had been still asleep and did not come immediately. This only increased his annoyance so that by the time Lamaxe arrived Trebird was cursing him liberally.

'Come, holiness,' Lamaxe oozed, 'I will help you to the

temple where you can pray quietly to Our Lady and ease your pain.'

This produced a 'harrumph!'

'Perhaps once you are there the Boy can fetch clean cloths and we will bathe your injured foot,' he continued as though he had received approval for his suggestion. 'In my hut I have some soothing herbs. The Boy can fetch those as well.'

Trebird merely nodded but he did allow himself to be helped to his feet and led to the semi-circular stone bench in the courtyard where he could sit in relative comfort in the sunshine. The Boy was called and went to fetch the cloth and herbs and Lamaxe attended to him. Once he had settled, Lamaxe had intended to go about his priestly duties but as he got up to go he heard a rhythmic whistling from inside the third temple. He looked up in surprise and met the High Priest's eyes. Trebird nodded.

'Oh, yes,' he said, 'she arrived late last night. Springox came to inform me very early this morning. I was going to send for her anyway.'

'Why didn't you tell me?' Lamaxe moaned inwardly, but he said nothing. He bowed his head to his superior and got to his feet, saying, 'Excuse me, holiness.' He then forced himself to walk sedately while he was still in Trebird's sight but as soon as he was inside the temple he rushed down the middle passage and found her in the paved square. She was whistling as she carved another spiral on the stone benches. So intent upon her work was she that she had not heard him enter.

Lamaxe, for all his yearning for her return, felt suddenly shy.

'Pebble,' he called softly. 'Welcome to the temple.'

She spun around, grinned broadly and, laying down her chisel, rose and put her arms around his neck.

'Lamaxe, I arrived too late last night to call on you. I was told that you were asleep but Springox, who it seems never sleeps, offered me a place. When I arose this morning all you priests were still in bed so I decided to start work in here.'

They stayed there for some time just holding each other, huge grins covering both their faces. Eventually, Lamaxe dragged his eyes off her face and looked at the stone bench in front of her.

'You are carving another spiral,' he said. 'Last time I saw you do that it was to honour the dance of the spring festival.'

'Yes, I am sorry to have been away so long. I must go where the work is.'

'What does it represent now – the spiral?' he asked.

She laughed and put her head on one side.

'The spiral can represent 'the dance,' she said, 'or the 'changing of the seasons', the 'passage of Our Lady across the night sky to the Southern Cross', or the 'movements of the sun', or even 'the unity of life'. Or whatever I like!'

He looked puzzled.

'You see, I like carving spirals. They are very satisfying.' She laughed again at the expression on his face. 'Typical priest! You are so straightforward in your thought processes, dear Lamaxe. Do you not see that this is art? It can represent what I want it to represent. And since I enjoy carving spirals, I have decided that they can represent many things.'

'I see,' he answered, though he was not sure that he did, and not for the first time.

She turned back to the stone and chipped away, the dislodged bits forming a mist which caught in her hair.

'I love to watch you work,' he said.

'And I love you to watch. However, I wanted to make this as a gift to Trebird for his injured foot. I am hoping that he will commission me to make more carvings and then I can stay a while with you.'

Lamaxe couldn't help but grin.

'I do hope so,' he replied.

'In that case,' she said, 'you must leave me to finish this while you pursue your priestly duties. Can you be free after noon?'

'I will make sure that I am,' he replied. 'Will you come to my hut?'

'Certainly not,' she answered, somewhat shocked, 'I am not a concubine or a wife to be summoned like that. We will meet at the compound entrance and walk in the fields.'

Lamaxe was on duty that day and with Trebird indisposed did not dare to skimp on his religious activities. First, he conducted a cleansing in the second temple, using the huge stone bowl which held the water. Then came the formal rites of the morning which he finished rather more quickly than was normal. He had also to offer a libation previously arranged on behalf of one of the farmers. Luckily for him, another couple who arrived unexpectedly wanting a reading of the entrails did so before lunch, so he was able to tell them the likely fate of their business venture and still have time to meet Pebble at the gate. The Supervisor of the Temple Compound, though a grey man, had a good heart and agreed to ensure that Lamaxe would not be missed for an hour or two.

'Thank you, Springox. If I am needed, say I have been called away on a mission of mercy,' the priest advised him.

'Do priests do missions of mercy?' the supervisor asked cynically, but it was a rhetorical question and Lamaxe had already begun making his way to the exit.

He took Pebble's hand and they walked away from the temples. It was a warm, dry day and he steered them away from the normal pathway, though he was careful to avoid where the muddy patch had been just in case. He thought that in his new skirt he looked very distinguished and he did not want splashes of dirt to spoil the effect. They walked for some time, not saying much but enjoying the sunshine and each other's company. Then Pebble lay down in a shady place in the grass and Lamaxe joined her.

'I love your new skirt,' she said. 'It suits you very much.'

'Thank you,' he said, preening himself somewhat.

'However,' she said with a smile, 'I hope your new found pride in it will not prevent your removing it at some point. It has been a long time.'

At this, he demonstrated the ease with which he could disrobe, and she reciprocated. They made love under the afternoon sun, the grass tickling their skin.

Afterwards, Pebble said simply, 'I have missed you, priest.'

'And I you,' he replied. 'Tell me what you have been doing and what has kept you so long?'

'All right!' she said and gave him a brief account.

'If you were at the Hypogeum you could have contacted me,' he complained.

'I saw you there at the funeral, but could not speak. I am so sorry. And, every day I expected to be able to return the next but they were very demanding.'

Lamaxe sulked.

'I couldn't say no, Lamaxe. It is a great honour to have your work judged fine enough for the Hypogeum. 'It is truly one of the wonders of the world.'

He said nothing.

'At Mnajdra they treated me very well and were so impressed with my work that they gave me a present to take away with me.'

'What do you mean?' he asked, still sullen.

She slipped her hand into the skirt lying beside her.

'Look,' she said, taking from it a beautifully carved stone figurine of Our Lady.

'You can carve as well as this,' Lamaxe answered examining the object.

'I can, but do you not see that this is a different style? This comes from Sicily or maybe even beyond. The workmanship is excellent, as is my own of course, but the style is different. I have been trying to practice copying it. And I saw other wonderful things. Do you know that at Mnajdra the Chief has a copper figurine that is so shiny that it glows in the sunlight?'

'Yes I saw one once. I do not understand how they are made.'

'I met a traveller while I was at Mnajdra who was trading something locally. He claimed that they melt rock to produce a liquid which is then moulded in some fashion. It seems fantastic. I would love to see it done.'

Lamaxe, whose interest in art forms did not extend

too far, was startled not so much by the explanation of technique as by the reference to an 'exotic' man.

'Who was this man?' he asked trying to keep the anxiety out of his voice.

She laughed, her face creasing up into deep laughter lines around her eyes.

'Are you jealous?' she asked. 'I am not your wife, you know.'

'I know,' he said miserably.

Pebble remained silent for a moment, not knowing whether to be angry that he should wish to control her behaviour or be flattered by his concerns. She was tempted to tease him but he was such a serious person and she was so fond of him that in the end she decided to allay his fears. Mind you, she had no intention of mentioning the farmer's son.

'Don't worry,' she said. 'I was much more interested in his trinket than in himself.'

Lamaxe was inwardly relieved and changed the subject.

'We should get dressed and return. I have duties to attend to. Could we meet again tonight?'

'We could,' she answered. 'We can come out here and stare at the moon and the great Southern Cross.'

He leaned over and kissed her.

'And,' she added, gently pushing him away, 'you can tell me all that you have been doing.'

It was only then Lamaxe realised that, after having wished so often to be able to discuss the lost girl with her, his joy at her presence had completely taken it from his mind.

'If you were at the Hypogeum,' he asked, 'perhaps you heard of a young girl, newly arrived there?'

'I did not,' she answered. 'What is your interest in young girls?'

'Nothing,' he replied. 'I will tell you later'.

Trebird was very pleased with the new spiral carving when he saw it. Indeed he was so impressed at the prospect that he made the effort to limp into the temple to inspect it. It was then that Pebble discovered that he also had an ulterior motive.

'You are a fine sculptor,' he said. 'You must show this talent to others.'

Pebble looked suspiciously at him. She knew Trebird appreciated her talents but it was unlike him to offer unnecessary compliments.

'I have a little job for you. Ab Headland has requested that you carve a panel for him to exchange for a special gift for the temple – one that will further enhance our fame and his reputation.'

'Of course,' said Pebble, cautiously. 'What does he require?'

'Ah, now!' he said. 'It is not so much what he requires but where.'

Pebble awaited further explanation. After a suitably dramatic pause the High Priest continued.

'You are to go to Sicily to carve a piece for one of their religious sites. Theirs are far inferior to ours, of course,' he continued sanctimoniously, 'and so want the prestige of owning something from our Sacred Isle. I am to come with you to finalise the agreement.'

Pebble was astonished.

She knew that one of the complexities of trade in a Neolithic society was the absence of a common currency of exchange so that without money everything has to be bartered. For big traders in a single product, like ab Headland and the vintner ab Graman this was not a problem. In ab Headland's case he exchanged raw wool for finished products but other exchanges were common. People accepted grain or beasts or stone or copper products, or slaves all of which were valued. For temples and their craft people it was more complicated. Pebble was able to travel from place to place to work and was generally looked after well as a result by the various temples and the local chiefs – well housed and fed. However, anything more than that had to be taken in the form of either grain or durable presents from an employer which either had personal value to herself or exchange value to others. For the temple, wanting an object already made elsewhere it was a particular problem. What might they exchange with a Sicilian craftsman that was fine enough and not readily available in Sicily? She could see what was coming.

Trebird explained that he and ab Headland had found a way of enhancing the temple's already outstanding reputation through owning an image of 'Our Lady' made of this new material called copper. It would establish Tarxian as far superior to all other temples on the 'Sacred Isle' and since ab Headland was their Chief, he believed that it would make him unquestionably the most important chief on the island. Of course, ab Headland could simply trade wool for it himself and then present it to the temple but Trebird wanted it to appear that the temple was so well respected, even abroad, that they would be given such a valuable and unusual object.

'This belongs to a temple, you say?' Pebble asked, her interest engaged.

'It belongs to a priest at Ragusa,' he continued. 'They claim to have a version of our Hypogeum there. Very inferior to ours, of course, and their temples are unspeakable but he wants to stress the similarities to the Sacred Isle and so is prepared to pay handsomely for it. Your style is quite distinctive. They will have nothing quite like it.'

Lamaxe was standing nearby and could see the spark of excitement in Pebble's eyes. The last thing he wanted was for her to disappear again, this time overseas.

'But Trebird,' he said, desperately looking for something to prevent it happening, 'Pebble has only just returned, and anyway, you cannot possibly travel to Sicily with your injured foot. The whole thing must be delayed.'

The High Priest looked down at his still bandaged foot and shook his head.

'But the exchange must be completed as quickly as possible,' he muttered. 'You delivered ab Headland's message. No, I must go. Your mother's herbal recipe, Lamaxe, will just have to work even more quickly.'

A glint came into Pebble's eyes and a smile played on her lips.

'Trebird,' she flattered, 'we cannot risk your foot on such a mission. I can go on my own.'

'Impossible!' replied Trebird and Lamaxe together, though each for his own reason.

'You cannot possibly go on your own,' continued Trebird. 'Suppose you were attacked on your way back and the copper piece stolen. No – quite impossible!'

Lamaxe looked at him aghast.

'Then,' said Pebble slyly, 'you can stay here and Lamaxe can come with me.'

Both Trebird and Lamaxe went to protest but she held up her hand to silence them. It still held her stone hammer and was covered in dust.

'It is the perfect solution,' she continued. 'Lamaxe is senior enough to negotiate the exchange on behalf of the temple but young enough and strong enough to protect me should I be attacked. I would hate to think of my being responsible for you, Trebird, receiving yet more injuries.'

Lamaxe had heard enough of foreign places yesterday to be unsure if he wanted to go, even with Pebble. However, he thought it politic to say nothing for the time being.

Trebird was silent in thought for a few moments. He was a brave man and would certainly give as good as he got in the event of an attack upon his person but he did take his dignity very seriously and hated the idea of being forced to brawl at the roadside, even for the sake of a valuable copper figurine. Also, his foot did hurt.

'Very well,' he said at last. 'That is the solution. You will both go. Let me see, how soon can you start?'

Pebble pretended to hesitate in case Trebird realised he had been duped, but only for a moment.

'I could carve a fine panel, like the animal panels which you have in the temples here but it would be better to carve it in situ. It would mean spending some days there. And, in exchange for my services,' she said, 'you can provide me with living accommodation for the whole of next winter, while I carve you a new panel or two as well. My own supplies of grain are due here soon so it will not even cost you very much.'

The two younger people watched as the High Priest weighed this up but they could see that he had little choice. Both he and ab Headland wanted it done as soon as possible and she would always be useful over winter. After all, she doesn't eat that much, Trebird thought, and he could get a great deal of carving out of her. The apse in the second temple needs repairing.

A broad grin gradually spread over his face.

'Agreed,' he said, at last. Then he hobbled back to his seat outside the third temple and the lovers agreed to meet again that same evening.

It was dark by the time that Lamaxe and the Boy had helped Trebird back to his hut and laid him on his straw. Lamaxe gained the impression that the foot was somewhat improved but allowed the old priest to continue to play the sick role as it was to his advantage that Trebird should stay in his hut for the rest of the evening. He wished the Boy good night and went to find Pebble. The conventions of courtship prevented his entering her hut so he knocked lightly on the door. She came immediately and they strolled out of the compound under the stars. At Pebble's instigation they made love and then lay back to stare at the sky. The Southern Cross dominated the blackness, as it typically did. Lamaxe was in contemplative mood.

'Do you believe that Our Lady lives in the Southern Cross and rides across the sky in the stars?' he asked.

Pebble considered.

'It is what I have always been led to believe,' she answered.

'But do you really believe it?' he persisted.

'You are the priest, so surely you should know. Why do you ask?'

Lamaxe made himself more comfortable, rolling his skirt into a pillow for his neck.

'I have been hearing strange tales about abroad. It seems that in Sicily and the mainland beyond, people worship Our Lady in other ways to us. I mean not according to the rituals that I have so carefully learned. In places they even call her different names. Worse still, it seems other peoples believe in quite different Gods and Goddesses.'

'So what if they do?' she asked. 'How does it affect us?'

'I have learned theology. I have always believed without question that Our Lady created us and the world around us and is the source of our continued lives. It is she who determines the harvests, the weather, our sickness and health.'

'I know no theology, Lamaxe, except what we all are taught, but does it matter if others believe something else?'

'I don't know.' The young priest shook his head. 'I have been taught that the rituals are crucial. That we must get them absolutely correct or disaster may befall us. Why then, would others have different rituals? Why does this not lead to disaster for them and their societies?'

'Maybe Our Lady tests different peoples in different ways?' she answered.

He thought about that.

'Yet, what about people who believe in different gods and goddesses?'

'Clearly they are wrong,' she answered pragmatically, already bored by theological discussion.

'I suppose so,' he answered, rather lamely.

Theological debate was not what Pebble had planned for this romantic evening so she tried to change the subject.

'Apart from theological doubts, what have you been doing with yourself while I have been away?'

Lamaxe turned and kissed her.

'I have been busy,' he answered, 'seeking a missing maiden.'

'Not me, I presume,' she joked.

'Not you. I knew where you were or rather thought I did. I just missed you.'

She couldn't help but smile at this while he proceeded to tell her about Ayya's accusation about his daughter's disappearance and Cloud's mother's request to him to try to find out what had happened to her.

'Why would she ask you?' Pebble demanded.

'Because I knew her, and her mother, in childhood,' he explained. 'Skycloud was always good to me and Ayya is a difficult man to live with.'

'So, you felt sorry for her. How well do you know the girl?'

Lamaxe explained that he had known her as a child and that she had had a crush on him and how guilty he felt now about how he had treated her. He reminded Pebble of the girl they had watched dancing at the spring festival, but she confessed that her interest had been in him not the dancing. This led to further embraces.

Pebble became interested when he explained how he had interviewed various witnesses and what they had said. However, she did not know the participants as well as he and his explanation became increasingly confused and confusing.

'Who are all these people?' she asked again and again.

Lamaxe tried once more.

'I'm sorry,' he said, 'I get confused myself with what happened when and who said what. If only we had a way of recording facts so that we could refer back to them.'

Pebble responded with one of her laughs.

'Well,' she said, 'I am an artist, perhaps I can oblige.'

She made him dress, took him by the hand and led him back into the temple compound.

'Get a torch,' she ordered as they entered the third temple. He did so, and she grabbed hands full of dust from the courtyard and scattered them onto the large entrance stone.

'There,' she said, taking up a sharp stick. 'Now, Ayya ab Featherstone. Tell me about him.'

As Lamaxe told his tale she sketched in the dust a feather and a stone. Under these she pictured a young female in a cloud which she then struck through with a slash.

'That is ab Featherstone's story,' she announced. 'Now, tell me about ab Flintrock.'

She began to sketch a flint chipping and a rock in the dust next to the earlier drawing. But as Lamaxe continued the narrative, he pointed to her pictures,

'No that won't work. How do we distinguish between a stone and a rock? The names will run into one another.'

Pebble moved her head to one side and looked at her handiwork. It was a gesture typical of her when she was thinking and Lamaxe couldn't help but smile.

'I know,' she said, more to herself than Lamaxe, 'I will draw a line around each name so that we can see when one ends and another begins.'

As she progressed she tried to link the characters together. She drew a linking line from the picture of Cloud to the ab Headland motif to show the link between Cloud and Cliff. They continued like this as Lamaxe reviewed the whole case. It still wasn't easy distinguishing the different signs and it took a long time but Pebble now began to see more clearly what Lamaxe had done and what had been said. She was also very pleased with her idea. She wondered if it could be adapted into her artwork. That way you could actually name the people that were being drawn. The idea excited her.

'So, that is what I have been doing,' he concluded. 'The question is what do I do next?'

'It is obvious,' Pebble replied. 'The girl didn't go to the Hypogeum or I would have seen her. She may have gone to the temples but no one saw her there either so she must have gone with one of the young men. So you must question Cliff and Red. If the girl is with them the problem is solved. If not, then she must still be on the island, alive or dead.'

'Yes,' he answered, 'I have been waiting for their return.'

'But you must go after them.'

Lamaxe looked a little shamefaced.

'I did not want to go,' he said. 'And anyway, Trebird would not release me. He disapproves of the search.'

Pebble smiled.

'But dear priest, now you have the perfect excuse to follow them to Sicily with me. We will go and I will make my carving, collect the copper piece, and you will find your boyhood friend and his colleague.'

Lamaxe's face showed a wide range of emotions. He didn't want to admit that the very idea of sea travel gave him palpitations. Yet the idea of being with Pebble appealed greatly and Trebird now seemed committed to the idea. And if he was there he might as well try to solve the problem of the missing girl. Pebble, seeing his confusion, kissed him lightly on the cheek.

'Let us go to our beds now,' she said. 'We can look at my

sketches again tomorrow and see if we can learn any more from them. A good night's sleep will help us to think.'

Lamaxe concurred and they went to their separate huts.

Unfortunately neither of them slept very well. Pebble was excited about her idea of artistically representing thought. If one could do that, one could keep records for a long time and no longer rely only on memory. Lamaxe was also thinking about the representational art but less enthusiastically. He wondered what impact keeping records of events over time might do to the passing on of tradition. Imagine if every error in a ritual were recorded for posterity? Our Lady must see every error, he thought, but she forgives and forgets. With records, we could never forget. However, what really kept him awake most was the idea of foreign travel. He had been fishing with his brother in the shallows but he had also seen the boats leaving the shelter of the harbour and they seemed perilously small compared to the size of the sea. However, as the night wore on and he still could not sleep, the idea took on a somewhat more positive aspect. If Pebble was to go to Sicily and negotiate the deal, he wanted to be there with her.

The next morning neither of them were at their best. Lamaxe and the Boy helped Trebird out of his bed again. He was not limping so badly now. Pebble helped herself to some porridge in the kitchen. As soon as they could they met up and went to look again at Pebble's drawings. Pebble was ahead of him and cried out.

'They are gone!' she said.

The stone had been swept clean. Lamaxe's hand went to his mouth. He was horrified.

'Our Lady's revenge?' he whispered.

'Hardly,' replied Pebble. 'It looks to me like a human hand.'

'Of course!' exclaimed Lamaxe; 'the Sweeper. He comes early.'

He looked at Pebble as a single tear made its way down her cheek.

'Not such a permanent reminder,' she said.

'Still it was a good idea,' he offered, 'and it helped to clarify the ideas last night, didn't it?'

Pebble responded with a weak smile. Her disappointment was obvious.

'I'll just get back to my carving,' she said. 'At least that is permanent. Make sure you get the idea over to Trebird that we are the ones to go to Sicily. I don't want him changing his mind.'

Lamaxe was still ambivalent but he couldn't disappoint her.

'Yes, Pebble,' was all he said as he made his way towards the temple door.

Both Lamaxe and Pebble, in their separate parts of the temple complex were disturbed by a noise outside. They put down what they were doing and went to look. There stood the Superintendent of the Temple Compound with two vessels, one of water and one of wine and a sack of food.

'What is happening, Springox?' Lamaxe asked.

'Trebird is preparing for his journey,' he answered.

'Journey?'

'Indeed. His journey to arrange a ship for you.'

'So soon?' asked Pebble, arriving from the other direction. 'He is keen,' she added smugly.

'But he can still hardly walk?' said Lamaxe.

Springox smiled.

'It is possible that his injury is less extensive than when you saw him yesterday. Our Lady can do remarkable things, can she not?'

'I thought he was exaggerating it,' whispered Pebble to her lover.

'In any case,' continued Springox, 'I have arranged transport. The Boy is fetching it now.'

'But surely, he could send a message?' Lamaxe said.

'He insists on making the arrangements himself,' came the reply, 'so he can take equal credit with ab Headland.'

Sure enough, a rumbling sound marked the arrival of Trebird, surrounded by woollen rugs, ensconced in a contraption pulled by an ox and led by the Boy. It was a kind of platform on skis which dragged along the ground.

'I shall be gone for about a day,' the High Priest announced. 'Lamaxe is responsible for all religious duties until I return. Pebble can practice her art.'

He turned to face her.

'Make sure it is good enough to justify the exchange,' he said.

With that, Springox handed over the food and drink, and the cart moved off.

The assistant priest and the sculptor looked at each other and burst out laughing. Springox tried hard to suppress his own hilarity and bid them goodbye with his usual suaveness.

'Well,' said Pebble, 'a whole day on our own and then a journey together. How exciting!'

Lamaxe grinned back at her, but he couldn't help the

sick feeling in his stomach at the prospect of sea travel, even with his beloved. He tried to mask this by being businesslike.

'I must attend to the daily rituals,' he said. 'I'm afraid I'm going to be busy on my own. Will you practice your carving?'

'It isn't technique I need to practice,' she answered. 'What I need to do is think of a suitable subject and how I'm going to carve it. Perhaps I'll go for a walk.'

Lamaxe kissed her lightly and went to prepare for the various worshippers and supplicants he expected to arrive soon.

Pebble collected a shawl from her hut and left the compound. She'd had an idea, but not about carving. She had decided to help Lamaxe with his other problem. He had said that he had interviewed various workers in the fields and that no one had seen the girl, but, thought Pebble, who would answer yes to a priest and risk being dragged into a serious case? If you are a field worker, it is usually better to play dumb. It was a pleasant afternoon and as she walked she found that she had time to think about the carving. She passed some piglets suckling on their mother and thought what a good picture that would make. The piglets represented fertility, which satisfied the religious bit, but they could be carved with real life and humour, which would satisfy her own artistic requirements. She was full of joy and found herself skipping along the path. At the sound of voices she stopped and looked around in embarrassment. There were women working in the fields.

# 8

When Pebble returned to the temple complex in the evening, Lamaxe was still busy. She found him reading entrails in the third temple. An elderly couple were watching anxiously but it appeared that the signs were favourable for whatever venture was envisioned by the supplicants, and they went away very pleased.

'Last one of the day,' Lamaxe told her. 'Let's see what the kitchens have for us.'

After eating, the pair went for a walk outside the temple gates. After a gentle bout of love-making they lay on their backs and starred at the Southern Cross.

'It is beautiful,' Lamaxe sighed. 'I wonder if Our Lady can see us down here now?'

Pebble frowned.

'You are supposed to be the theologian,' she said. 'I thought that Our Lady was only interested in big things, not in individuals?'

'So it is said,' he replied, 'but I do call on her help with my own problems from time to time. She doesn't seem to mind.'

'I hope she isn't looking now,' Pebble said, covering her

nakedness with her skirt. Then she rolled herself up in it, turned over and poked him in the stomach.

'Well,' she said, 'never mind theology, tonight you can rely on me to help with your other problem. On my walk today I met several workers in the fields. They told me that your missing Cloud was seen heading for the temple. At least a young woman of her description went that way.'

'Then why didn't they tell me?' Lamaxe asked. 'Surely people will tell the truth to a priest?'

Pebble giggled.

'Don't you see, dear boy, that priests represent a sort of power. If you are a poor worker in the field priests mean authority and that means trouble. Gone are the days when all were equal and worked alongside each other and with the temple. Now there are rich men who, they think, conspire with the priests against them.'

Lamaxe was affronted.

'I don't conspire with rich men!' he said.

She said nothing so he changed the subject.

'If Cloud was really seen heading in the direction of the temple, was she actually going there or was she on her way to the Hypogeum as she told her father?'

'That I don't know and neither did they. If no one saw her there, she could just as easily have been heading for the coast and a rendezvous with Cliff as her father suggested. Or, for that matter with one of the other lads.'

'Yes,' he mused, 'I'd almost forgotten about Tornbark and Blackwing. I suppose I ought to interview them as well.'

Then he shook his head.

'It's all so confusing. What am I to tell Sky?'

Pebble thought that with any luck they would have

left for Sicily before Sky came to the temple again so he wouldn't have to tell her anything but all she said to Lamaxe was, 'Wait till we get to Sicily and you can ask Cliff yourself.'

The next morning Lamaxe was busy again in the temple. It was the middle of the morning when Trebird returned. He heard the scraping of the cart as it entered the courtyard, even over the sound of his own chanting. He continued with the ceremony but it didn't take too long as there was no blood sacrifice. Even so, by the time he left the building Trebird and the cart had disappeared. He went searching for them but found instead the Superintendent of the Temple Compound. Springox greeted him with: 'Ah, good! You are ready. Get your possessions together for the journey. Trebird has arranged your transport. You must leave at once.'

'But I have ceremonies to perform this afternoon,' he replied. 'What is the hurry?'

'Trebird will take the ceremonies with the help of the Boy. He has arranged for you to take a boat at dawn tomorrow morning to Gozo. From there you will transfer to a ship which will take you to Sicily. All is arranged. Now hurry or you will not get to the coast in time.'

Such impatience from such a patient man surprised the assistant priest. He had no worries about packing his possessions. After all he had so few. He decided that he had better find Pebble and have some food to sustain him for the journey. He found her in the kitchens already eating.

'Come eat,' she called with her mouth full. 'Trebird insists we must leave immediately. He has sent messages that we are arriving this evening so the boat can leave at first light.'

Lamaxe sat down and began to eat, though his appetite had suddenly disappeared. He couldn't help thinking how pleasantly peaceful life had been before Cloud went missing and Pebble returned to the temple but instantly felt guilty for thinking such a thing and ate his food, though still without relish.

Before leaving he put on some leather sandals to protect his feet. He changed into old clothes for the journey but very carefully packed his best green priestly skirt and his cap. If he was going to represent his temple abroad he must be sure to look as impressive as he could. Pebble was waiting in a sensible tunic and pleated skirt, her head covered to keep off the sun. Her bundle, secured to her back, seemed considerably larger than his own. At this point, Springox came hurrying and presented them with more food and water for the journey which Lamaxe packed away. Then Trebird, looking very grand, bade them farewell. He gave Lamaxe the carved bead which he always wore around his neck on a length of sinew. It was, he said, a token of the authority of the temple. The assistant priest was quite touched. The gesture was only slightly spoiled when Trebird warned him not to lose it. He placed the cord carefully around his neck and dropped the bead inside his tunic where it should be safe. With that the two travellers walked out of the temple compound and waved goodbye.

They were to go north and make for a little inlet on the east side of what seamen referred to, partly ironically, as 'the grand harbour'. This was the shortest distance to the sea which is why Trebird had arranged for the boat to meet them there. However, Pebble decided on reflection that whilst they were due at the inlet that evening, the boat would not leave before the next morning so she insisted that they take a diversion to the Hypogeum.

'But why?' asked the priest.

'I have been thinking,' she said. 'I could ask my friend Chisel if he has had any news about Cloud.'

Lamaxe shook his head.

'Why do you masons have such strange names?' he muttered.

Pebble laughed.

'Because we are such strange people,' she answered. Then she leaned across and stroked his hair.

'And also because carving stone can be a noisy business. Nicknames are easier to shout.'

They walked on in silence, hand in hand.

However, when they arrived at the Hypogeum there was no sign of Chisel. Pebble sought out the other masons and made enquiries.

'He left this morning,' he told her. 'The work is finished and he has a girl back home who he wishes to marry so he hurried away.'

She then asked all the other masons for news of Cloud but no one had seen any young girls'

'I think this is a dead end,' said Lamaxe.

'Well,' Pebble replied. 'I suppose that we can always take it up again when we return from Sicily.'

So, they strolled on towards the coast. Lamaxe was very quiet and it took some time for Pebble to realise why.

'Don't worry about Chisel,' she said, 'he was just a nice bloke.'

Lamaxe knew roughly the place they were to go because he had occasionally been there to fish with

Oyeh. He remembered quite enjoying the fishing in the protected inlet, but not the one time his brother had taken him into deeper waters. Deep water was something he feared, though nothing seemed to worry Pebble so he kept his concerns to himself. He remembered that Tornbark ab Treefall, one of the boys pursuing Cloud, lived on his father's farm not far from their route so they made a detour to see him. His father's farm was small in comparison with Ayya's but well kept. The son and his father were in the fields so they approached and asked him about Cloud. He had heard of her disappearance and seemed visibly upset by it.

'I am very fond of her,' he told them, 'though she seems not to care for me.'

'Where were you when she disappeared, two days after my father's funeral?' Lamaxe asked.

'I remember your father well,' interrupted ab Treefall senior. 'A man worthy of great respect.'

'Thank you,' replied the priest, determined not to be distracted. 'But where was your son?'

'Why, here with me,' the father replied. 'We had taken a day to attend the funeral and had to catch up with our work.'

'It is true,' Tornbark added. 'I remember that day. I weeded the upper field.'

They nodded in unison.

'What about your friend Blackwing?' Pebble asked. 'Was he also at the funeral and did you see him afterwards?'

'Blackwing ab Stonecrop?' the father asked. 'He had injured his ankle and could not walk.'

'Poor Blackwing,' Tornbark replied. 'He did it several days before and couldn't even go to the funeral.'

They thanked them and left. Then they stopped shortly and shared the food and water.

'What do you think?' Lamaxe asked.

'The lad seemed genuine,' she answered.

'I thought he was genuine as well. Of course, he could just be lying. What about the other one?'

'Well, you can't fake an injured ankle for long. Not if you are a working farmer,' Pebble replied.

Lamaxe nodded.

'I agree. It seems hopeless.'

After a brief interlude they continued on their way. Even so it was nearly nightfall when they reached the coast and they failed to find the boat anywhere in the gloom. Pebble was quite unconcerned about this.

'There is nothing to worry about,' she said. 'If they have been commissioned by the temple they will not leave without us.'

'But you said earlier that they must not be delayed,' he responded.

'Oh that!' she answered. 'That was just for Trebird's benefit. Of course they will not dare to leave without us.'

They found a sheltered spot and settled down for the night. The air was warm. Despite the stars and the familiarity of the Southern Cross looking down, Lamaxe felt strangely isolated away from his familiar temple complex.

They found the boat early the next morning moored in a small inlet. To Lamaxe's eye it seemed little bigger than the boat in which he used to go fishing. However, the two men in it seemed full of confidence and they left forthwith. The plan was to head to the mouth of the 'grand harbour' and then turn west following the coast along the whole of its length until they reached the most northerly tip of the island. From there they would head out into more open waters towards Gozo where they would meet up with the larger trading ship that would take them all the way to Sicily. These little boats were designed to hug the coast. Indeed, in the absence of proper roads, it was a normal form of travel to sail from inlet to inlet. However, this made it no more attractive to Lamaxe. He sat in the centre of the boat and, once they had left the 'grand harbour,' he resolutely kept his head down and looked neither to his left nor to his right. The sound of the sea, the oars swishing through the water and the rocking of the boat were upsetting enough for him. He found himself unconsciously stroking Trebird's stone bead until he realised, felt embarrassed and put it away. Pebble, on the other hand, loved every minute of the journey. She constantly asked the boatmen the names of places seen along the coast, admired the sandy beaches to be seen in some of the coves and even leaned over the side in an attempt to observe fish swimming alongside. The boatmen laughed and joked with her, pointing out other items of interest that she had missed. Some of the scenery was spectacular. Normally, the boat would have pulled into various inlets to deliver goods and see friends but today they had been set the task of getting these two to Gozo and, since the temple had instructed them, they were determined to do so in time.

As the sun warmed his back and nothing dreadful happened, Lamaxe began to relax sufficiently to think about the task ahead. It occurred to him that the programme that Trebird had set would leave him no time in Gozo to visit and interview Rocksand ab Graman, Red's father and the winemaker, to see if Cloud had travelled there. He didn't know where the ab Graman lands were but it was obvious to him that they would not arrive at the smaller island until evening and were expected to leave early the next morning. Maybe, if necessary, they could call on the way home. He consoled himself that at least they would get to Sicily and so see Cliff and Red, that much sooner. He wanted to get it over with.

At last they reached a wide bay with two tiny islands at its far side.

'Not much further now,' the boatmen told them.

They rounded the head and then cut across the mouth of another bay. Although land was always in sight, the shore seemed to Lamaxe to be a long way away. Pebble loved it and marvelled at the birds flying around the cliff head. Eventually they reached the other side of the bay and at the next headland turned north into open sea. Lamaxe closed his eyes completely. Strangely, he felt better, although the continuous movement of the boat was a constant reminder of where he was. Pebble was excitedly pointing to an ever enlarging Gozo directly ahead. After a while Lamaxe opened his eyes and saw for himself that they were almost there. He could see clearly the coastline and a sort of harbour where the larger ships were berthed. It was comforting. He could even see the moving dots of people along the shore.

It took them longer to land than Lamaxe had expected. Distances are misleading on the water. They entered a wide bay and pulled to the west to land on a small beach. The boatmen helped them off the boat and they collected their luggage, such as it was. Pebble thanked the boatmen with great animation and they smiled and waved as the two adventurers made their way along the beach. The next job was to find the ship they were to use. Trebird had been very efficient in finding and commissioning a ship so quickly but he had omitted to give them any indication of how they were to recognise it. After several false starts, at least two of which resulted in offers to Pebble 'to ditch the priest and come aboard' they came upon a rather rundown looking vessel, the captain of which was loudly cursing his crew. The crew joined in the vulgarity and Lamaxe was disappointed to hear a number of serious blasphemies. This didn't seem to bode well for a ship commissioned by the temple. Nor did it settle his worry about the open sea. What if Our Lady was angry at the words and decided to punish them? Nevertheless, it turned out that this was the correct ship. Pebble and Lamaxe discerned that Captain Crowfish's curses arose from the fact that crucial repairs on the ship were still not completed and it could not embark until they were done.

At the first break in his invective, Pebble shouted to attract his attention.

'Captain! Is this the boat commissioned by the Tarxian temple?'

He turned and stared down at the two on the quay.

'I expected a priest and a sculptor,' he said. 'I can see what must be a priest. Are you the sculptor?'

'I am,' she replied. 'What is the delay?'

'I was determined to leave early in the morning, but repairs are not completed. We need new cleats and will have to wait until the day after tomorrow before we can leave.'

Lamaxe spoke.

'Do you mean that we have dashed here only to now be delayed?'

He said this with apparent indignation but secretly it occurred to him that he might yet get to see Rocksand ab Graman before they left the island.

'Indeed. It is more serious for me,' the captain continued bad-temperedly. 'As well as you two, I have a cargo I have promised to deliver on time. The sea is unpredictable enough without this.'

Then he shrugged his shoulders and stepped down onto the quay next to them.

'No matter,' he said, calming down and holding out his hand in greeting. 'My name is Crowfish, captain of this fair vessel. In truth, the delay is not really the crew's fault either. It is poor materials. But they must be replaced. You'll have to kick your heels for a day while we finish preparing the ship.'

Lamaxe returned the greeting but also expressed his anxiety.

'Does this mean that the boat isn't safe?'

'Ship!' replied the captain grumpily. 'Boats are tiny vessels that work the coast. This is a ship. Of course it is safe. Well, it will be once the repairs are complete.'

Lamaxe did not find this entirely reassuring.

'I have a message from the temple for the winemaker here – ab Graman,' he explained. 'I am seeking a missing woman.'

'So have I – all my life,' the captain laughed.

Lamaxe ignored the poor joke.

'Would there be time for us to visit the winemaker before we leave?' he asked.

The captain considered this.

'I know of him. His farm is in a deep valley, near our Gozo temples. It is a good walk but if you are fit and you start early enough you could make it there and back before nightfall, as long as you make your visit brief. But I will leave the morning after, with or without you. I can't delay any longer'

Lamaxe looked at Pebble who nodded in agreement.

'We have enough food for another day. You must show us the way and we will start immediately'

The captain showed them how to reach the farm, scratching a crude map in the sand. He also pointed out the location of an old shelter near the beach where they might rest overnight on their return if it was late. However, he warned them against travelling in the dark because, like Malta, the paths were very rough and few and far between so that it was dangerous to travel without being able to see your footings.

'And be careful. Pirates dock here as well as traders,' he added.

Now he had calmed down he seemed prepared to play the host and offered them water to wash in and a skin of clean drinking water to take with them. Finally he insisted on accompanying them as far as the shelter. They made a cursory inspection but it seemed dry and there was reasonably fresh straw. They thanked him and, then, refreshed, were ready to proceed on their next journey.

# 9

They started out early in the morning. Ab Graman lived some way inland in a pleasant valley not far from the old Gozo temples and the local Hypogeum at Xaghra. It was a long walk and much of it uphill. The paths were reasonably well kept as far as the temple site but thereafter were pretty rough and frequently disappeared altogether. Lamaxe was used to walking but found he had some difficulty in keeping up with Pebble. Maltese girls were strong and fit and he presumed that it must be all that work in the fields that caused this but then in Pebble's case she spent most days crouching down chipping stone. This meant that her arm muscles were well developed but he was surprised to discover that her calf muscles were similarly so. He had only looked upon her calves from an aesthetic point of view before.

They came upon the temples first. They were remarkable, dwarfing his own temple complex by their size. They were much older and dominated by a huge surrounding wall. He begged Pebble to stop and explore them but she insisted that they didn't have enough time so after a quick look inside, they continued on their way. Lamaxe was interested to see that the inside walls were painted deep red. This gave him ideas that he might put to Trebird when he got home. Then they passed by the local Hypogeum, very like the Tarxian one, but smaller.

The shallow valley itself, when they got there, was well worth seeing. The setting was very attractive and the sight of the vines was unusual in a country dominated by mixed cereal and meat production. It was quite unlike any farm Lamaxe had seen on Malta. The river strolled down the middle of the valley, wandering as it did so. The vines stretched out along the hillside in rows in contrast to the meandering of the river. He noticed that the bulk of the vines were planted on just one side of the valley and wondered why this should be so. The farmstead itself was very like the ones at home except for an absence of larger animals. There were a few pigs running around the yard but apart from that only cats and dogs. Clearly, this was a specialist farm.

Rocksand ab Graman greeted them pleasantly enough, after Lamaxe had introduced himself as a childhood friend of Cliff. Pebble smiled sweetly at him but said nothing and sat in the corner. However, when Lamaxe explained that he was following up the accusations made by Ayya, the vintner's expression turned cold.

'I am obliged to do business with that man,' he said, 'but that does not mean that I like him. Now, had he disappeared, you might have reason to view me with some suspicion, because I would not weep were he himself under the ground.'

He laughed to indicate that this was intended to be humorous. 'However,' he continued, 'any accusations against Red are absurd. As to Cliff, I cannot believe that he would threaten his father's trade by such an action. Both he and my son are responsible men.'

Lamaxe offered an ingratiating smile and raised his hands in front of his face in a gesture of submission.

'I merely wanted to clear the air,' he said. 'May I ask a few simple questions to help me to clarify where the girl might be now?'

Rocksand inclined his head in assent.

'First, I take it that you have not been visited by the girl, Skycloudyoung? That she has not been staying here?'

'I have never met her to my knowledge unless possibly as a child. I used to go to her father's farm on business occasionally when younger. Now I prefer not to meet him. He is not a pleasant man to do business with. But business is business. These days, Red goes or I send messengers for his orders.

'So she has never been here?'

'No. I know of her because the boys have spoken of her. They call her Cloud. Cliff often comes here to visit when his ship docks on his way home from Sicily.'

'So Red has also met her regularly?

'From time to time only, when he goes to visit Cliff in Malta. Three, maybe four times a year at most.'

'Thank you,' the assistant priest continued. 'Am I correct in believing that your son, Red, has sailed to Sicily on business?'

'You are!' he answered. 'He left a few days ago. It was two days before the last time I attended the temple. I celebrated the rituals down the road.' He gestured vaguely in the direction of the temples. 'He is visiting some business contacts of mine to discuss the sale of some of the coming vintage.'

'And does he often go on your behalf?'

'He does. Over the last two years he has begun to do so

regularly. I enjoy the comfort of my own home nowadays and anyway I am getting a little too old for sea travel. He enjoys it, as I used to do when I was younger.'

'I see,' continued Lamaxe, '... and please forgive me for asking, but is there someone in Sicily who could confirm his presence there?'

Rocksand became irritated.

'You are rude and persistent even for a priest.'

Lamaxe said nothing and after a moment the vintner answered the question.

'Of course there is. My business associates. But if you want the evidence of someone you would already know and trust, then Cliff is also there now on business. I gather they usually lodge together when they are there, which, as I said, is quite frequently.'

'Thank you,' said the priest. 'And Cloud is not with either of them?'

'I am sure she is not. It was a regular business trip. However, I did not see Cliff leave, so I suppose anything is possible.'

'So, have you any idea why Ayya should make such an accusation against Cliff?'

Rocksand hesitated for a moment but then replied in the negative. Lamaxe raised an eyebrow quizzically.

'Well, only that he likes to make trouble,' was the final answer.

Lamaxe could think of nothing further to ask so thanked him profusely and apologised if he had upset him.

At this, the vintner relaxed and his attitude began to change. He stood up and walked over to a shelf where there was a clay jug.

'I am being a poor host,' he said. 'After all, you are a priest and a guest. I insist that you both try some of my wine.'

Pebble had sat quietly during the whole of this discussion and was pleased and a little surprised to be offered wine alongside the men. Lamaxe had no desire for wine but was afraid to offend such an important man by saying no. After all, the wine was the man's livelihood. In any case, he understood that this was good wine and his opportunities for imbibing it were very limited. He thought that at least he ought to be able to say that he had tasted it.

'Thank you,' he replied. 'That is most kind.'

Pebble also smiled and inclined her head in agreement.

The vintner poured the wine and then tasted it himself with evident pleasure. Pebble was unused to wine but found it an interesting change from water. It tasted vaguely of fruit with a strong acidic aftertaste, not entirely pleasant. Even so, she thought it wise to praise it highly and Rocksand smiled as he resumed his seat.

'So you have no idea why Ayya made his accusation against Cliff?' Pebble asked, smiling sweetly.

The winemaker hesitated once more but he seemed to have relaxed now.

'I am told that Cliff was seen to spend much time with Cloud at your local spring festival. I was unaware of this myself, you understand, but Red told me of it later. It appears that they danced together a great deal. Red was teasing Cliff about it. Ayya apparently did not like it. He wanted no distractions from her alliance with Chitah ab Flintrock.'

'Was the relationship continued after that?'

'I have absolutely no idea. Red and Cliff laughed about it

so I do not think that Cliff took it seriously. Also, Cliff works hard. He has taken a lot of responsibility for the business off his father's hands. He frequently goes near Ayya's lands on business, but I have no reason to believe that he sees a lot of her. Frankly, I think, like Red, he is far too busy to have much free time. Even at home they both work hard in the family businesses so their main free time would be between business meetings when they are in Sicily or beyond. What the two do there, apart from business, I can tell you little about.' He laughed. 'I know what I did there when I was younger.' With this he dug Lamaxe in the ribs. 'What I do know is that they are both very good at business.'

Lamaxe pondered his reply.

'So, he could have taken her?'

Rocksand looked as though he was about to lose his temper but then chuckled.

'Curse you priest, you are persistent,' he said, humour in his voice. 'I do not believe that he has but we will only know for sure when the two of them return.'

Lamaxe thought that an honest answer and could think of little else to ask.

'Another wine?' the vinter asked instead. 'Do you like it?'

In truth Lamaxe was not sure how much he did like it. It seemed to leave sediment in his mouth when he drained the cup and the aftertaste was not entirely pleasant. He also knew enough about alcohol to realise that it was pretty strong and he needed to keep a clear head. However, he could not say as much to an important man who he had just had the cheek to question.

'Thank you,' he said. 'It is very fine, and shows the quality of your produce.'

This proved to be exactly the right thing to say. The vintner beamed at him and turned to Pebble. After her initial uncertainty, she decided that she liked it and the feelings it generated. It made her feel warm inside and more than a bit giggly.

'I like it very much,' she answered, holding out her cup for a refill, 'it makes me feel jolly.'

This greatly pleased the vintner who then called for a servant to bring bread. Lamaxe was grateful for the bread as the wine was so strong and he was unused to it. The bread itself was freshly baked and of a far better quality than that to which he was used. Pebble declined the bread but accepted yet another cup of wine.

After a few more cups they found that they were enjoying ab Graman's company. Once his guard was down he proved to be a pleasant though serious businessman. Lamaxe couldn't help contrasting his seriousness with the dreadful jokiness of Lamool ab Headland. He settled down to forget his current tasks and enjoy himself in pleasant conversation. Too late Lamaxe realised how much Pebble had been drinking. She began to hiccough. He decided that they had better leave as soon as possible before she disgraced herself. They still had time to make the return journey but he had no desire to have to carry her all the way. The vinter seemed almost sorry that they were leaving and Lamaxe wondered if, now that his son had taken over the work of the business, he might be rather lonely. Ab Graman insisted on offering them more bread and fruit for the journey.

Lamaxe thanked him but assured him that they would not take long to return to the port.

'No,' said ab Graman, 'I meant for your journey tomorrow. It is a long journey.'

'Is it?' asked Lamaxe. He had been sufficiently worried about the idea of travelling at all on a ship that he hadn't really thought about how long it would take.

'Yes. The distance is about three times the total length of the Sacred Isle.

Lamaxe looked appalled.

'Do you mean that we could be on board overnight? How does it steer in the dark?'

'By the stars of course. It is perfectly safe, I assure you. In fact,' he added, 'it is really rather beautiful at night.'

Lamaxe looked amazed.

'But it can be rough,' the vintner told him.

'Rough?' He was aghast.

The vintner nodded. Pebble was finding it hard not to giggle all the time now so Lamaxe had no choice but to graciously accept the food and water and make their goodbyes.

Pebble waved cheerily as they left and at first they made reasonable progress but gradually she became less and less steady on her legs. She stumbled a couple of times and began to drift away from the path even after they had passed the temples where the way was clearly marked. Lamaxe, the leather water flask slung over his shoulder, firmly grasped her arm and led her. He was becoming more than a little annoyed with her. He knew from personal experience the effect of alcohol and was concerned both about getting her back that evening and about how well she would cope with the sea journey tomorrow. Indeed, if truth were told, he was worried about how he would cope with the sea journey, especially if she were ill. Their progress became slower and slower and he found himself taking more and more of her weight. The day was progressing and night came suddenly in that part of the world. They were within about quarter of a mile of the quayside when she begged to be allowed to sit and rest. Much against his better judgement he agreed to a short respite. She sat crossed-legged on the ground and closed her eyes. Lamaxe opened the bread and cheese and ate a little. He also drank deeply from the water flask.

After a short rest he insisted that they go on. He hauled her up by putting his arms under her shoulders and forced her to walk but he found that he was having to take nearly all of her weight now. As a result he had to concentrate on her rather than where they were going so it came as something of a surprise when they were verbally challenged.

''ey priest!' came a call.

Lamaxe looked around.

'You gotta be de tempule priest come to trade. Tha' right?'

The accent was thick and at first Lamaxe was uncertain what was being said.

There were two of them, dressed rather strangely to Lamaxe's eyes. He supposed they must be sailors since their clothing was a bit like Captain Crowfish's men and they had that same general swagger. One was small and wiry with spiky hair and the other quite large – nearly six feet tall, broad of beam and swarthy. The small one spoke again.

'Come on, you give! Yeh?' He gestured with his hand.

Lamaxe wasn't used to foreign accents. They were clearly not from Sicily although they spoke the language after a fashion. He found it even more difficult to pick up the implications of their words. Theft was almost unknown in the Sacred Isle. What did exist there was largely petty and pretty much restricted to sharp practice in trade. Had these sailors misunderstood his mission and thought that he was carrying valuables? Were they really trying to steal something from him? Him – a priest?

'I am a priest of the Tarxian temples,' Lamaxe said in his most sonorous voice. 'How can I help you?'

The bigger one began to fidget with the large piece of wood he carried which suggested to Lamaxe that their intentions were clearly not amiable. Although violence between individuals was not uncommon in his own island, it was mostly the result of quick tempers so that he had never come across deliberately planned violence, except ritually in the temple, of course; certainly never robbery with violence. Indeed, there was no word in his language for it. The nearest he could come to a word which described what they were doing was 'piracy'. But pirates only robbed at sea.

The small wiry one scratched himself.

'We 'ear, you 'ere t' trade? You 'ave valuables to barter, yeh! Show us.'

Lamaxe dropped the water container and let Pebble sink to the ground. She flopped cross-legged as he deliberately placed himself between them and her. Then, pointing to her, he said, 'She is the only thing of value I have.'

'If tha's true, maybe we 'ave 'er,' the wiry one said.

Lamaxe was confused. Could they be after Cloud and had mistaken Pebble for her? He had to concentrate. But no, he decided, they were looking for valuables. They had mistaken the purpose of their trade with Sicily. The larger one gave an ugly laugh and played with his cosh, slapping it into the palm of his hand. This confirmed to Lamaxe that he wasn't going to be able to talk his way out of this one. He had to think fast. He surmised that, being foreigners, they would not know much about priests from the Sacred Isle. They wouldn't know, for example, that a priest always carried a flint knife when away from home in case he was asked to make a sacrifice or read some entrails. He always kept his secure in his loincloth. By appearing to scratch his hip, as he talked he was able to carefully work it loose and into the palm of his hand so that it didn't show.

'We have nothing of value,' he repeated.

The two men exchanged glances and then the larger one stepped forward with his cudgel swinging.

'We see 'bout that!' he said.

Lamaxe didn't hesitate. He braced himself awaiting the onslaught and then kicked out without warning, hitting the big man squarely between the legs. It hurt his own toe despite the protection of the sandal so he thought that he had struck home. The big man's eyes went wide and his mouth puckered comically as he groaned and fell, clutching himself. Spiky hair moved forward threateningly waving a large knife in front of him. It glinted of copper. Lamaxe stepped forward himself and before his opponent had time to think he lashed out with his own flint knife aiming it towards the throat. He missed but slashed across the cheek of the smaller man who, gasping, clutched his face. For a few seconds they were both rooted to the spot staring at each other. Then the man's cheek gushed blood from near his neck right up to his nose. As he brought his hands down from his face they instantly dripped bright red. The man looked down at his hands and then at his companion helpless on the floor. He turned and ran. Just to be safe, Lamaxe turned to the other one, who, still breathless, was just beginning to raise his head from the ground. He kicked him again, this time in the mouth. There was a cracking sound and he went down groaning. Then Lamaxe turned to help Pebble to her feet. She appeared to have slept through the whole thing. He gently awakened her and pulled her up, keeping his knife hand free and pointing it at the injured man. He waited, holding her, while the thug spat out teeth and crept quietly away until there was sufficient distance for him to rise and run towards the temples.

'Come on,' Lamaxe said to the sculptor. 'We have to get back before it gets dark.'

The rest of the journey was uneventful though very slow. It was becoming seriously dark by the time they reached the coast and Lamaxe was very watchful for any return of their attackers. But he saw nothing and eventually decided that they had gone to lick their wounds, literally in the case of the spiky-haired one. He soon found the shed they had been allocated for sleeping. Pebble began to gag as they walked so Lamaxe led her into a bushy area behind the building where she couldn't be seen. There she began to vomit violently. This she did several times. When she was empty, he used the water from their flask to gently wash her face and then trickled some drops between her lips.

'Better?' he asked.

'Ugh!' she replied.

He laughed at this and gently led her into the building

where he found some bedding straw. He laid her down on her side on the straw in case she was sick again and sat next to her until he thought she was asleep.

His heart was still racing so he wasn't sleepy himself. After a while he went outside again to look at the Southern Cross and talk to Our Lady. He was anxious about two things. Firstly, he wondered what kind of a world he had wandered into where people were attacked for their property. Never mind that he was a priest and so should receive extra respect. It seemed quite wrong. He was worried about his own reactions as well. He couldn't reconcile the unthinking and fearless way with which he had dealt with their attackers with his foolish but genuine fear of the sea. He had felt no great fear of the knife and the cosh although the attack was clearly real and personal. Of course, his unthinking response had been partly to protect Pebble who was in no condition to protect herself at the time. Even so, it did not seem to fit with his strong irrational fear of going on water. Why should he be afraid of crossing the sea? The sea had no argument with him. It posed no special threat. He didn't believe in Gods other than Our Lady, but if there was a local Sea God, surely it couldn't hold a grudge against him. He was a stranger to the area. He called on Our Lady for help. He needed to be especially strong tomorrow when they sailed because Pebble was going to have an awful hangover so he was going to have to be in control. As usual, Our Lady gave no response to his prayers but he felt better anyway. He wasn't sure why. He usually felt better for having prayed, though he never seemed to get any answers.

After a while sitting quietly and listening to the water

lap against the quay, he began to feel sleepy and returned inside. It was dark in there but enough moonlight crept through the cracks for him to see that Pebble had turned onto her back. She was snoring noisily. He gently pushed her onto her side again until her breathing eased and then lay down behind her. He put his arms around her and snuggled his face into the back of her neck. She murmured something in her sleep as he held her tight. It had been a strange day but he was happy. He couldn't help smiling. Pebble, with her strong sense of independence and concern about protocol, would be very annoyed in the morning to discover that they had shared a roof all night. The morality of the island firmly forbade that outside marriage. Sex was fine but only out in the open.

*'It's just as if we are married,'* Lamaxe whispered to himself, his face breaking into a smile.

Pebble moaned in her sleep. This was perhaps not the most romantic introduction to the joys of wedded bliss, he thought, but he decided that he loved it and that everything would be all right in the end. Once she had finished her sculpture and returned with Trebird's copper figurine and he had solved the mystery of the missing girl, they could return home and settle down to a peaceful life again, only this time, they could do it together. He gently kissed the back of her neck. She groaned again and, very gently and quietly, broke wind. He smiled thinking of Lamool ab Headland's awful joke.

# 10

The next morning the young priest woke early. He was still lying with his face buried in Pebble's neck. He carefully extracted himself from the embrace and stood up, wondering why his big toe hurt so much. Limping outside he examined it in the sunlight. It was a beautiful day and the sea glittered in the sunlight. His toe however was a deep blue; deeper even than the colour of the sea – the nail broken and almost black. It must have been the big fellow's teeth, he thought. Thank the Goddess that he had been wearing sandals or the damage might have been much worse. He sincerely hoped the toe wasn't broken. He twiddled it painfully and decided that it probably wasn't but to be on the safe side he bound it tightly to its neighbour. Then he limped back inside to wake Pebble. She looked and sounded dreadful. What is more, she soon made it clear that she felt terrible. The only good thing about this from Lamaxe's point of view was that she didn't even notice last night's sleeping arrangements. He insisted that she drink plenty of water. She declined to eat anything saying her mouth tasted awful, so he coaxed her onto her feet and gently insisted on leading her towards the quay and the waiting ship. She co-operated but was obliged to divert on the way and disappeared behind the shed to empty her bladder. After that she consented to be led the rest of the way.

They stumbled down the shore with Lamaxe carrying both sets of belongings over his shoulder. At the ship the captain was again shouting at his crew, but this time in a much more enthusiastic and positive way. The crew was also moving more purposefully than before. It looked as though the repairs had at last been completed.

'Hello!' Lamaxe shouted to the captain.

'Ahoy!' came the reply.

Lamaxe took this to be the sailor's equivalent and asked if they should come on board. The captain swung across and landed next to them on the sand. Lamaxe was impressed though Pebble seemed not to notice. She just stood there with her eyes staring fixedly at the ground.

'Bad night?' laughed the captain, pointing towards her.

Lamaxe merely smiled.

'Should we come aboard?'

'My barque awaits you,' Crowfish replied with a flourish of his arm.

He led the way up a plank and pointed to an area on the deck, separate from most of the cargo, in front of the rudder and behind the oars.

'We've made a kind of nest with animal skins,' he told the priest. 'You should be comfortable there.'

With that the captain strode off over the deck and began again shouting at his men who were messing about with ropes. He had never seen a ship so close up before and was surprised at its size and how many oars it had. Even so, it seemed perilously small to cross so much sea.

However, he had other things to worry about at the moment so with only a slight shudder he turned to Pebble and made her as comfortable as he could. She groaned a bit but soon settled down among the pelts and went to sleep. She was still asleep when the captain called out to his crew to cast off and one of them released the ropes so that they floated away from the shore. He would dearly have liked her to be awake to give him courage but he couldn't bear to disturb her so he quietly took her hand in his as the ship lurched, turned away from the shore and headed out into the harbour. Their passage seemed quite smooth until they left the protection of the bay but thereafter the sea became a little choppy. This bothered him at first but as they progressed his feelings settled into a mild disquiet. He tried to think of other things. He wondered how, despite all his priestly training, he could have missed the attacker's throat with his knife. After all slitting throats was an important part of a priest's training. He supposed it showed how important the Boy's role was in holding the sacrificial animal still. He must remember to tell him that when he got home. If he got home!

Of course, he told himself, it wasn't that he had intended necessarily to kill the man. Our Lady had never required human sacrifice, as far as he was aware, so his experience of killing people as opposed to animals was non-existent. It was just that he had acted automatically – without conscious thought – just as though it was a sacrifice in the temple. Would he have worried if he had killed the man? He thought not. After all he was only defending Pebble and himself. Had he done so what would the Fat Lady Goddess think? It was not Our Lady's place to get involved in individuals' problems, he told himself. Even so, a small voice in the back of his head thought, I am on Her business, and a little support wouldn't come amiss! Shocked by his own near blasphemy, he tried to think of more practical things. Why hadn't he grabbed the attacker's knife? It had been made of copper, or at least it had shone dully as though it was. He had been told that metal was much stronger and sharper than flint so it might have been useful.

'Never mind, next time perhaps!' he said out loud, then clapped his hand over his mouth disturbing Pebble in the process.

'Oh Lady!' he said. 'Must there be a next time?'

Pebble began to stir so he found their water flask and dribbled some onto her lips. She smiled weakly at him and then lay back. Sitting there side by side he got used to the pitching of the ship and the sound of the oars. As they settled into a rhythm the crew relaxed. Pebble woke up. She began to feel a bit better and took a small amount of Lamaxe's supply of bread as well as some water. He began to relax as well.

Later the captain came and sat with them. He offered them water, which they declined, and they offered him some of their bread. This he accepted.

'Good bread!' he said his mouth still full with it. 'I have been hearing that you had an exciting time on shore.'

Lamaxe said nothing.

'I take it that it was you who was set upon?'

'It was,' Lamaxe acknowledged, 'but no harm was done.'

'That isn't what I hear,' the captain replied. 'One of my crew tells me that someone returned to port last night with a hole in his face. Did you do that?'

Lamaxe merely nodded.

'There is more to you than I thought, priest,' Crowfish said approvingly. 'He is going to have a fine scar. You will know him when you see him again.'

The captain laughed at this but Lamaxe just nodded again and added nothing. He wasn't sure what the captain's point was. Perhaps it was another joke.

'I'm just offering a warning. The man you scarred is known around the harbour. They call him 'Skinny'. He is reputed to be vicious and has a strong sense of his own importance as well as a nasty temper. Now everyone will see his face and remember who won the fight. He will remember that you did it. Should you ever see him again, beware.'

Lamaxe nodded silently. At last he spoke.

'I did not seek the confrontation. I merely defended us.'

'Life on the seas doesn't work that way. He will want his revenge.'

Lamaxe nodded sadly.

'There was a second man; a big man. Do you know him?' he asked.

'His accomplice,' the captain answered. 'He's known as 'Fatso'. Sailors don't have much imagination when it comes to nicknames, I'm afraid.'

Lamaxe smiled.

'He was a powerful man,' he said. 'I didn't see much fat on him.'

The captain nodded in acknowledgement. Then he rose.

'Thank you for the bread,' he said.

So much for relaxing, the priest thought to himself. Even so, he settled down next to his sculptor who snuggled into his shoulder. In order not to think of any more unpleasant things, he studied the darkening sky as he had done so many times before. As he watched it, it dawned on him what had been said earlier about steering by the stars. He could see that it was true. Once you knew how the stars moved, which as a priest he did, you could set your course by them. Strangely, this comforted him. Sailing was not so very different from being a priest after all. You studied the sky and the environment all around you and you behaved accordingly. He just wished he was back in his own environment.

It was about then that a squall blew up. Not a very fierce one, the captain told him afterwards, but enough to concentrate his thoughts and to loosen his bowels. He huddled down as close to Pebble as he could and covered them both with some of the animal pelts to keep the water off them. He realised that he had been unconsciously fingering Trebird's bead around his neck again. It seemed to give him some comfort.

It was dawn by the time the weather had settled. The captain came back to sit with them once more.

'That kept us on our toes,' he laughed as he offered them a swig of wine from his leather flask. Pebble declined but Lamaxe accepted. He felt that he needed something. The wine was weak and bitter; very different from that of ab Graman. Nevertheless, he thanked the captain.

'Has the storm taken us much off course?' he asked.

'This is a dangerous sea,' Crowfish told him, 'especially at this time of year. The prevailing winds tend to push us back to the Sacred Isle. You study the stars – look for yourself. Fortunately, the squall was not bad and the wind has blown us not too far off course. The Sea God must approve of your mission. We will be only a little late arriving.'

'Excellent!' the priest replied with genuine relief in his voice. Then he caught the captain's arm, drawing him towards him. Lowering his voice he changed the subject. Despite himself, he had been thinking about this during the stormy night.

'Tell me, captain, the man I injured? He had a strange accent. Foreign? Do you know where he comes from? I would like to be ready if I am likely to come across him again and if so to know where that might be.'

The captain didn't answer immediately. His head nodded slightly as he thought about it.

'I could not say for certain where he comes from. He is a sailor, though I will not employ him. My men do not like him either. He is not Maltese or from Sicily by his accent. He is indeed foreign and must come from farther along the big coast. Beyond Sicily, across a narrow strip of water, there is a narrow piece of land which juts out into the long sea. Then there is the coast which stretches beyond that along the length of the long sea itself as well as several islands with which trade takes place. There are increasing numbers of people coming from both to Sicily. I have been there sometimes myself to trade, though the cliffs beyond Sicily are very high and steep. Many different peoples live there. But Skinny is a sailor which is why he speaks our language, however poorly. Once his face heals, you will see him again somewhere if you travel this coast. He may well come looking for you.'

Lamaxe had too much time to think about the implications of that. However, as the hot sun beat down upon them and Pebble's condition improved, he tried to think of other, more pleasant things. Soon they could see the Sicilian coast rising in the distance. It was most dramatic with deep inlets and it glistened in the bright sunlight. Crowfish had explained that they would land on the southern coast, but not at the nearest point to Gozo. They would head around the headland and a short way up the coast until it became more sheltered so that they could land in safety. There was a favourite harbour there which was near the river up which they would need to go to reach Ragusa.

'Not more boat travel!' the priest had exclaimed.

The captain explained that the river meant that he had less distance to transport his goods on land. Sicily had steep hills so going by water was hard but walking with heavy loads was even harder. Also it was much easier for them to travel to the 'temple' that way. Lamaxe noticed the emphasis that Crowfish put on the word 'temple' and asked why.

'Their society in Sicily is very technologically advanced compared to yours,' he said, 'but the religious places do not compare. In that you will be disappointed. Not though in their copper work which is very fine.'

To Lamaxe's way of thinking, the captain seemed to know far too much about their mission. He wondered how many others had heard the story of their journey to exchange treasures. He hoped it didn't mean more trouble.

The captain also told him a little about the island and with the proximity of the shore, Lamaxe began to relax and chat happily until Crowfish had to return to his duties. The priest sat quietly cuddling Pebble as she drifted in and out of sleep. Gradually details of the coastline became clearer. The ship turned so as to be side-on to the coast and he had a good view of the deep inlets and the green of the land. It shone in the sunlight.

'It's very beautiful,' said Pebble unexpectedly.

'Oh, you are awake! Isn't it?'

'The way the land in the distance seems to disappear into the sky.'

'Very poetic. I presume you are feeling better?'

Pebble wriggled deeper into his shoulder.

'Much better, thank you. Have you been praying for me?'

'Don't mock!' he replied.

Then changing the subject he said:

'The captain was telling me about the island. He says that they have a mountain which stretches right up into the sky. Perhaps that is what you can see. It is supposed to be in the north-east of the island so we are at the right end to see it. However, we are on the south coast.'

'Umm!' was Pebble's only reply. 'It's lovely.'

'Crowfish tells me that the mountain sometimes belches smoke and fire, even rocks from time to time.'

'Oh come on,' said Pebble. 'This is the stuff of tales told to children. Now you are mocking me.'

'I think not,' he answered. 'It truly is a remarkable island.'

'It seems so close. Will we be landing soon?'

'Soon! Then we will start to head for the temple. Apparently we have to travel by boat again.'

'Very well,' she answered, unimpressed with the concern apparent in his voice. 'Do we have any food? I'm starving.'

Lamaxe carefully unwrapped the remains of their bread and cheese. The cheese was getting a bit ripe by now in the heat and the bread more than a little stale but both were still edible and they made a feast of it in their nest. Once the oars had stopped and the ship lay still they both lay back and stared at the sky. The crew was noisy at first as they relaxed after a day's hard work but eventually they fell still and the only sound was the gentle lapping of the water. Lamaxe thought it quite idyllic. He felt that he was not so far away from home.

Then everything was hustle and bustle. The crew jumped ashore and began unloading their cargo. Lamaxe and Pebble remained in their nest during the initial frenetic activity. However, once the frenzy had died down they grabbed their luggage and sought out the captain to thank him.

'We transfer to that boat. We will take you with half of our cargo – the rest will remain here under guard. No nest for you this time,' he laughed.

They climbed aboard. The river boat seemed very small after the ship and was heavily overladen with goods so that it lay very low in the water. Lamaxe hated being so close to the surface but Pebble was by now feeling recovered and thoroughly enjoyed every minute of the way.

They disembarked but could see no sign of a large settlement. The two of them stood around, rather lost, as the crew began the process of unloading. Eventually Crowfish was satisfied with the crew's progress and was able to turn his attention to them. He used a stick once again to scratch directions in the dirt.

'Just make sure that you complete your business and return within five days or I will have to leave without you.'

It was a timely warning. Pebble had a lot to do. First

to negotiate what she would carve and then finish the agreed article within the time allowed. With instructions from the captain they set off immediately on the road to Ragusa. It was a short walk but a hard one because of the climb, especially as they were so stiff from their time on the ship. The countryside by the river had been green even at the end of summer but as they climbed higher they came across some of the most barren land they had seen anywhere. It was in sharp contrast to Lamaxe's first impression of a green island.

They came upon the settlement suddenly. Before they were noticed by anyone Lamaxe stripped off and changed into his best priestly attire. The settlement was composed of wattle and daub huts much like at home. These were spread around within a large circular enclosure. It seemed to Pebble that it consisted of a number of separate families each with its own round house. Always interested in the new, she wanted to investigate further but Lamaxe insisted that there was not time to do so now as they still had to find the temple. There was no sign of any monumental buildings anywhere so in the end they asked some of the local people where to find the priest.

Lamaxe was pleased to find that they were reasonably friendly and that he had no difficulty understanding their speech.

'What is this place?' asked Lamaxe.

'This is Ragusa,' they said.

'And pray tell me, where can I find your priest?'

'You want the temple or the tombs – the Hypogeum,' they said, and indicated the way to the outskirts of the settlement.

The two pressed on through the dust until they saw

another wooden building, nondescript but slightly larger than the norm. Dressed in his impressive new green skirt and priestly cap Lamaxe felt very superior to the frankly rather bedraggled priest who came from within to greet them. This gave him confidence. Pebble did her best not to show her disappointment at what they saw and Lamaxe tried to be especially pleasant to the priest for Pebble's sake.

'Greetings, holiness,' he began. 'I am Lamaxe ab Tarxian from the Sacred Isle come to visit your island. Here is my official sign, brought from my High Priest, the great Trebird ab Tarxian.'

So saying, he pulled out Trebird's stone bead from under his tunic and displayed it proudly.

'We come to offer exchange.'

The elderly local priest inspected the bead vaguely, bowed and muttered his own welcome.

'I am Mountsea ab Ragusa,' he replied, in a quiet but quite refined voice. 'I was expecting you though I knew not when. You are welcome.'

'May I introduce the famous sculptor, Pebble, come to prepare a work for you,' Lamaxe continued.

Pebble bowed and the local priest waved his arms about in greeting to her.

'What can you do for us?' he asked, getting straight down to business.

'First, I must see the location,' replied the sculptor, 'and see the quality of the light. Whatever I do must be appropriate for the conditions.'

'Of course,' the elderly man said, indicating that Pebble should follow him.

Lamaxe coughed pointedly.

'However, first,' he said, 'I am obliged by my temple to agree a suitable exchange.'

The man bowed his head.

'Indeed,' he said. 'I sent news through our network that we required a sculptor of some quality and were prepared to barter in return.'

'Yes, I believe Lamool ab Headland made the agreement.'

'I know the son better,' Mountsea replied. 'It was he who passed on the message. However, we did not know precisely when you might arrive.'

'Have you previously seen our metalwork?' the old priest asked.

Before Lamaxe could reply he drew from inside his cloak a small statuette of the Fat Lady Goddess. It twinkled in the sunlight. Lamaxe gasped. It was beautiful; so finely worked that Lamaxe had never seen the like before.

'We thought that this might suffice,' the local priest replied. 'We make copperware locally so can spare it to exchange. It is superb, of course. It will, I think, enhance even your own magnificent temple.'

Pebble's eyes opened wider than Lamaxe had ever seen them before. He could have sworn that she was drooling at it. He pulled himself together.

'It is indeed a fine piece and greatly honours Our Lady,' he finally answered, 'but wait until you have seen our sculptor's work.' He indicated towards Pebble with his arm as he said it.

'Indeed,' replied the priest.

Then, turning to Pebble: 'Do come with me.'

Pebble and Lamaxe were shown the location. The 'temple', as the captain had implied, turned out to be even less impressive close up. The layout was not dissimilar to that of his own but, made only of wood and daub, it lacked the grandeur. To Lamaxe this was not a temple at all. A temple was a glorious free-standing stone building designed for communal prayer. This was a wooden hall.

'Do you not build in stone at all?' he asked the older priest.

'We do,' he replied. 'Come, see our Hypogeum.'

So saying he led them further up the path towards a rocky outcrop. The front, carved directly from the rock, looked well enough but inside was a disappointment; like a smaller, less impressive form of the upper floor of their own Hypogeum. It was more of a rock tomb. They entered through a series of doorways carved around the cave mouth. Inside it consisted of three large rooms with numerous catacombs off to the sides. This was an admittedly complex chamber tomb – a burial place with integral spaces for prayer. Afterwards Pebble told him not to act so superior. However, even she admitted that the 'temple' was a terrible disappointment compared to the Tarxian temples or to the Hypogeum at home.

Nevertheless, she made the best of it. She liked the nature of the light, she told Mountsea. This pleased him enormously. She suggested to him that her sow and pigs motif would fit very well. She could cut deep into the stone and the light would be strong enough to enhance the detail. Mountsea was less sure.

'I had thought to ask you to carve a free standing piece at the entrance in a Maltese style.'

'A kind of 'homage'' she said, privately doubting that anything she could carve would allow equal comparison.

They debated this for some time discussing styles and location and Lamaxe quickly became bored. He wandered off to examine the 'temple' in detail. Again he was not impressed. He wandered further off to explore the chamber tomb again. Clearly it was a series of catacombs but not much like the one back home. The exchanges between the islands ensured some similarity of culture. In any case, if you were going to bury bodies in underground tombs it seemed logical to make places to pray and leave offerings within the same complex. How could it be, he wondered, that a society capable of creating such exquisite copper artwork did not lavish that quality of style on its religious buildings? Pebble cynically explained to him later, that it was a matter of priorities. The caves had been partly excavated for flint which had been the main basis of their trade in the past. Otherwise, they built in wood and daub because that was plentiful. However, there were other differences. Mountsea appeared to recognise the Fat Lady as the Goddess. Yet there were detailed differences in the layout of the temple and particularly in the altars which appeared to be due to more than the difference in scale. In short, it all looked slightly unfamiliar to him. What he had learned from the textile trader appeared to be the case. There were serious differences in ritual even within their shared religious beliefs. He was genuinely perturbed.

Eventually Pebble and Mountsea agreed on what she would attempt and they went on to examine possible pieces of stone. Pebble rejected several of those offered until she was satisfied. The only question now was, could she complete it to a satisfactory standard in the time available? Lamaxe heard them calling to him so he made his way back to where they had been standing. Pebble had brought with her a tiny example of her work to show – an exquisitely tiny carving of a goat. This was deemed to be of good quality and of a lively style favoured by the local priest. It was finally agreed that the Tarxian temples would receive the copper figurine of Our Lady plus a fine skirt pin for Trebird in exchange, providing the large scale work of Pebble proved to be as good as her sample. Then Mountsea, nodding to Lamaxe, shouted, 'Boy!' at the top of his voice. It echoed around the chambers and contrasted strangely to his whispered conversation. After a few moments a young lad came running.

'Yes, holiness?' he said.

The local priest patted him on the shoulder in a patronising way.

'Boy,' he said by way of introduction, 'show our visitors from the Tarxian temples how we make our copperware.' The Boy nodded enthusiastically, and led the way.

He took them back towards the settlement to a small, rather dilapidated outhouse. There was a small pile of broken shiny ware piled near the entrance where one grubby workman was working over a very hot fire. Another man was busy working inside the hut. They could hear thumping as though of a hammer. The Boy carefully explained to them what was going on.

'The copper-ore,' he said, 'originally comes from special rocks which are crushed and heated until something in them melts and so can be extracted. This is a complicated process; too complicated for us. It is done abroad.'

'So where does your copper come from?' Pebble asked.

'We lack both the equipment and the skill,' he admitted.

'However, the metal is very pliable when heated so we are able to rework damaged or unwanted copperware into something new. This is what they are doing here. We get our raw material from our own damaged ware and we also trade for it especially from Crete.'

Lamaxe had never heard of Crete but said nothing.

As they watched, one of the men heated some broken bits in a small pot. Once melted, the liquid was transferred carefully in a cup which was held in a specially fashioned wooden handle. The Boy explained, unnecessarily, that the handle had to be long and made of wood because of the heat. Lamaxe and Pebble could feel the heat on their faces. The workman then carried this cup over to the hut and disappeared inside.

'I cannot show you the precise process,' the Boy continued. 'You will understand that this is our livelihood. However, I can tell you that the melted copper can be worked in two ways: either by pouring it into moulds to make objects or into thin flat sheets which can be beaten into shape.'

Pebble was fascinated but had to accept that seeing the process was forbidden.

'Wait here,' the Boy continued and entered the hut himself.

They could hear a discussion going on inside. Then he returned holding a small shiny object.

'See,' he continued, opening his hand. In his palm was a small model of a calf. The two visitors gasped. It was beautiful; so beautiful.

In all honesty, Lamaxe did not really understand the process but Pebble appeared to grasp the essence of it. As they stared, one of the men came out of the hut wiping his hands. He took the small object from the Boy and held it up, twisting it round so that it gleamed in the sunshine.

'Here's one I made earlier,' he croaked. He spoke their language but his mode of expression was so guttural that they had difficulty catching the words. Lamaxe supposed his voice was affected by working constantly in the fire and smoke.

'See,' the old man continued, 'we clean off any excess metal and polish it.'

He gave a laugh from deep down in his throat: 'A perfect calf!' he said.

That evening they slept comfortably on fresh straw. The food had also been good though the herbs were slightly different from what they were used to at home. They lay in each other's arms. Pebble decided that this was acceptable because they were on another island.

'You must leave tomorrow and solve your mystery,' Pebble told her priest. 'That way I can get on with my carving without distractions. I have a lot to do and now only four days left in which to complete it.'

Lamaxe reluctantly agreed. He wanted to find Cliff and Red and try to solve the mystery of Cloud's disappearance, but he did not want to leave Pebble.

'How on earth will I find Cliff and Red in a foreign land?' he complained. 'They could be anywhere.'

Pebble thought about this.

'You will ask the Boy to guide you,' she said. 'He seems a bright lad and would probably be glad to escape the watchful eye of his priest.

'Very well,' answered Lamaxe doubtfully, 'I will ask the priest if he will spare him.'

Mountsea was not very keen to do so but Pebble cleverly

suggested to him that when Lamaxe was elsewhere, she would be able to work much better and quicker without the distractions caused by his presence. So in the end the priest agreed that the Boy would show him the way and try to find their friends. The Boy himself was delighted but did not show this to the priest.

'Oh course, holiness. I will do as you require,' was all that he said, his eyes downcast. However, when the priest's back was turned, he winked at Pebble.

# 11

Lamaxe and Pebble had an early breakfast with Mountsea consisting of some kind of rather tasteless slop. The Boy arrived, bowed to the priest and deferentially indicated to Lamaxe that he was ready whenever he wanted to leave.

'We need to find their ships, holiness,' the Boy told Lamaxe. 'I think they will be near to where you landed. We must then trace your friends.'

As he said this he turned to Mountsea.

'It may take some time. I trust that his Holiness will release me for the whole day and if necessary the night as well?'

'Very well,' replied the old priest. 'But first our good friend the priest will join me in a small sacrifice to cement the relationship between our two religious communities.'

The last thing Lamaxe wanted was to undertake a sacrifice but he bowed to the inevitable and nodded his head.

'How do you know the ships' whereabouts?' Lamaxe enquired of the Boy.

The Boy smiled at this and touched his finger to his nose.

'Holiness, I have my contacts,' was all he said.

Pebble said goodbye and went off merrily, waving vaguely at them as she left. Her mind was already taken up with her carving. Mountsea told the Boy to bring them a very small lamb – clearly the runt of the litter – which had been tethered to a stake near the temple entrance and indicated to Lamaxe to follow him. They all entered along with the lamb. The ritual was sufficiently similar to his own for Lamaxe to usefully participate but sufficiently different in detail to worry him. There was no large statue of the Goddess. What is more the priest made no attempt to conceal the knife, although there were in truth few people there to see. Even the business of slitting the beast's throat seemed to Lamaxe to lack any real sense of occasion. He noticed that Mountsea's hand trembled as he held the weapon. Was this nerves in the presence of another priest or was it a natural tremor? Lamaxe couldn't decide. The blood spilled satisfyingly from the slit throat but onto the ground not the altar and when they came to disembowel the animal the omens did not seem to him to be particularly good. The intestines were flawed. Mountsea did his best to disguise it but Lamaxe could see clearly a small growth on one part of the acres of tubing. He said nothing. Indeed, though he didn't like to admit it even to himself, he found himself trying hard to avoid the blood and keep his official dress clean. Out of politeness he thanked Mountsea for allowing him to participate and managed to excuse himself from any further involvement. The Boy went off quickly to wash the worst of the blood off his hands. It was now mid-morning.

Lamaxe and the Boy made their way back along the

path towards the river. As soon as they had left the vicinity of the holy site, the Boy's attitude changed. He seemed to discard the deferential manner as easily as a cloak.

'So, tell me what it's like on the Sacred Isle?' he asked Lamaxe.

Lamaxe was somewhat taken aback, both at the suddenness of the change in attitude and at the manner of address. He had put up with a great deal on his journey so far, but he still expected a bit of deference from inferior religious functionaries. He imagined what Trebird would have said if their Boy had spoken like that to him.

'Who are you to ask a priest?' he said. 'A Boy should only speak when spoken to.'

The Boy grinned at him.

'Come on,' he said. 'That's all very well inside the temple, but you know as well as I do that I'll soon be a fully fledged priest just like you. You're not much older than me. I bet you were a Boy not so long ago.'

'That is immaterial,' replied Lamaxe, at his most pompous. 'The niceties of tradition must be observed.'

The Boy laughed bitterly at this.

'Tradition!' he exploded. 'What kind of a tradition is it that says I can't use my own given name because it isn't important enough? I've got a name you know; and a family. So have you. Why must you use your temple name instead of your family name? It's stupid!'

Lamaxe took a moment to compose himself. He was unused to unruly adolescents.

'When you join a temple you dedicate yourself to the Goddess. You know that. You always remember your own family and may even return to them in old age, but the temple and its people become your family. That is why you do not use your own family name. You are known by your role because you are in a process of transition.' He paused for a moment. 'Surely, you know all this? Surely you have been properly taught?'

'Of course I know it,' answered the Boy. 'That doesn't make it right. My real family were successful farmers, well respected in the district. They have recently become successful traders as well. That's what I'm good at: wheeling and dealing. I was sent to the temple. I didn't ask to be. Neither did you. It isn't fair. Trade's the future.'

Lamaxe couldn't think of anything useful to say after that so they walked on in silence for a while. Not another tradition being questioned, he thought. We have been happy with our traditions for thousands of years. Where does this change come from all of a sudden? It confused him.

'I have seen many strange things in the last few days,' he said quietly, speaking to himself as much as to the Boy. 'Trade has always been important. It was the surplus from trade that made possible the building of our magnificent temples. From what I have seen recently though, you may be right. It may be that trade will dominate the future even more and will bring changes. No doubt it will bring advantages but it will also bring disadvantages as well – new customs threatening old traditions; new forms of violence never seen before.'

The Boy said nothing.

'Anyway,' Lamaxe continued, 'we still have Our Lady. She is important – to me anyway. There is no antagonism between Her and the idea of trade. On the Sacred Isle, traders have been amongst the temple's most important benefactors.'

'Perhaps it is different on the Sacred Isle,' the Boy replied, 'but here we increasingly see foreign traders who have different religions; people who don't worship the Fat Lady.'

Lamaxe winced at the open use of that term. The Boy continued, 'We've even got competition between religions now! You saw the metalworking? The copper calf is for some eastern religion. They worship a beast.'

'Then they are in error,' Lamaxe replied sanctimoniously, 'and Our Lady will punish them.'

They boarded a tiny boat somewhat to Lamaxe's dismay and rowed down the river. In truth they mainly went with the fast current and Lamaxe had to acknowledge that the Boy handled the craft well. After a while the Boy suggested that they land to avoid some rocks and eat some lunch. He gently brought the boat to rest against the river bank. He had brought bread and fruit as well as drinking water so Lamaxe sat on the bank and drank the water willingly. He ate some of the bread as well although it was not to his taste; not like the bread back home.

'Why do you want to find these friends?' the Boy asked.

'I don't mind the questions so much,' replied Lamaxe, 'but you might address me properly.'

'Sorry, your holiness,' he replied without contrition.

Lamaxe decided that that would have to do. He also felt that he might as well tell the Boy his reasons. Maybe he really had contacts and could help.

'I have been asked to seek a missing girl,' he answered. 'Why need not concern you, but my friends, the traders, may have some information about her.'

'It must be important information for you to come all this way to find it,' the Boy replied.

'I came here with the sculptor to ensure her safe passage,' he replied. 'The other matter is secondary. It is merely convenient that they should be here also.'

'Hmm!' said the Boy, clearly not convinced.

They were not alone on the bank and the Boy called once or twice to other islanders to stop and ask for information. He chatted to each at great length and Lamaxe had some difficulty in following their local accents when they spoke to each other. Despite these lengthy conversations nothing very useful appeared to be forthcoming. They finished lunch and returned to their boat. As they continued down river Lamaxe began to relax a little in the warm sunshine. He even let his hand trail in the water, and they started to chat fairly informally.

'Where do you propose we look when we get there?' Lamaxe asked.

'I believe that Cliffsound ab Headland's ship has been sitting on the beach for some time guarded by one of his crew. It was there when you arrived. Didn't you recognise it?'

'As far as I am aware I have never seen it,' replied Lamaxe. 'He is a childhood friend of mine and in adulthood I only ever see him at the temple or occasionally at my family's home. I have certainly not noticed it. Sea travel is not my favourite activity.'

'Me neither,' grinned the Boy. 'That's one of the few disadvantages of trade. Anyway, it seems that Cliff – is that what you call him? – and his friend Redstone continued their trading sharing Redstone's ship.'

'That seems a strange way to trade, if Cliff left behind his goods.'

'Not necessarily,' the Boy explained. 'You need to know something about trade, you see. Were they trading cloth? That is the normal import here.'

'Yes, Cliff's father produces cloth. Red would be trading his father's wine.'

'Ah well,' the Boy continued. 'It's too early in the year for the new wine crop so I guess Red would be bringing samples and negotiating sales for next year. There is probably not enough time for another trading journey before the winter storms. Cliff would be carrying actual cloth to be exchanged here for new wool. That would be stored on Cliff's ship under guard. He probably took some samples as well to try to build new trade links. They will have gone on to the other islands, or even the main coast with samples to find new markets.'

'That sounds very dangerous,' Lamaxe said, thinking of his childhood friend.

'A bit,' answered the Boy. 'There are pirates but it's not as dangerous as you might think. There's increasing trade overseas. That's why there are so many new gods appearing. Do you know, someone turned up the other day saying they worshipped a man with a bird's head. Ridiculous!'

'Absurd,' Lamaxe agreed.

Despite the Boy's attitude and lack of respect, Lamaxe found that he couldn't help liking him. He had a natural charm and an infectious grin.

By now it was nearly evening but they had almost reached the beach. When they arrived the Boy told Lamaxe to wait by the boat while he sought information.

He disappeared into a rather dilapidated hut and came back a few minutes later wearing his biggest grin.

'Hey! We're in luck!' he shouted as he ran across.

Lamaxe shuddered again at this relaxed way of addressing a priest, but found himself caught up in the Boy's enthusiasm.

'Well?' he asked.

'Red's ship returned last night. If we walk over to the far end we should find it.'

Lamaxe sighed in relief. At last he was getting somewhere. Please let the girl be with them.

'Come on!' the Boy called, waving his arms.

Lamaxe hurried towards him in as dignified a way as he could manage and the two soon covered the ground. The Boy was rushing on ahead but Lamaxe was too aware of the damp sand underfoot and the danger of slipping and spoiling his clothes. As a result the Boy was already hailing one of the crew by the time he arrived.

The crew member was a small wiry man but with bulging muscles.

'Hail!' Lamaxe called. Then he remembered what Crowfish had said. 'Ahoy!'

The man, standing on a pile of wool on the ship, towered over him, his arms folded, thus emphasising the size of his muscles.

'Ahoy, holiness,' he said.

Lamaxe was pleased that Red instilled a sense of respect for the temple in his crew, though he wondered if this was simply the difference between men of the Sacred Isle and elsewhere. Then the man spat on the deck. Lamaxe inwardly shuddered.

'I am Lamaxe ab Tarxian,' he said in his official voice. 'I seek Redstone ab Graman and Cliffsound ab Headland. I am on a mission from the temple.'

The crewman relaxed a little.

'I'm the bosun. I've heard of you,' he said. 'Cliff mentioned you.'

'I am a childhood friend of Cliff's. I seek them about an important matter. Can you tell me where I might find him?'

'He and Red have gone off to relax. To eat and drink with friends after their voyage.'

'But where?'

The man shrugged his shoulders.

'They are staying with a local friend. They will lodge with him for a night or two. It makes a pleasant change from the ship.' He said this with great irony, since he himself was clearly stuck on board. 'But, I don't recommend you try to find it in the dark,' he added. 'The farm is some distance inland.'

'Thank you. I will seek them out tomorrow. You can give me directions?'

The crewman nodded.

The Boy took his arm and led him away.

'It is nearly dark,' he said. 'I will find you someone to feed you before night comes, then I intend to visit some friends nearby.'

Lamaxe concurred, though the thought of spending a night here on his own did not appeal very much. The Boy took him down an overgrown path leading from the beach to what looked like a hovel and shouted, banging on the door. An elderly woman opened it.

'I bring a holy guest from the Sacred Isle,' he said.

'Provide us with a meal and you will be rewarded by our temple.'

Lamaxe had difficulty following their accents but the woman bowed and muttered, 'Your holiness.'

Lamaxe doubted that she could have much food to feed herself but was amazed when they were provided with two substantial wooden bowls full of a very acceptable fish stew and some clean water. The stew was fine but the bread hard and gritty. Still, he thanked her and they sat outside in the fading light. As soon as the Boy had eaten he got up from his haunches and spoke.

'Well, I'm off!' he announced. 'I've performed my task and I'm now going to make the most of a free night. The chance doesn't come often. I'll return for you in the morning.'

'But where can I sleep?' asked Lamaxe, looking unhappily at the hut behind.

The Boy shook his head at the unworldliness of the priest.

'Do as the sailors do,' he answered. 'Why not sleep on the ship you came on? I don't suppose the captain will mind.'

With that he left, laughing and waving in Lamaxe's direction by way of goodbye.

Lamaxe finished his bowl in silence. He supposed the ship was his best bet. He thanked the woman again and made his way along the beach. Some ships were tied up properly alongside a wooden platform. Smaller boats were simply beached. Although there were several craft there, there were very few people. He supposed that they all had more sense and were staying with friends in one of the settlements nearby. The only people still there were those on lookout to protect their own or their captains' property.

He found Crowfish's ship without much difficulty. There was a crewman on board whom he vaguely recognised and he asked permission to spend the night on board. Lamaxe was distinctive enough in his priestly dress for the crewman to recognise him but he pretended to be reluctant at first. He soon recognised the seaman's motives and agreed to guard the ship for some of the night so that the crewman could go and find his mates. Once this was settled, the man agreed quite readily. Lamaxe's stomach felt full from the meal and he had drunk well on clean water so he happily settled down in the 'nest', pulled some skins over him as much for comfort as to keep him warm, for it was a pleasant night, and stared up at the stars. As always, the Southern Cross dominated the sky and he found himself talking to his Goddess. As usual she didn't answer. Nevertheless, he tried out all his new found doubts on her. He decided in the end that no response to his queries was perhaps a positive sign and settled down in his bed. Instead of religion he thought of his Pebble and was soon asleep. The crewman returned in the middle of the night, almost sober, but Lamaxe did not hear him.

True to his word, the Boy arrived the next morning. Lamaxe had thrown off the skins and was luxuriating in the warmth of the sun when he heard whistling. Looking up he saw the same cheery head bobbing along the beach. The Boy smiled and waved at him so he raised himself and climbed on to the shore.

'I stopped to ask your seaman friend for further directions on my way so we can start at once if you wish.'

'Is it not a little early to be calling on someone we do not know?'

The Boy grinned.

'They are staying at the home of a man called Highsow ab Hinterland. He is a wool farmer and trader with a farmer's ways. I am sure his household will be up and about already. However, his demesne is quite a walk away. It will not be morning when we arrive.'

'Then we had better start straight away. I am sure that he will welcome a priest, especially one who is a friend of his friend.'

They set off inland climbing all the time. From time to time they passed small farmsteads with small round huts, the animals' freedom of movement bounded by a circular ditch. Neolithic farming settlements are such that there is very little variation between the houses. Some are bigger, some smaller, some are rectangular rather than round but all are essentially similar and made of wattle and daub. Even at home Lamaxe occasionally got lost, but the homesteads here were even more spread out, the sheep being allowed to forage on the hills on the fairly barren soil. The Boy seemed to know the people that they passed and gave them a merry wave. Lamaxe had anticipated suspicion from the locals towards a strange priest but the company of the Boy seemed to favour him. They climbed all day. Travelling by foot took much longer than the boat journey had. Eventually they approached a largish settlement of houses surrounded by a semi-circular ditch.

'Here it is!' said the Boy with a flourish.

Lamaxe thought it a large holding. There was a substantial area within the compound and three separate houses. However, the Boy explained that most of Highsow's productive lands were spread about the island. Clearly he was a man of substance.

The young priest looked about. Someone in a soiled tunic was cooking hunks of fish in the ashes of a fire in front of the house. It smelled delicious. The man took each fish and wrapped it in leaves before burying it in the ash.

'Hail!' he called to the man. 'I am Lamaxe ab Tarxian and I seek Cliffsound ab Headland and Redstone ab Graman. I understand that they are staying here if this is the house of Highsow ab Hinterland.'

'It is,' the man replied, barely looking up from his task.

'And you are Highsow ab Hinterland?' Lamaxe asked. The man looked like a servant but Lamaxe was unsure of the ways of Sicilian farmers so was playing safe.

'Not I,' laughed the man. 'He is out with the sheep.'

'And my friends?'

'They are in the guest house, but I cannot leave the fish just yet to announce you.'

'I can find them myself,' Lamaxe replied, pushing ahead.

'No, please, my master requires me to announce you.'

'No matter,' replied Lamaxe. 'Stick with your fish. I am a priest. I can find my own way.'

The man appeared about to insist but then shrugged his shoulders and pointed to one of the houses.

'If you must,' he said. 'I suppose I had better prepare two more fish.'

Lamaxe wanted to speak to his friends alone so he turned to the Boy.

'Perhaps you would like to help him with the cooking while I speak to them.'

The Boy and the slave both shrugged their shoulders this time.

'Inside that house on the left,' the slave called after him.

As he strolled past he asked over his shoulder:

'Do they have a girl staying here with them?'

The man burst into laughter and shook his head. Lamaxe wondered if he would ever understand the disrespectful attitude of servants here.

He walked over to the house. Although not very large it was sturdily made. He pushed open the door. There was no response so he knocked on the wooden post. Still nothing so he knocked again. He had closed his eyes on entering. This was normal procedure in order to allow one's eyes to adjust to the differences in light.

'What's the matter?' a voice called out.

Lamaxe opened his eyes in the semi-darkness and called 'Hello!'

'May the Goddess strike you, Bentwood,' came a reply. Then a pause and, 'Oh, is the fish ready?'

Lamaxe recognised the voice as Cliff's so he pulled aside the curtain guarding the internal partition and called his name in greeting. The word died on his lips. There in front of him were the two friends. Both were totally naked, the coverings having fallen off them. Cliff was astride his friend Red with his back to the entrance. Lamaxe could not describe what they were engaged in, because he had no word for the activity. Of course, he had seen oxen in the fields engaged in it, but he knew of no such thing among humans. The Goddess approved of sex as part of the round of fertility but this was something new to him.

'Bugger, it's a priest,' said Red speaking a language

Lamaxe did not understand and looking up from underneath his friend.

Cliff turned, anger on his face, but almost immediately the anger turned to embarrassment.

'By the Goddess, it's Lammy,' he cried.

Lamaxe dropped the curtain. His jaw had fallen open.

Cliff quickly draped himself in the bed covering and came out through the curtain.

'Well by all that's strange,' he said holding his arms wide in greeting. As he did so the bed covering slipped and he had to grab it quickly. Lamaxe automatically stepped back and Cliff laughed, throwing his head back as he did so.

'You're perfectly safe, you know. I'm not after your body.'

Lamaxe relaxed a bit and Cliff took his arm.

'Wait two moments while we dress and you shall join us for some excellent fish and then you can tell us what brings you so far.'

Lamaxe was still finding speech difficult but he nodded.

'Oh, and we'll explain the rest,' added Cliff, waving vaguely in the direction of the curtained cubicle.

Within moments the two friends appeared, properly dressed this time and they all went down the hill.

'This is Bentwood,' said Red pointing to the slave. 'The one thing he can do really well is cook fish.'

Bentwood smiled and nodded. He lifted the chunks of fish onto wooden platters which he distributed among them, the Boy included. Cliff guided them to a small clearing next to the house where they could sit and talk without the slave or the Boy hearing.

'Good fish,' said Red. 'It comes from the great sea over

to the West. The local fishermen lure them in to the island shallows to catch them in traps.'

Lamaxe eventually found his voice.

'It is good,' he answered. 'It has the quality of meat.'

'Yeh! The fishermen call it tuna,' Cliff said.

The two friends relaxed as they ate though Lamaxe remained quiet.

'Well, what brings you here?' Cliff asked him.

'Cloud has disappeared. Her father blames you, Cliff, for stealing her away.'

Cliff chuckled.

'Now you know that that is one thing that you cannot accuse me of. Nor Red, eh?'

Lamaxe shook his head.

'It seems this part of my journey was wasted,' the priest replied.

'Don't say that,' said Cliff, 'for it is good to see you.'

'Hmm,' was all Lamaxe could manage in reply.

There followed an embarrassed silence.

'It's the blasphemy, you see?' Lamaxe finally uttered, trying to explain. 'The Goddess – Our Lady!'

Cliff and Red looked at one another and turned together to the priest. They answered him in turn.

'There is no blasphemy.'

'Of course not! We know our duty.'

'When we cease our travelling and return to the Sacred Isle to settle down we will do what is required of us.'

'Like everyone else, we will find the daughter of some local well-off farmer and settle down and have children.'

'It's reproduction that that Our Lady requires of us, isn't it?'

Lamaxe was rather taken aback by this two-pronged

salvo. He had been horrified at first but now felt unsure of his theology. If they intended all along to settle down and help produce the next generation perhaps it didn't matter. After all, the oxen in the fields obliged with calves eventually. It didn't affect their fertility. Perhaps when he returned, he should discuss it with Trebird. He shuddered at the thought. Perhaps not Trebird, but it would be good to ask Pebble her opinion.

'Come on, relax,' Cliff said, holding out his hand in greeting. Lamaxe grasped his palm and smiled.

'That's better,' Cliff said. 'Had you asked, I would have told you earlier, but I don't see much of you now, not like in childhood, and it is not the kind of thing that comes up in conversations in the temple.'

He laughed at this and Red joined in.

'Do your fathers know?' asked Lamaxe.

'Of course,' they both replied. 'What do you think they did when they were at sea?'

They lapsed into silence again until Red passed around some fresh water and they all drank. Then Cliff insisted that Lamaxe tell him the full story of Cloud's disappearance and his own journey to Sicily. While he offered his narrative they asked questions and made suggestions. However, none of them could think of a solution as to where she might have disappeared. It got later and they begged him to stay with them overnight so that they could reminisce about old times and also meet their host Highsow ab Hinterland. Lamaxe was keen to get back to Pebble but their entreaties eventually persuaded him. After all Pebble would be busy carving and would not welcome his intrusion if he arrived back too early.

Better to stay here with friends than to kick his heels in Ragusa getting in her way while she worked. He also secretly admitted to himself that he really didn't want to be dragged into helping Mountsea with further rituals. He preferred his own way of doing things. Eventually, he called the Boy and told him that he was staying the night.

'Excellent, holiness!' he said. 'Then I have the perfect excuse to stay as well.'

# 12

Pebble had been working hard all day when she became conscious of eyes on the back of her neck. Assuming it was Mountsea watching her from behind, she took no notice. He had already come a number of times to see how she was progressing but had passed no comment on the work. Then, as she continued to chip away at the stone, she heard the mumbling of a conversation behind her. It can't be just Mountsea, she thought, so she contrived to stand back from her work and surreptitiously survey the area behind her. Sitting just a little way away were the two copper workers. As she turned they smiled shyly.

'Hello,' she said, 'can I help you?'

The younger one stood up and walked towards her.

'I am Smithyoung,' he said, holding his hand up in greeting in the appropriate manner. 'My father you have already met.' He indicated the old man by his side, who then rose slowly to his feet.

'Smith,' he croaked, introducing himself.

Pebble raised her hand in greeting.

'Pebble,' she said.

There was an awkward silence.

'We came to see your work,' the younger one explained with an embarrassed cough. 'Craftsman to craftsman.'

After her previous unpleasant experiences, she sighed in relief and encouraged them to examine what she had done so far.

'It is interesting to observe your technique,' said Smithyoung running his fingers over the indentations she had produced. 'We do similar carvings in clay for the mouldings, but in reverse'.

Pebble turned to the old man and, thinking of what the Boy had said to her, laughed.

'This is my living, you know. I was not allowed to see your technique.'

The old man croaked something but she could not catch the words.

'My father says that the Boy merely repeats what the old priest says. Priests know nothing. They are afraid to lose their market. We are craftsman to craftsman.'

'Well,' said Pebble, rather coquettishly, 'I'll show you mine if you show me yours!'

They spent some time examining her carving in detail; and then escorted her down to their shack and showed her their processes. First they modelled clay into the shape of the object they wanted. Then they smeared it in beeswax and, once that had set, did any fine carving necessary on the wax.

'To inscribe the delicate finishes,' the younger one explained.

'What has this to do with copper?' Pebble asked.

'You saw us smelting the copper,' he stated. 'Once we have finished carving the wax we smother it in clay leaving small drainage holes. Then we stand the object carefully on the ground and we pour in the molten copper. The hot copper melts the wax which then runs out through the drainage holes. Once it is cooled we remove the clay and, if we have done it right, we have the copper object perfect in every detail.'

Pebble was amazed.

'It is a straightforward technique,' he continued, 'but it does require great skill. Copper does not run freely so it does not always fill the mould and we have to make repairs.'

'It is remarkable,' she said, enormously impressed.

The young man warmed to his explanation.

'We have been experimenting,' he said confidentially. 'We have discovered that when, sometimes, impurities get into the copper, it can flow more easily. We wondered if we dare deliberately mix it with other metals.'

Pebble could not have been more impressed.

'Could I try?' she asked.

'Oh no!' the old man croaked.

'The priests would never allow us to let an outsider work on it,' explained his son. 'But at least you know now how it is done.'

Pebble looked more than a little disappointed but was pleased to have been shown it.

'Anyway,' said Smithyoung, as they turned to leave, 'It is men's work!'

*

Highsow arrived in the evening and proved to be a jolly host. He reminded Lamaxe of Cliff's father in that, in the priest's view, he had a very poor sense of humour which he enjoyed inflicting upon other people. However, he did it in such a charming and generous manner that Lamaxe could hardly complain. He was a big sheep farmer and a major supplier of wool to Cliff and his father. He explained that his family had originally had a mixed farm with something of a penchant for pigs – hence his personal name – but that his own grandfather had discovered the attractions of wool and so the family had put the bulk of their effort into that. They had extensive holdings in the district and, of course, like all prehistoric farmers, they continued to grow a range of things for their own use. His fine clothes demonstrated the effectiveness of his ties with the ab Headlands and when they ate they were served a good quality wine –'in honour of Lamaxe's visit', his host told him. This had clearly come from ab Graman's estate. He and the two young traders were obviously good friends as well as business colleagues and the whole experience was thoroughly enjoyable for Lamaxe. After all that travelling he began to relax.

Highsow explained that he had returned late from inspecting his sheep because he had not been able to resist engaging in his other favourite activity – hunting. He called it 'pig-tickling'. Indeed, they ate roast boar which he had killed that very day. He arrived with just one servant dragging the boar's body behind them and his dog. It turned out that Red was also a particularly fine hunter and they discussed the merits of their various bows. Highsow had acquired some new obsidian arrow heads from Lipari with which he was very pleased. He claimed that they were extra sharp and Red seemed impressed. Lamaxe had hunted with his brother Oyeh when he was younger but he had never been very good at it and Oyeh had been nearly as bad as he was. While all 'Copper Age' farmers did some hunting to supplement what they grew, Oyeh treated it as a necessary nuisance rather than a sport. The idea that you could really enjoy hunting as a leisure activity surprised Lamaxe somewhat. Mind you, he didn't care for fishing too much either if the water was at all rough. Highsow however was keen to convert Lamaxe and he encouraged him not only to stay the night but the next day as well and try it. Lamaxe declined saying that he had a duty to return and insisted on leaving early in the morning.

At this point the Boy had wandered over and tried to speak. Lamaxe was getting fed up with his cheekiness and waved him to silence but Highsow laughed and said, 'Oh, let the Boy speak. We are not in a temple now.'

'Thank you, sire,' the Boy said, bowing slightly in his pseudo-obsequious way.

'It occurred to me that his holiness could stay for tomorrow morning for a hunt and still return by the late afternoon if you gentlemen' – here he turned to Cliff and Red – 'would escort him back. You could show him the much shorter way on foot while I returned to the coast to collect the boat. You would probably be back even before I and the boat arrived at Ragusa.

'Excellent idea,' boomed Highsow, 'there you are, Lammy, the Boy has the solution. That's settled then. Thank you, Boy.'

So it was settled. Lamaxe was not very enthusiastic but didn't want to offend his host by showing it. Reluctantly he agreed to stay and go hunting with the others in the morning. It was not the kind of opportunity that came often in the daily life of a priest and he couldn't see that it would do any harm. The Boy would leave early and return on his own to collect and return their boat. Lamaxe secretly suspected that the Boy had plans of his own for the day.

Before it became too dark that evening Highsow insisted that they practise with bows and arrows so that Lamaxe had some experience before the hunt. He had an old pelt set up on a wooden frame surrounded by straw and they each took turns in shooting at it. Red proved to be by far the most efficient, though Highsow was not far behind him. Cliff came a poor third. Lamaxe himself was a real novice and showed little in the way of natural aptitude. He missed the target altogether on his first attempt seriously endangering Highsow's hunting dog. It wasn't until his third attempt that it could be said that he might at least have injured the prey. Nevertheless, it was all done with such good humour that he found with some surprise that he was enjoying himself.

By the time Lamaxe rose in the morning, the Boy had already left and Bentwood was preparing a breakfast of Emmer porridge and spelt biscuits. The meal was filling but not like the porridge at home, Lamaxe thought. The others emerged from their huts and Bentwood and the other slave collected together the equipment. They set off in good spirits climbing east to where there was more cover.

'I suggest that we try our luck with some birds today,' Highsow suggested. 'I killed enough boar yesterday to last us some time.'

The others nodded their agreement though Lamaxe privately thought that he would prefer the bigger target if he was not to make a fool of himself. As at the practice session, Red proved himself a brilliant shot with a bow and Highsow also killed several birds. Lamaxe missed altogether at his first three attempts. This led to an ignominious search for the precious arrows.

'Don't worry,' whispered Cliff, 'I'm not much better. We each have our talents, eh?' With this he nudged Lamaxe with his elbow. Lamaxe persevered and by the end of the hunting session he had managed to wing two birds which Red finished off for him. He was secretly pleased that he was getting at least as good as Cliff.

'You must take your spoils with you,' laughed Highsow, 'though a few birds will hardly make a meal. Take some boar as well'

So, the morning passed enjoyably enough and after a light midday meal, served by Bentwood, they returned to Highsow's domain and the young men prepared to leave. They waved goodbye to the sheep farmer and went on their way. The Boy had been right. The walk was pleasant with a good view on that clear day of the huge mountain that dominated the island. It was very hot but there was a slight breeze and they laughed and chatted as they walked. This was much pleasanter than a hard paddle upstream in a boat. As the sun warmed his face and the insects buzzed around his hair, he secretly thanked the Boy for saving him from yet another trip on the water and hoped that he too was enjoying his stolen freedom.

As promised, they arrived in the late afternoon. The old priest came forward to meet them and was very pleased to receive the boar joint as well as Lamaxe's birds as a gift. His hands shook badly as he greeted them all.

'We shall eat them tonight,' he declared, 'just as soon as the Boy returns to prepare them.'

'Holiness,' explained Red after the introductions, 'the birds would benefit from hanging for a few days. It brings out the flavour. Perhaps you should stick to the boar.'

As soon as he could Lamaxe made his excuses and went to find Pebble. As always she was hard at work. The carving looked magnificent to Lamaxe's eyes.

'Mountsea must be very pleased,' he said. 'It is beautiful.'

'Mountsea is a wily old priest and will admit to nothing,' she answered wryly. 'However, I do believe that he is pleased. As you can see I have roughed out the design and must now finesse it. It will not take too much longer to bring it to perfection so soon we can return home.'

The light glinted in her hair highlighting the tiny chippings from the stone. He kissed her. Then he took her hand and gently led her away from her work to meet his friends outside.

They all got on well and chatted happily until Pebble noticed Mountsea's unease.

'Holiness, what is wrong?' she asked.

Mountsea smiled but looked concerned.

'The Boy is late returning with the boat. He is a willful child and often manages little escapes to enjoy himself, but even so, he should have returned by now. Perhaps the current is particularly strong today.'

'You don't think something could have happened with the boat, do you?' Lamaxe asked, his own dislike of water making him very conscious of its dangers.

'The Boy is not one of nature's sailors,' came the reply, 'but he is very competent and it is a good boat. No doubt he is out enjoying himself. However, he will be foolish not to return before dusk.'

They continued their conversation and thought no more about it. The two traders agreed to stay the night rather than return that evening and Red produced a skin of his father's wine which they all sampled with pleasure.

It was nearly dusk when their conversation was disturbed by shouts and a general clamour. They all rose and made their way along the path towards the river. Two men, strangers to Lamaxe but clearly known to Mountsea, were gently lifting a cargo onto the ground.

'What is it?' called the local priest.

'It's the Boy,' one of them answered. 'We found him at the beach, near your boat. He has been gravely injured.'

On instructions from the old priest they carried his limp body and placed it near the fire. Mountsea examined him. He had cuts and grazes all over his body but the worst was a huge bruise on the side of his head.

'Bring water and herbs,' Mountsea ordered, and one of the men ran to obey.

'How is he?' asked Lamaxe.

'Not good. He has been hit with something very heavy. He has a massive bruise and an indentation in the bone but that is not the worst of it. I fear that he is bleeding inside his skull.'

Lamaxe shook his head, not fully understanding the implications. Pebble held his hand.

'I have seen such injuries among masons at the quarries,' she told him. 'The pressure of the blood will destroy his brain. There is nothing we can do. At best, he will live to be an idiot. I'm sorry.'

Mountsea was in tears. He brushed them away with

the sleeve of his garment, his hands shaking even more so as he did.

'There is something we can do. We are priests. It is dangerous but we should try.'

Pebble raised her eyebrows curiously.

'What?' asked Lamaxe. 'We can only pray for him.'

'We could trepan his skull' Mountsea whispered.

Lamaxe looked confused.

'We cut a piece out of the skull to relieve the pressure. All priests are trained in this.'

He looked at Lamaxe.

'I know nothing of this,' Lamaxe answered in panic. 'I have heard of it being done on the dead but on the living? I have never known it actually to be done nor ever seen it. Surely it is one of ab Headland's stories.'

'It is part of a priest's role. We must try,' the old priest said, though his hands were now shaking uncontrollably. 'I have performed this act myself in the past. Only once, but it was partly successful. However, now, it needs younger hands than mine.'

Lamaxe returned his look with horror.

'I couldn't,' was all he could reply.

Silence followed as each thought about the implications. The traders withdrew slightly from the others, making it clear that this was priestly work. Eventually, Mountsea spoke.

'If we do nothing then the Boy will die. If we try we might just save him.'

He gave Lamaxe a hard look.

'It is part of being a priest. You should learn.'

'How is it done?' asked Pebble, a calm voice in the storm.

'You take a knife and cut the skin to expose the bone. Then you grind the bone with a sharp implement to remove a small piece. This allows the blood to flow out and so do less damage to the brain.'

'And if you cut too far?' she asked.

'Then he dies.'

She nodded.

'And even if it works the wound can turn bad and still kill him,' Mountsea added as a tear rolled down the old priest's cheek.

'I cannot do it at my age. My hands shake too much. It is Lamaxe or nothing.'

Lamaxe said nothing. He sat there with his head in his hands.

'If I must, I must,' he whispered.

'Good,' replied Mountsea. 'Let us get on with it.'

Pebble looked at Lamaxe. She could see him suffering.

'Wait,' she said quietly. 'I am the one skilled with tools. I will do it.'

Mountsea looked horrified.

'This is priest's work!'

'And a priest – no – two priests would be supervising,' she continued in a reasoned tone.

'But…' exclaimed Mountsea.

'Look,' she replied. 'I am good with tools; with carving; with a chisel. Stone on stone! Can stone on bone be very different?'

'But you are not a priest. There are incantations to be said; prayers to be offered.'

'You do those. I'll do the cutting. Now let's get on with it before he dies.'

Lamaxe had been quiet so far. Now he gently touched Mountsea on the shoulder and spoke.

'I think perhaps Pebble is right. That way, you will supervise and ensure that everything is done properly. I will learn the technique and so improve my priestly functions, and the Boy may yet survive.'

Mountsea thought about this for a while.

'Well,' he said finally with a shrug of his shoulders, 'I suppose the Boy will probably die anyway.'

With the help of Cliff and Red they prepared the patient making sure that as much light as possible fell on the Boy's skull. Pebble would have preferred to wait until morning when it was light but the old priest told them that by then it would be too late and the damage would be done. She honed her tools and Mountsea send his people to gather certain herbs which he prepared into a poultice to cover the wound afterwards. He muttered incantations while he mixed it. Lamaxe insisted that they all washed their hands though Mountsea assured him that there was no religious precedent for this. Nevertheless, he complied, anxious to keep the other priest on board. They worked all night. Lamaxe, using his sacrificial knife and on Mountsea's instructions, carefully cut and peeled back the skin. The skull was white and glowed in the firelight. Then Pebble working with her chisels slowly augured a hole in the skull. The end result was not neat. She would have been ashamed of it had it been in stone, but once she was through the blood oozed out of the wound and Mountsea seemed satisfied. Once the blood had been reduced to a trickle he sealed the wound with the poultice and wrapped a clean cloth around the Boy's head.

'There is nothing more we can do,' he said, 'except wait.'

They wrapped the body up in a warm woollen blanket and placed him by the fire. Then they all returned to the fire where Red and Cliff were waiting.

'Now we need your wine, Red.' Pebble said.

She realised that now it was over she was shaking too. Lamaxe put his arm around her shoulders.

'You were brilliant,' he whispered in her ear.

'I know,' she whispered back, 'but next time you do it, you're the priest.'

Red poured each of them a generous helping. After a while food, mostly the wild boar, appeared from somewhere. No one remembered preparing it, and they decided that it must have come from neighbours concerned about the Boy. They had little appetite.

'It's funny,' mused Lamaxe. 'We see so much illness and death and yet it always hurts when it is someone that you know.'

'Did you know him well?' asked Cliff. 'You haven't been here long.'

'That is true but we had spent time together and I liked his spirit.'

'Like!' Pebble pointed out. 'He isn't quite dead yet.'

The wine skin was passed around and the conversational hum rose as they began slowly to relax and talk of other things. Lamaxe remained quiet. Pebble noticed this and drew him aside.

'What is it?' she asked. 'Don't feel guilty that it was I who did the deed. I have the most skill.'

Lamaxe dropped his head.

'You do,' he answered. 'Being a priest seems to have taught me very little that is useful.'

She laughed, though it was rather forced.

'No one does an incantation like you.'

This produced a very wan smile on his part.

'Actually, I'm also feeling guilty that I may have been the cause of the attack.'

Pebble looked shocked and he continued.

'Well, what harm had the Boy ever done to anyone that he should be attacked so viciously? He has a witty tongue which might have brought him a slap or two but not surely such an horrendous assault?'

She nodded agreement.

'Why would anyone attack a priest, especially a junior one? It wouldn't have been robbery.'

'Do you remember on Gozo?' Lamaxe asked, 'When you got drunk on ab Graman's wine and we were attacked on the way back?'

She shook her head, slightly embarrassed.

'You and the wine know that I remember very little about it.'

'Well,' he said. 'We were attacked by two seamen – pirates really, I think. One of them was skinny and used a knife. I won. I must have given him a vicious scar. The other man was huge and wielded an enormous mace; just the sort of thing to do that damage to the Boy's head. They attacked us because they had heard that we had valuable things to exchange. I can't help wondering if they were looking for me this time and finding the Boy thought that any priest would do for revenge in the absence of the one they wanted.'

Pebble didn't speak but put her arms around him.

'You see,' he continued, 'Anyone from Red's or Cliff's crew might know I had been there and that I would return. After all that had been the original plan and they had no reason to suspect an enquiry about me even from those two. It wouldn't be difficult for the two of them to work out that I had used a boat to come down river. If they had waited there and the Boy turned up in priestly garb they might even have thought that he was me. We are not so very different in age, as the Boy himself pointed out to me, and I don't suppose either Skinny or Fatso got a good look at me last time. They were too busy defending themselves.'

They sat for a while just holding each other and thinking terrible thoughts. Then Pebble took Lamaxe's hand and led him back to the fire.

'We must tell the others,' she whispered.

The others' reactions were completely in character. Cliff and Red were all for hunting the two miscreants down next morning.

'I've brought some arrows and my bow with me,' Red informed them.

Mountsea was more cautious.

'This is not like Malta or Gozo,' he warned. 'It is a big island with many harbours and beaches. They could be anywhere by now. We have done our best for the Boy. Now we can only wait and see what happens to him. That will be my job. The best thing that all of you can do is to go about your business. You must return to your own island. Lamaxe and Pebble, you must take the treasure I will give to you back to your temple in exchange for the fine workmanship Pebble has done here. Red and Cliff you should return home also. Go back to your families and concentrate on the spoils of trade.'

'He's probably right,' said Cliff. 'We are unlikely to find them without great effort. Better to go home and secure your own safety and that of the temple's property.'

'In fact,' added Red turning to Lamaxe, 'Why not return with us? Your captain sails the day after tomorrow but we can wait until the next day. That way, you can stay to see how the Boy does and then come back with us in our two ships. We can afford you protection.' He waved his bow in the air.

Lamaxe was about to protest but Mountsea interrupted him.

'This makes good sense,' he said. 'Cliff and Red can return to their ships tomorrow and gather their crews together. They can check out the beach area to make sure that the villains have left. You can stay and see if the Boy improves and then use our boat to return to the beach. I will arrange for one of my congregation to collect it later.'

And so it was agreed. Red produced another skin of wine and they drank and told stories around the fire. In the morning Cliff and Red left and the others waited anxiously for news of the Boy. For the whole of the morning he lay still and silent. It was only when the sun had passed its apex that they saw the first flicker of his eyelids. Mountsea called them over.

'There is sign of consciousness,' he told them, 'but do not expect much further improvement before you leave.'

'Poor Boy,' Pebble said, 'I would like to know if we have had any success.'

'Yes,' added Lamaxe, 'please let us know how he gets on.'

'Of course, I will send word. Meanwhile, complete

your finishing touches to the carving today and tomorrow and then we will enjoy the remains of the boar meat and your birds for our meal before you leave.'

The next day Lamaxe went with Pebble as she returned to her task. She was intent on finessing the carving to produce her best work but her heart really wasn't in it anymore. She scraped a little and smoothed here and there. Lamaxe stood behind her watching but she became irritated by this and sent him away. So, while she worked he inspected again the inside of the Ragusa Hypogeum. It just wasn't anything like as impressive as the one back home in Hal Soflieni or even the one in Gozo. It wasn't a Hypogeum at all really, just a chamber tomb. Thinking about Hal Soflieni then made him think about his own Tarxian temples and he began to feel very homesick. He wanted to go home. Sicily had not been a success for him. He had failed in his primary mission to find Cloud. He had probably been responsible for the Boy nearly getting killed and he hadn't even been able to operate on his skull when the need arose. Pebble, on the other hand, had successfully completed the whole of her mission, or soon would. The carving was there in front of her and it was beautiful. And she had successfully (he hoped) operated on the Boy's skull. He really didn't deserve her.

He returned to see how she was getting on. Hearing him behind her, she put down her tools, turned and smiled at him.

'Come on,' she said. 'I can't do any more here. Let's go and see about some food. I wonder if that boar and those birds are cooked yet?'

Lamaxe snorted.

'The Boy would have made some joke about it being a fowl meal,' he said.

She embraced him and then led him back into camp.

'It isn't your fault,' she insisted.

The news that evening was better. By the time they returned to Mountsea the boat had been returned and was in good condition. Even better, the Boy had stirred and begun to utter some sounds. Not moaning but rather what appeared to be some attempt at speech though quite indecipherable. Mountsea seemed pleased with his progress and lavished attention on Pebble as the architect of the improvement. Though still anxious for his wellbeing they enjoyed a pleasant enough evening. They were prepared to leave early in the morning so Mountsea took them to inspect the boat. He was concerned that Lamaxe didn't seem a very competent sailor. The young priest assured him that it had seemed straightforward enough watching the Boy sail it and Pebble quietly confessed to having herself steered a small boat before. That was yet another talent that the sculptor had which Lamaxe didn't know about. They had an early night in preparation for the journey ahead.

# 13

The morning showed further improvement in the Boy. His breathing was even and he had begun to toss and turn in his sleep. Though still unconscious it seemed now much more like normal sleep than a coma. Mountsea's face showed his relief.

'I hope that all will be well with him. I have already this morning sacrificed a piglet for his recovery, albeit the runt of the litter.'

'Please send word to us when he awakes,' Pebble pleaded.

Lamaxe said nothing but stared intently at the Boy willing him to improve. Mountsea shared his porridge with them and saw them safely into the boat. They thanked him profusely for all his kindnesses. Last of all, with still trembling hands, he took off a bag strung around his neck under his tunic and placed it carefully in Pebble's hand. She opened it even more carefully. The copper glinted in the sunlight.

'Guard it well,' he said, 'and when you look upon it, think of Ragusa and our poor selves.'

'We will,' promised Pebble and kissed the old man lightly on the forehead. He blushed.

'Thank you, daughter,' he said. 'And here is the pin I promised for your High Priest. May peace follow you on your journey.'

'We will ensure that Trebird receives it safely,' Lamaxe told him, 'and please be sure to send us news when you can of the Boy's progress. I have become very fond of his cheeky ways.'

The old priest nodded his head. His hands shook now with emotion as well as with their natural tremor.

'I promise that as soon as he improves I will send news via the very next traveller to the Sacred Isle,' he said.

They climbed into the boat and with much waving pushed it away from the shore. Lamaxe held the paddle but once the current had taken them he found that he only needed it to steer. To his amazement he discovered that his fear of water had withered. A slight queasiness in his stomach was all that remained. Pebble noticed his new found confidence too but dare not mention it. She wondered if the fear of water had paled into insignificance after the excitement of their adventures. She had always enjoyed travelling and liked to experience new things but the injury to the Boy, more than anything, had deeply shocked her. Now she was just grateful that it would soon be all over and they would be home. She leaned against the young priest and closed her eyes, letting the warm sunshine fall on her face. She couldn't help smiling at herself when she thought how brown her face had become of late. In Copper Age society most women were weather-beaten from working in the fields but Pebble, who as a sculptor was often working inside and always with her head down away from the sun, was unusual in having a lighter skin. She had always thought that this contributed to her distinctive appearance. She knew that she was not traditionally beautiful, but she was striking. I'll just look like everyone else by the time we get home, she thought.

They were in no hurry and managed to land the craft safely part way along the river to avoid the rocks and climbed onto the bank where they lay in the sun for a while. There was no one around so they found themselves making love in the grass. They had been so busy of late that their opportunities had been few. It all seemed quite idyllic. As the sun passed its apex Pebble became aware of the time and was concerned that they should reach the ship in good time. She turned to Lamaxe who was sound asleep. At first she couldn't bear to wake him and lay there just staring at his sleeping face.

'It's no good,' she said to herself. 'We must get on.'

She took a blade of grass and gently brushed his cheek. No effect! She kissed him gently on the forehead. He tried to brush her off as if she were a fly but did not properly wake. Despite the beauty of the moment she began to be irritated.

'Right!' she said out loud and began to tickle him. This worked and he opened his eyes.

'Oh, hello!' he said, smiling, 'was I asleep?'

Showing what she thought was great restraint, she kissed him lightly on the cheek and told him that they should continue their journey. He leaned across to take hold of her but she pulled away from him.

'No,' she said. 'Now! We need to leave now or we will be late!'

Back in the boat she offered to take the paddle so he moved over and they sat side by side as best they could.

Lamaxe put his hand over the side and let the water swoosh through his fingers which made Pebble smile. Noticing it, he began to smile himself.

'Yes,' he said, 'I'm learning the attractions of water.'

Then he raised his legs and wriggled his toes.

'See, by boat I can travel without my feet hurting so much.'

She laughed, though she noticed that most of the nail was still missing from his big toe. Travel they did and in no time they arrived at the landing stage nearest to the beach. They clambered out and working together pulled the boat ashore. It would be collected later by someone sent by Mountsea from Ragusa. It was now only a short walk to where the ships were waiting so they strolled enjoying both the sunshine and each other's company. They linked arms and stopped frequently to admire the few wild flowers under foot and to watch the insects that buzzed constantly above their heads.

'This would make a wonderful carving,' Pebble said, her arm sweeping round to take in the view.

As they watched a bird of prey swooped down across their path. They stood still watching it first kill and then disembowel a mouse. Lamaxe pointed to it.

'Should I read the entrails?' he joked.

They strolled on arm in arm thinking of little else but themselves, making the most of this rare opportunity to be alone together. They were so lost in each other's company that at first the voice didn't register.

'So dis is wot dey do outside de tempule, eh!'

The voice was harsh and the accent foreign. They walked on oblivious.

''ey! priest!' the voice shouted. 'Who's yur friend?'

This broke their reverie. Lamaxe turned around and his heart sank. The still oozing wound was gradually beginning to develop scar tissue and was very obvious: a bright red line going diagonally right across the face. Lamaxe recognised it immediately. Skinny had never been attractive but the scar was so dominant that it was the only thing about him that you now noticed.

'Hello. Skinny, isn't it?' Lamaxe said, trying to keep the anxiety out of his voice. He looked around seeking the other one. There he was blocking their path to the beach, his cudgel in his hand. Lamaxe could have kicked himself. He had let his guard drop and now the consequences could be very bad indeed.

'Back to back' he whispered to Pebble and she obeyed, not recognising the men but sensing the danger and guessing from the scar who they must be. Each of them felt under their clothing for a weapon; Lamaxe for his sacrificial knife and Pebble for her sharp chisel and her stone hand hammer.

'So, you know ma name!' Skinny called. ''ow you know that, priest?'

Lamaxe forced a smile on his face.

'Oh, you're famous,' he answered. 'People recognise your face anywhere.'

'Tha's true,' the hoodlum replied failing to recognise the sarcasm and looking pleased. When he smiled his face seemed to split in two as the red lines crossed, one his mouth and the other the scar.'

'I'm sorry,' the priest whispered to Pebble, 'My fault! Be ready to run.'

Then he called to Skinny.

'I just asked the rats,' he said, 'They say you follow them everywhere picking up the scraps they won't eat.'

Pebble grabbed his hand.

'Don't antagonise him' she whispered.

'Too late,' he replied. 'They aren't going to let me go. Not after I gave him that scar. Watch the one with the mace. He's slow but he's very effective. When I jump them you run. It's your only chance. Cliff and Red can't be so far away. Get help.'

Skinny scowled and spat on the ground.

'Me, I'm a generous guy,' he said. 'You wanna pray 'fore I kill you? Ain't tha' wha' priests do?' He laughed. 'Tha's all they good for.'

Fatso joined in at this point, laughing loudly and thumping his club in the palm of his hand.

'Woman's OK though. I think I 'ave 'er, no? For a little fun?'

Lamaxe started to sweat with fear. He could feel it running down his back. Trying to look as calm as possible his gaze passed from one to the other seeking out their eyes as he imperceptibly turned Pebble so that she was facing away from the two of them. Then he gave her a slight push away from him and shouted at her to run while he rushed forward towards the two villains. They both set themselves.

'Come on, then,' he said. 'Who wants to die first?'

The big man began swinging his club as he walked slowly forward. Skinny drew his big copper knife from inside his clothes grinning as he did so and also headed towards Lamaxe. They were converging on the young priest but the big man arrived first and swung at his victim. Lamaxe dodged, stabbed with his knife into the other's arm and then ran to face Skinny. As he did so, a rock flew through the air over his shoulder and struck the thin man on the side of his head. He stumbled. Lamaxe looked behind him and, to his initial dismay, saw Pebble still standing there.

'How's that?' she shouted. 'A pebble from Pebble!'

'Run,' he shouted.

'Not me,' she said. 'I'm not leaving you.'

He turned again to face the big man. Fatso was furious. The wound was very slight; little more than a prick, but it angered him. He began to swing the club wildly at Lamaxe, who was forced to back away. He knew he wouldn't have long before Skinny got up again and attacked him from behind. As the big man lunged towards him he balanced on his toes and suddenly threw himself full length under the swinging mace, grabbing his assailant around the knees and pulling him to the floor. They landed with a thump that knocked the air out of both of them. Lamaxe could taste dust in his mouth. Fortunately for him, he recovered first, thrust his knife into the nearest body part available and then jumped back ready to face Skinny. The big man roared and held his lower leg which began to bleed profusely. Lamaxe hoped it would slow him down as he moved forward to engage with Skinny. As he did so, Pebble ran forward and leapt on Skinny's back, hitting him repeatedly on the head with her hand hammer. He was so surprised that he dropped his knife but quickly recovered and rolled with her on the ground.

'Oh, Our Lady, help us now,' Lamaxe called as he ran towards them. By this time Pebble had dropped her hammer and the two rolled around in the dust, seemingly locked together. He couldn't separate them. What should he do?

'Pebble, let go,' he ordered, hoping that for once she would obey him. She tried but as she rose Skinny grabbed her hair and dragged her down again. Lamaxe chose his time carefully and kicked with all his force at the hoodlum's head, terrified that he would hit the wrong one. His aim was good. Skinny's head went back, his arms went loose and he moaned. Blood gushed from his damaged scar. Lamaxe grabbed Pebble and pulled her to her feet. Then he half carried, half dragged her away. She was exhausted and for once stayed where he put her. Then he turned again to face Fatso, who, though limping, was still a power to be reckoned with. His face was filled with sheer fury.

'I gonna beat you to a pulp,' he said as he moved towards the priest, 'and then I gonna rape yur girl and then I'm gonna cut out yur guts and hang them on a bush.'

Lamaxe was by now too out of breath to reply. He just stood there waiting, hoping that Skinny hadn't recovered yet. The big man swung the club again and Lamaxe dodged but he was tiring and the huge piece of wood caught his shoulder. The pain was intense and he fell, rolling as he did so to try to get away. He could taste blood in his mouth now and realised that he must have bitten his tongue. Fatso kept coming. Lamaxe could see the determination on his face. He really meant to kill.

The young priest rose yet again spitting out the blood. He feared it would be his last time. The blow had torn all his remaining energy from him. He grasped the knife tighter. At least he could take the big hoodlum with him, he thought. He just hoped that Pebble could outrun the other one. He set himself as the man approached. He could feel the air displaced by the swinging club. This was it, he thought. And then, quite suddenly and unexpectedly the expression on the big man's face changed. The fury was replaced by surprise and then by pain. At the same time, a protrusion appeared at his throat. Lamaxe stared at it in fascination.

What on earth was it? he thought even as he braced himself for the final blow. Then the big man's arms gradually lowered and the club dropped from his limp hands as his body buckled and fell to the ground.

'Good shot, Red.'

Lamaxe was almost too tired to work out where the voice was coming from.

'Thanks. Better than hunting,' came a reply. 'You try the other one, Cliff.'

Lamaxe lifted his head and stared in amazement. Walking towards him were Cliff and Red. Cliff's bow was still cocked but Red's was empty and carried at his side. He had fired his arrow from some considerable distance and hit the big man through the back of the neck so forcefully that the arrow head must have passed right through and now protruded from under his chin.

'The other one!' thought Lamaxe, coming to his senses. He turned back once again towards Skinny who was still on the ground but rising. Lamaxe watched as, bleeding profusely from his face, he took one look at the body of his friend and then at the bowmen, turned and fled.

'Now, Cliff!' Red ordered and his friend released an arrow. Cliff really was a very second rate shot in comparison with Red. It was a good shot by Cliff's standards but hit the running man in the shoulder. Skinny stumbled and clasped the wound with his other hand but managed to stay on his feet and kept on running.

'By Our Lady,' cried Red, 'You've let him escape.'

With that Red reloaded his bow and let loose his last arrow but Skinny was by now too far away and it landed short, kicking up dust.

Pebble had got her breath back. She rushed to Lamaxe and though she only caught him gently the force of her arrival knocked him to the ground, so exhausted was he. They lay there hugging each other.

'You really should have got him, you know,' laughed Red, mocking his friend. 'What you need is more practice.'

'Yeh! yeh!' was all Cliff replied. 'Are you two all right? It looks as though we arrived just in time.'

'You certainly did,' said Pebble. She got up and gave each of them a big hug.

They sat Lamaxe and Pebble down and gave them water from their skins. Cliff offered them wine as well which Lamaxe accepted gratefully.

'I need the energy,' was all he said, 'and it takes away the taste of blood.'

Once they had begun to recover, they wanted to know what had brought the friends out to meet them.

'It seemed a nice day for hunting,' said Red with a smile.

Cliff was a bit more serious.

'Some of the crew had heard rumours that a stranger with a very bad fresh scar on his face had been hanging around asking questions about a priest. Others said these two had been noticed the day the Boy was attacked. It seemed a sensible precaution to walk over to meet you just in case.'

'We are awfully glad that you did. I couldn't have lasted much longer.'

'That's the trouble with you priests,' joked Red. 'No stamina! You are very good with a knife but the best weapon by far is the bow.'

'Yes,' said Cliff, 'taking up the theme, 'Red doesn't mind what kind of pig he shoots, be it wild boar or pirate.'

'What about the one that got away?' asked Pebble.

'Not much chance of catching him I'm afraid,' Red answered. 'That was only a flesh wound. It will heal soon enough if it doesn't go bad and they must have a ship somewhere. He'll probably live to fight another day.'

'Still,' added Cliff, 'thanks to Lammy here he'll always stand out in a crowd.'

Despite their jocularity their minds soon began to turn to more practical matters. They needed to get back to the ships and sort out their travelling arrangements. They must be ready for embarkation soon. Also they had the problem of what to do with the dead body? It was the end of summer but the weather was hot.

'It is rather heavy to drag along with us, isn't it?' said Pebble sensibly.

'He was a foreigner. I have heard lately of so many foreign religions. Do you know what his religion was?' asked Lamaxe, thinking like a priest. 'What burial practices he followed?'

Red laughed at this.

'He is a common murderer,' he said, 'and a pirate. I propose that we string him up here as an example to others. There's a tree over there. He'll be seen easily from the path.'

'But in a few days he will stink,' Cliff added practically.

'Then we can send a messenger to Mountsea who will come in a few days and cut him down.' Red bowed theatrically towards Lamaxe. 'He is a priest so I am sure he will think of a suitable burial practice,' he added sarcastically in an aside. Red laughed at his own joke. Although the man had tried to murder him Lamaxe was not very comfortable with the idea of hanging his body up as an example to others. Nevertheless, he couldn't think of a better solution and he didn't want to offend his friends, so that was what they eventually agreed. Lamaxe and Pebble were so exhausted from the fight that they left it to Cliff and Red. The two traders managed to start a friendly argument over the best way to do so but finally agreed. They left him swinging there as they returned to the ships.

After much discussion they all agreed that it would be best if the two passengers travelled on Red's ship since it had the lightest load. Cliff's ship was full to overflowing with raw wool. Indeed, extra wool had been pilled in part of Red's ship also. However, there was room behind the rowers for Lamaxe and Pebble to construct a small nest as on Crowfish's ship. It was too late in the day by now to set off so they agreed to spend the night there and leave in the morning. Some of the crew lit a fire on the beach and they held small fish over it on long sticks to cook. They were delicious. Indeed it would have been a jolly evening had not Lamaxe and Pebble been so tired and full of aches and pains. As soon as they politely could they gave their excuses and retired to the nest on board. As they lay quietly in the dark, Lamaxe asked the question he had wanted an answer to all evening.

'Why didn't you run when I told you?'

'Don't expect me to obey your orders.'

'But seriously, if Red and Cliff had not come along when they did I would be dead and so would you. You know you should have run to save yourself. If nothing else you could have gone for help.'

'You heard what they said they would do to you. I couldn't have got help before they had tortured and killed you.'

'And raped and killed you!'

'I can take care of myself. Anyway, Lamaxe, if I had escaped, what would be the point? Life would be no fun without you.'

There was silence after this while Lamaxe digested it.

'You mean…?' he said.

'Of course!' came her reply.

He leaned back on the warm skins and stared up at the sky. Did this mean that Our Lady had heard his prayers after all and, for once, had acted upon them? Both sets of prayers, that is: the one about saving their lives and the one about the future. That was the trouble with prayers, he thought. You never knew.

'I think it is time we got some sleep,' said Pebble.

They both snuggled down and were soon fast asleep. The Southern Cross looked down on them unconcerned.

# 14

The trip home was surprisingly uneventful. The prevailing winds made it always easier to sail from Sicily to Malta than the other way. Lamaxe's shoulder was very sore and his other limbs all ached from the strenuous fight. He still had the taste of blood and grit in his mouth. Pebble was stiff as well but, being fitter than he, recovered more quickly. As agreed they travelled in Red's ship so they were supplied liberally with skins of his father's wine to assuage their thirst. However, Pebble declined all offers and stuck to water. Lamaxe found that the wine eased his pain a little. He had begun to acquire quite a taste for it by the time they reached home.

Because both ships were laden with the ab Headland wool it had been agreed that both would sail to Malta and unload there but because they had been gone so long they decided to call first at Gozo on the way in order to see Red's father and reassure him of their safe return. They landed the ships and set a substantial guard, given the value of the goods on board, and then made their way to ab Graman's house. They received an astonishing welcome which included, quite literally, a fatted calf. The celebrations went on into the night but both Pebble and, especially Lamaxe, were not really in the mood. Pebble disappeared off to the edge of the compound to relieve herself and on her return had difficulty in tracking down her lover. She found him sitting quietly on a fence post staring at the skies.

'What's the matter?' she asked.

'Just thinking,' he answered.

'About…?'

'Oh! I was thinking that there is not a cloud in the sky.'

'Hmm?'

'Perhaps I should say, not even in the sky. I've completely failed to find any trace of her. When we get back I will have to tell her mother and father. I don't know what to say to them.'

Pebble put her arms around his waist. She had to reach up to do so as he was on the fence post.

'You have done your best. It is clear that Ayya was completely wrong when he accused Cliff. The girl must still be on Malta somewhere – whether she is dead or alive.'

Lamaxe shuddered. He didn't like to think of her as dead. He couldn't help thinking that if he had found her sooner she might still be alive. He stroked Pebble's hair thinking how he would feel if she were dead. A tear squeezed out of his eye and made its way down his cheek. Not wishing to let Pebble see this he changed the subject.

'Look,' he said, pointing, 'The Southern Cross is so clear tonight. Do you think that Our Lady is looking down upon us?'

Pebble raised her head and grinned at him.

'I hope she has better things to do,' she replied. 'After

all, we're all right now. We're nearly home. She doesn't have to look after us any more.'

Lamaxe ran his hand gently through her hair.

'I think we can presume that She was looking out for us the other day. How else could Red and Cliff have arrived so fortuitously?'

'The Goddess helps those who help themselves,' was all Pebble said in reply. They both continued to stare silently at the night sky, lost in their individual thoughts.

They stayed there in comfortable companionship for some time. Then Lamaxe's shoulder began to stiffen again and he slipped off the post and onto the ground.

'I will have to try again to find her when we get back,' he said.

'They may have found her already,' Pebble replied.

Lamaxe brightened.

'Do you really think they might have?' he asked.

'No, not really,' she said. 'You are the only one who is looking for her. Anyway, I suspect that she has disappeared for good. But don't worry, I'll help you look. Trebird will be so pleased to receive the copper figurine that he will surely not begrudge us a little time to ourselves.'

Lamaxe laughed bitterly at this.

'You don't know Trebird as well as I do,' he said.

Then, taking her hand gently, he led her back to the centre of the compound.

The next day they set off again for the Sacred Isle. They landed safely, though it took Cliff some considerable time to organise the unloading of the bales of wool. These were placed on sledges and dragged along to the ab Headland household. Cliff's welcome by his father was if anything even grander than that for Red had been. After all, a local chief must outdo everyone else even in his celebrations. This time, of course, it was accompanied by a stream of rather coarse and mostly unfunny jokes from the Chief himself. For politeness sake, Lamaxe and Pebble joined in with the laughter, but they had by now wearied of celebration and just wanted to get back to the temple compound. They made their excuses and left after first thanking Cliff and Red profusely for all they had done. The two friends walked back with them part of the way and even offered to help with the search for Cloud if they were needed.

By the time the two had reached the temple compound it was dark and everyone except Springox had retired to bed.

'Welcome, holiness,' he greeted them, not at all fazed by the hour. 'And you, miss,' he added, addressing Pebble.

'Hello, Springox,' Lamaxe replied. 'Are there beds ready so we can go straight to sleep. It has been a very long and tiring few days.'

The Superintendent raised one eyebrow.

'Beds?' he enquired.

'Yes, two beds,' Pebble answered with a smile. 'Arrangements may alter, but for the moment I retain my independent status. Thank you.'

The old man bowed his head, masking his own smile.

'I will see to it,' he said.

Soon they were tucked up in their separate beds and both fell fast asleep in minutes.

They rose separately but at approximately the same time and bumped into each other as they headed for some food. A good night's sleep had given them an appetite. They saw the Boy in the distance frantically waving to them and waved back but were waylaid by Trebird before the Boy could speak to them.

'Ah! You are returned. Good. Where is the figurine?'

Lamaxe was taken aback a little at this abruptness. Even he expected some kind of welcome from his High Priest. Pebble decided to play a little game with the old man.

'We have had some success, holiness,' she answered.

'Only some success?' came Trebird's anxious reply. 'Do you have it? Where is it?'

Pebble smiled sweetly at him.

'Allow me to tell you the whole story,' she answered. He nodded so she sat down at the table and slowly helped herself to some porridge. Lamaxe did the same. Then, as she ate leisurely, she recounted some of their adventures in as long-winded a way as possible. She could see the sweat breaking out on Trebird's brow. Did she have it? Was it not right? What could have gone wrong? She could see the questions fleetingly appear across his face as she ground on with her tale. Eventually, she described how Mountsea had presented her with the packet from around his neck.

'So where is it?' he demanded, any lingering politeness having dissipated. She smiled, and slowly withdrew the bag from around her own neck and bent to allow Lamaxe to untie the string. Trebird fumbled in his haste to open the bag. He first pulled out the skirt pin and looked quite forlorn.

'That is a personal present for you from Mountsea,' Lamaxe told him. 'Look deeper.'

He did so and then he let out an enormous gasp as he saw the object for the first time. He held it up and turned it in the light to see it sparkle.

'It is truly magnificent,' he said.

Pebble was still enjoying her minor torture of the High Priest but Lamaxe felt a surge of relief that the old man was pleased. Trebird simply stared at it for some moments muttering to himself. The others strained to hear.

'Truly, this is as great as anything which ab Headland possesses,' he whispered. Then he turned to address them directly. 'You have both done well. Now we must arrange a great ceremony to announce the acquisition and display it in the temple. Ab Headland, as Chief, will have to publicly acclaim it.'

'I thought ab Headland had arranged this?' Lamaxe asked.

'We both arranged it,' he replied. 'But it is for the glory of the temple not the chief.'

'Does it matter?' asked Pebble.

Trebird gave them a sly smile.

'It matters to me,' he said.

Lamaxe and Pebble looked at each other. Had they risked their lives in some petty power squabble over who had the most impressive figurine? Surely not! In private Lamaxe would admit to himself that he found ab Headland very irritating but he had been very generous to Lamaxe, and his son Cliff had been magnificent. He wanted nothing to do with petty squabbles.

By this time, Trebird was calling for the Superintendent of the Temple Compound.

'Springox, quickly, let us discuss the ceremony.'

As Springox slid into view the old priest rose and would have disappeared into the temples to make arrangements. Lamaxe called him back.

'Trebird,' he said. 'Before you go, I must tell you that I

have also been searching for the missing girl. I have found no sign of her. I must go and tell her parents of my ill-luck. Will you excuse me duties for a while?'

'Oh!' called Trebird irritably. 'You can forget about that. It is history. Besides, Ayya is desperately ill. He is likely to be dying. Forget all about the girl. Nobody cares any longer.'

Lamaxe's face fell. He had tried hard. It hurt for his efforts to be dismissed so cavalierly. He was about to protest when the Boy, who had by now arrived but was hanging around on the edge of their conversation, intervened.

'Holiness,' he said to Trebird. 'I feel that Lamaxe should be made aware that one of his brother's children is seriously ill. He may wish to have time to visit him.'

Trebird was now completely consumed with the new figurine.

'Indeed. Indeed,' he said dismissively. 'We have had an epidemic of the choking disease while you have been away. Several children are ill and likely to die.' He waved his arm vaguely in dismissal. 'If one of your brother's children is among them then you may go to him.'

'Thank you, Trebird,' he said already heading for the door. Pebble went to follow.

'No,' he said to her gently. 'Let me see how bad it is first. Oyeh and Moonlight will need some space if this is true.'

'I would like to come,' she continued.

'Then come later and offer to help my mother.'

She nodded her assent. As Lamaxe left he called a thank you to the Boy who waved back in turn.

Pebble took the Boy aside.

'Was the old swine really not going to tell Lamaxe about the child?' she asked.

'He has been so wrapped up in awaiting your return that he has paid little attention to the epidemic. When Crowfish returned without you, he was nearly hysterical with concern. Not for your wellbeing, you understand, but for the figurine.'

'I'm sorry,' he added after a pause.

'Don't be,' she answered. 'I know well enough what he is like, but I am surprised that he should regard rivalry with ab Headland as so important.'

The Boy hesitated but when she gave him her warmest smile he relented and decided to tell her his thoughts. He explained that Trebird had been in discussion with other priests from other chiefdoms on the isle and that they were concerned with the growing importance of trade with other peoples and its impact upon religion. There had never been any serious conflict before between the traders and farmers and the priests. Indeed, it had been the chiefs, mostly rich traders like ab Headland, who had generated the wealth and organised the work parties to build and to repair the temples so that there had always been a strong alliance. However, as the farmers became richer and more wanted to trade outside the island they had found themselves more open to other cultural influences. Traders from outside brought their own gods and goddesses. The priests didn't like this. In Trebird's case the anxiety had been exacerbated by ab Headland's tendency in private to make fun of so many things which Trebird held dear. The High Priest had begun to distrust his Chief. What better way to show the Goddess's power and importance than to outdo the chief in terms of wealth and prestige; and what better way to do that than to display that wealth openly in the temple.

'I see,' said Pebble. 'And thank you.'

'You won't say anything?' the Boy asked anxiously.

Pebble winked at him.

'Just between the two of us,' she whispered.

Lamaxe hurried to his brother's farm. His mother saw him from the house doorway and came running. She looked very old as she fell into his arms and wept openly on his shoulder.

'You are returned and well? Thank the Goddess!'

Lamaxe just nodded.

'Tell me what has happened, mother?' he asked.

She told him about the sickness. First it had developed within the family of a single trader but soon escaped into the wider community. Several children were now ill. One had died already. Ossay, Oyeh's son, had become ill two days ago. He was finding it difficult to breathe. His sister, Seacloud, was still well but they all feared that she would be next. The parents were devastated. They had already lost one of their three children and now it looked as though they might lose them all.

'But you must have food?' his mother said, suddenly recognising her duties as a host.

'No, mother. I have eaten.'

'Then come inside.'

'Is Oyeh there?'

'No. He cannot sit still. He is out working the fields.'

She led him across the compound and inside Oyeh's house where Moonlight sat hunched in a corner cradling her sick child. He kneeled beside her.

'Pray for him,' she said.

He did so. Then he asked to take the child and carried

him outside into the light where he could see him better. His little body was limp and his breathing laboured. It did seem to be the choking disease, as the Boy had suggested. His mother came to the door.

'Don't hold him in the sun,' she said, 'he is hot. He needs the cool of the shade.'

Lamaxe acknowledged her concern but asked that she wait one moment while he examined the child. He opened Ossay's mouth and could see clearly the swelling at the back of his throat. He had never understood illness. It arose from nowhere and spread for no obvious reason. Why, he wondered, did some die and others appear to be unaffected? Still, Ragusa had taught him something. Priests could do more than just use prayer and potions. The trepanning had shown that people were not completely helpless against illness and injury. He was beginning to feel that trying to cure people was part of a priest's job just as much as praying for the Goddess to intervene. Perhaps the Goddess could intervene through the actions of the priest?

'Go inside,' he told Moonlight. 'I will bring him in shortly.'

Once the woman had gone he reopened Ossay's mouth. Think logically, he told himself. The swelling in the back of the throat seemed to be partly blocking the airway so he poked at it with his finger. Some of the gung surrounding the opening appeared to come away on his finger nail. The boy choked with a coughing fit. Lamaxe tried again. The throat was very swollen. Then he had an idea. He searched around for a flexible hollow reed. Laying the child on the ground he took his knife and cut the stalk smoothing it until it had no sharp edge but was quite hollow. Then he picked up the child, opened his mouth and tried to insert the tube down his throat. This caused much coughing and choking in Ossay as he panicked and he had no success. He waited until the child had calmed down again. He tried again and partly inserted the reed. The breathing improved slightly. Perhaps if it could be kept clear he might survive, he thought. The child coughed again and out came the reed along with some vomit. Lamaxe cradled him in his arms and walked back into the house where he returned him to his mother.

'I will pray for guidance,' he told her, an idea flickering through his mind.

Then he went outside and carefully washed both his hands and the reed. His mother came out and offered him clean water to drink which he accepted. Then he returned indoors and ostentatiously prostrated himself on the floor as though praying. He had participated in the Oracle event at the temple long enough to know the value of theatre. He mumbled incoherently to himself as he lay there. Occasionally he muttered the Goddess's name. He was still there when Oyeh came in from the fields to eat. Oyeh walked around his brother without comment and went to Moonlight and the child.

'He seemed to be breathing a little better for a moment when Lamaxe held him,' she told him, 'but now it gets worse again.'

Lamaxe remained prostrate for some considerable time longer. He had been thinking hard. Dare he attempt it? What would Oyeh do? As a priest he knew something of the body and its internal organs. He had opened up enough of them. It seemed to make sense. The problem was not with the child's lungs but with his throat. He wished Pebble had come with him. She had more courage. Eventually, he arose with a serene look on his face, hiding the turmoil inside.

'The Goddess has spoken to me,' he said. 'The child is very ill and may not survive but if we do exactly what the Goddess tells us, he may recover.'

'What do we do?' they asked anxiously in unison.

'Wait!' he said. 'First, I must follow my instructions.'

He went outside, cleaned the tube again and also carved another one. Best to have a spare, he thought. Then he sharpened each of them to a point using his flint sacrificial knife. Finally, he went back inside and sat down opposite the two parents. He waved to his mother to join them.

'The Goddess says that an evil thing has put a blockage in his throat. This is meant to kill him. Our Lady has instructed me as to what to do and this I will follow however strange it seems. Do not interfere.'

He held the reed in front of him.

'This is a holy reed,' he announced.

With that he took the child in his arms and carried him outside for greater light. Turning his back on the parents so they couldn't see he took out his knife and very carefully used it to pierce the child's throat. He wasn't at all sure what he was doing but he knew from the sacrificial animals that there was a tube in there through which to breathe. If he could bypass the blockage perhaps the air could get in and out. He tried very carefully to insert the reed through the hole. If he pushed too hard or the cut was in the wrong place then his nephew would die.

Once the cut was made and the reed was in place there was an immediate improvement in his breathing. Moonlight cried out.

'The Goddess has done a miracle! She has saved his life.'

Then Lamaxe turned around. When she saw the reed sticking out of his throat she screamed. Oyeh tried to grab the child off his brother but was restrained by Starbright.

'Wait!' she said. 'The child's breathing is better.'

Lamaxe raised his hand, still holding the stick in place and chanting quietly.

'See how the holy reed counters the evil swelling. Do not thwart me in this. It is Our Lady's work.'

Oyeh was suitably chastened. They sat as in a frozen tableau for some time.

When Lamaxe felt that Ossay's breathing had eased sufficiently he carefully handed back the child to its mother and went again to thoroughly wash his hands. He had no idea if this would work, but it seemed to ease the child's breathing and he knew that children who suffered from this illness usually choked to death.

'If the reed comes out then a new one can be inserted. I have one here. I have already blessed it in Our Lady's name.'

He showed them his spare.

'You must learn to do this ritual yourselves when I am not here. I have offered a very powerful prayer which means that this will work for you as well as me even though you are not priests.'

The two women looked terrified but as the breathing continued to improve their faces began to show relief. Oyeh still looked in shock.

'You must do it exactly as I say or you could injure

his throat and make him worse. It is imperative that the reed enters the correct hole in his throat. Oyeh, you are a farmer and hunter – you know which hole is used to breathe. You must also believe that it will work or it will not. Do you understand?'

His brother nodded his agreement. They managed to keep the reed in throughout the morning. The child remained very ill, still running a temperature, but his breathing continued to improve.

Pebble had waited until mid-morning before leaving the temple compound. It was a warm summer afternoon and, despite her anxiety at the fate of the child, she strolled enjoying the sunshine and the peace and quiet after the bustle of Trebird in the temple. As she walked she stopped to chat to the women working in the fields or picking wild fruit and herbs from the wayside. She had always found it easy to talk to other women but now her skin was nearly as weather-beaten as their own they were even more forthcoming. During the course of her short amble she found two women, one of them was really only a young girl, who remembered seeing Cloud on the fateful morning of her disappearance. Both remembered it because it was just before the day of the ritual and because of the fuss that Ayya had made about the chief's son at the community meeting. It was not every festival at which the Chief's son was accused of kidnap. The woman told Pebble that she had seen Cloud on the path, apparently walking towards the temple compound. She had been concentrating on her work and so had not actually seen her enter.

The young girl had been sent by her mother to find a particular herb and this had proved to be difficult. She had walked all the way up to the walls of the temple compound before she had located some growing in Trebird's garden. She had not spoken before because she knew it had been wrong to take it. She claimed to see Cloud actually pass through the temple entrance. Pebble noted their names in her head and where they lived and began to feel that she had done a good day's work. Cloud must have got as far as the temple although no one there had seen her. Where had she gone from there? There had been suggestions that she had been heading for the Hypogeum, which certainly remained a possibility but no one had reported seeing her there either. Had she met Tornbark, the farmer's son, after all despite what his father had said? Had she met one of the masons? Or had she mysteriously disappeared between the two places? That seemed the most likely but why? She would report it all to Lamaxe when she saw him.

When she arrived at Oyeh's farm she went straight to find Starbright. As usual she was cooking, leaning over a clay cooking pot, dropping hot stones into it and sprinkling it with the occasional herb. It smelled like some kind of stew. She greeted Pebble as she might a daughter, sat her down and offered her food.

'Land Tortoise,' she said pointing at the pot.

Pebble accepted a mouthful but politely declined the rest and asked about Ossay.

'He seems a little better,' she answered. 'Lamaxe has said prayers for him and they seem to have had some good effect. But it is early days. The choking sickness is a killer.'

'And his sister, Seacloud?'

'She is still well. We wait...'

With that she hung her head. Pebble could see that

she was completely exhausted both physically and emotionally.

'Why do you not rest and I will tend the pot?' she said trying to lead the old woman by the arm.

'I cannot sleep,' she said. 'You go to Lamaxe and help him help the child. Pray for him.'

So Pebble rose and went in search of her priest. She found him once again holding the child and gently rocking him. His eyes were closed so she touched his arm lightly and he jumped awake.

'How goes it?' she asked.

'Well enough, I think. We must just wait.'

He smiled weakly at her. Then, indicating that she should crouch beside him he passed her the child. She looked askance at the reed still protruding from his throat.

'Is it not the choking disease?' she asked, 'sometimes called 'oxethroat'. Usually the throat becomes blocked and they die.'

'Yes. See his throat.' He smiled at her. It was a weak, tired sort of smile but with a look of real satisfaction.

'I have never seen this before,' she said. 'Is this your doing? It is horrific.'

'It is,' he replied, 'but listen to his breathing. You are very observant. See, the throat was blocked but now he can breathe through the tube. It has been in all night. He seems much better.'

'Remarkable,' she replied.

He laughed.

'No, not remarkable! I thought about you trepanning the Boy: that was remarkable. I thought why should we lie down before death? We should fight it. So I followed your example.'

'Your mother only said that you had prayed for him.'

'I did. I feared that Oyeh would not let me do such a crazy thing so I pretended that the Goddess had ordered me to do it.'

'Perhaps she had!'

Lamaxe laughed again at this.

'Yes,' he said. 'Perhaps it is like the Oracle room. We have to help Our Lady get her message over to the people.'

They sat in silence after that.

They stayed the night, eating with the family and retiring to their separate beds. Oyeh was very silent throughout. The women were more voluble. Ossay was not yet out of danger but they could now see a chance for him. What was more, the girl Seacloud was still well. Of course, sometimes this sickness took several days to spread so there was still reason to worry but with the Goddess's help there was hope. At the end of the meal Oyeh disappeared for a while but then returned carrying a handful of reeds.

'See brother,' he said to Lamaxe, holding up the tubes, 'I am prepared. Will you bless them for me?'

Lamaxe rose and embraced him.

'Brother,' he said, 'Of course I will. I must leave in the morning but I will do so knowing that the children are in your capable hands. Remember, be very careful, pray in between times, and believe.'

Over his brother's shoulder he winked at Pebble.

# 15

In the morning Lamaxe and Pebble set out for Ayya's farm. They were both deep in thought and said little. Lamaxe was still anxious about Ossay's condition but couldn't shirk the responsibility of visiting Ayya and telling Sky of his failure to find her daughter. Then, as they walked Pebble remembered what she had forgotten to tell Lamaxe about her discoveries the day before. She explained her walk and her conversations with the woman and the girl.

'So,' Pebble concluded, 'Cloud was definitely seen going towards the temple by at least two people and the girl insists that she saw her actually go inside. This doesn't mean that she didn't go on to the Hypogeum as she intended, but surely someone from the temple must have seen her.'

'It is a new lead,' said Lamaxe gratefully, 'but as far as we know only Trebird was near the temple at the time. I and the Boy were collecting the sacrificial beast and Springox had gone to see the mason. Trebird assures me that he did not see her and there was no one else.'

Pebble thought about this.

'What about the servants?' she asked. 'We tend to forget about servants.'

Lamaxe nodded.

'There is only the cook and she is only there for meals when we are there. Springox tells me that she saw nothing while she was there. In any case, she is far too busy with her cooking to notice comings and goings.'

'Not that day she wasn't, if only Trebird was there,' Pebble insisted.

'True, but why should she interfere with young Cloud?'

Pebble had no answer to this.

'And there was no one else?' she asked, somewhat forlornly.

Lamaxe shook his head.

'I will have to ask the neighbouring farmers and check on their sons' behaviour but we have already eliminated ab Treefall and ab Stonecrop. The other person whose farm is near is ab Speltland but he has no sons, only daughters.'

They found Sky kneeling outside the house nibbling in a desultory fashion on some flatbread and staring at her porridge. She said nothing but indicated to them with her hands that they should join her and partake of a meal. They had eaten before they left Oyeh's house but it was rude, outside of the immediate family, to refuse such a welcome so they indicated acceptance with a nod of the head. Sky passed them a wooden bowl each. They took some bread, Lamaxe eating very slowly in order to put off what he had to say. He could think of no kind way to express it. Sky saved him the trouble.

'You have not found her.' It was more of a statement than a question.

Lamaxe shook his head.

'We found Cliff and Red but it is clear that they have not seen Cloud. I fear that she did not leave the island.'

'So, she is dead.'

Again it was a statement not a question. Lamaxe made no reply. Then Sky erupted into a coughing fit. Pebble leaned forward and put her arm around the woman's shoulder.

'Truthfully, I do not know', Lamaxe replied at last. 'We believe that she went to the temple and we think she may not have reached the Hypogeum. Other than that we do not know. I could still interview the farmers whose land lies in that direction but I do not know where else to look'.

Sky's head went down and she stared intently at the ground for some time. Then she looked up and indicated with her hand over her shoulder.

'Tell him,' she said.

'How is he?' asked the priest. 'I had heard that he was ill.'

She shook her head.

'He is old and he is dying.'

'I'm sorry,' Lamaxe replied.

She shrugged her shoulders.

'He will not beat me any more,' she answered matter-of-factly, 'but to lose a daughter and a man so close together is hard.'

She buried her head in Pebble's shoulder.

Lamaxe stood up and entered the house. Ayya was lying on his straw mattress, his head raised. There were traces of blood on the bed covering. It took a while for Lamaxe's eyes to adjust to the darkness and at first he thought the old man was asleep but, as his eyes adjusted he realised that Ayya was staring ahead, his eyes round and still, almost as though he were already dead.

'Well priest?' he croaked. 'Have you found her?'

He erupted into a bout of coughing and spat blood onto the floor.

Lamaxe kneeled by the bed, avoiding the blood.

'I have not,' he said.

'Cliff?' the old man asked.

'Cliff and Red were together the whole time. They and their crews confirm that Cloud was never with either of them.' He paused briefly. 'I fear that she never left the Sacred Isle.'

The old man groaned.

'You must find her!' he said as loudly as his failing voice would allow.

'I do not know where else to look,' Lamaxe replied.

Tears came to the old man's eyes.

'I would be happy now for her to have been with Cliff, son of the chief that he is. She must be alive. She must have children.'

Lamaxe raised an eyebrow. Why the sudden change of attitude he wondered.

'What about Chitah?' he asked.

There was silence for a while except for his further coughing. Then the old man spoke again in a whisper.

'Things have changed,' he said. 'I had ambitions to be the famous ancestor of the greatest farming family on the island. But now, I see that I may not have issue at all. Yet I must become an ancestor!'

His voice rose suddenly at this and there was pleading in it. It was now loud enough for Pebble to hear outside.

She left Sky and entered the building. As she did so the old man laughed bitterly.

'I had hopes of being remembered by the community as a great man, revered as an important ancestor. Now it seems I may not have anyone to remember me at all and my shade will fade into oblivion. You must not let that happen. You must find her.'

Lamaxe looked across at Pebble. She blinked but gave no indication of how he should respond.

'You must!' the old man pleaded from the bed. The coughing began again worse than before.

'Very well,' said Lamaxe. 'I will continue to try. I have promised your wife that I would.'

'Thank you,' Ayya replied sinking back onto the mattress. There was a note of such humility in his voice that it almost brought a tear to Lamaxe's eye. He brushed it aside. How could he feel sympathy for this horrible old man who had apparently beaten his wife and driven his daughter away? He thought of himself and Pebble. He wanted her as a friend and a companion as well as a lover. He had not thought about children. They were a given. But he supposed that he also would want to be remembered as an ancestor.

He stood up and leaning over towards Pebble, took her hand. He gave her such a look of tenderness that she blushed. She squeezed his hand in return and they went outside into the sunshine. Sky was still bending over the food but she wasn't eating.

'I will continue the search for Cloud,' he told her. 'I do not know if she is alive or dead but I will try to find her anyway.'

As he said it, he thought of the further disapproval he would get from Trebird for saying so. Nevertheless he thought that it should be part of a priest's job to try to comfort people. It was not just about making rituals and ensuring that the seasons changed. Sky raised her head and offered him a half smile, but it was a smile of little hope.

Pebble leaned over the old woman and hugged her. She looked up but then began coughing again, holding her hand to her mouth. As she withdrew it, Pebble saw the blood.

'You are also ill,' she said.

Sky offered her a weak smile.

'I too am coughing blood. Perhaps we will both soon be gone?'

The young couple sat either side of her and Pebble stroked her hair.

'He is not all bad,' Sky said pointing inside the house towards her husband. 'He had a wild youth but settled down when I eventually agreed to have him. It is only in recent years that he has been so unpleasant.'

'I always wondered,' Lamaxe intervened,' why everyone calls him Ayya? That is a diminutive, normally used only for children and within the family. He is an important farmer now yet everyone uses that name.'

The old woman gave a genuine chuckle.

'As I said, he had a wild youth – women, drink, foolish things. His father thought he would never grow up. So, everyone kept on using his childish name. I refused him several times, you know. Eventually, he settled down and worked seriously on the farm. It was only then that I agreed to have him. But by then, it was too late. The name Ayya had stuck. Everyone carried on using it.'

'But the way he has treated you and Cloud...?' Pebble began.

Sky raised her hand for silence.

'It is only in recent years,' she said. 'I think he was frustrated. Cloud is our only living issue. He always wanted to start a dynasty. Our two sons died in infancy. He blamed me for not having more children. And then Cloud refused to agree to his plans with Chitah. He had thought that by aligning the two families he would create the greatest farming family on the island; more important than the chief's.'

She began coughing again in earnest. They offered her water which she accepted. Then she waved to them to leave.

'Go! Find my daughter if you can.'

They arose and hand in hand they left.

They had walked nearly as far as the temple compound both lost in thought when suddenly Pebble had an idea.

'Wait!' she said. 'Remember my drawings? The ones I did to try to represent your account of who the various people were and what they were doing? They were destroyed early in the morning by the work of the Sweeper.'

Lamaxe looked surprised.

'Yes, the Sweeper,' he said. 'He is so quiet and unassuming that we never think of him. The Sweeper must have been there for some of the day at least.'

'I will ask him,' Pebble insisted.

There was tremendous hustle and bustle within the temple compound when they returned. Trebird was giving instructions about the requirements for his ceremony and the Boy was rushing about trying to fulfill them. Even Springox indicated some sense of urgency in his movements. As soon as Lamaxe was noticed by the High Priest he was waved over.

'Come, come,' he said. 'Where have you been? I need you to discuss the details of the ceremony. Hurry now.'

In other circumstances it would have been amusing but Lamaxe was too full of concern for his sick nephew and with the missing Cloud to take his superior's pomposity too seriously. How dare he not ask about his nephew? How could a copper bauble be more important than the child's life? He bristled and was about to protest when Pebble tapped him lightly on his behind and whispered, 'Go with him and I will speak to the Sweeper.'

So Lamaxe held back his protest and went silently along.

Lamaxe and Trebird discussed the arrangements while the High Priest bustled about, frequently calling for the Boy and Springox to move this to there and then back again. The Boy ran about in confusion while Springox glided from task to task.

'I want a special ritual,' Trebird told the assistant priest. 'It can be quite short but it must be very different from the normal rituals. This is a very special occasion.'

Lamaxe, although he had benefited by being praised for his work in bringing the figurine to Tarxian, found it very difficult to take the figure seriously. Perhaps it was because he and Pebble had met the men who made it? Perhaps it was that they knew that the same men had also produced the gilded calf? Perhaps it was that the copper had been melted down from a broken dish? Somehow the knowledge undermined the object's sanctity. Of course, even the great stone statue of Our Lady which stood at the entrance to the third temple had been sculpted by a human hand, but that had been carved from a solid block of stone by someone who had really cared. One could believe that the Goddess had guided the sculptor's hands. It was more difficult for him to see the Goddess's hand in the industrial process in Sicily.

Lost in such thoughts Lamaxe became aware that Trebird was talking to him again and not just shouting at the Boy.

'Sorry, holiness,' he said.

'Ah!' exclaimed Trebird. 'You too are overwhelmed by its majesty, eh? I said that I think we will start with a short ritual in the third temple which is the grandest. I will explain that Our Lady is making special demands and needs to be placated. I will ring their hearts with threats.'

He smiled at this.

'Then we can go in procession to the Oracle room where the Oracle – that's you – will tell them that if we promise to comply, Our Lady will give us a special gift in thanks. Lamaxe, are you listening? Then as High Priest I will guarantee that the community meet all her demands, placate her and so save us all. The congregation will be greatly relieved and they will be thankful – to me!'

He placed great emphasis upon the word 'will'.

'The Oracle will then add that Our Lady is pleased with my response and will give us an image of herself that will ensure that we have great fortune. Have you got that? Lamaxe, I am depending on you.'

'Yes, Trebird,' he replied without enthusiasm. 'But is this what you agreed with ab Headland?'

The High Priest didn't bother to reply to this.

'Then I will display the new image to the congregation who will be in awe.'

Lamaxe nodded.

'After that,' Trebird continued, 'we will process back to the third temple where the Boy will have an animal for sacrifice. It had better be an ox, I think.'

He broke off to yell at the Boy.

'Make sure it is an ox for sacrifice. Try and get a white one.'

Lamaxe nodded his head in agreement once more and tried to smile ingratiatingly. He hoped that he was showing enough enthusiasm despite his personal feelings. Trebird chuckled to himself.

'I can't wait to see the expression on ab Headland's face,' he said.

Meanwhile Pebble sought out the Sweeper. He was not the easiest person to find. Normally she would never have considered speaking to him directly without the presence of Springox, but the Superintendent was busy with the hustle and bustle generated by Trebird's enthusiasm. She found the nondescript man in the kitchen eating a bowl of something. He was embarrassed to speak to her but after she had reassured him that she only wanted information, he reluctantly agreed. She omitted to tell him that he was a suspect. His story was a simple one. He had seen the girl as he was leaving the temple complex to collect new brushwood for a broom. She had been seeking Trebird but he didn't know why and hadn't asked. It was not his place to ask questions. He did not normally expect to be noticed by either priests or worshippers and prided himself on his invisibility. He had been particularly embarrassed to be spoken to by such a beautiful young girl so he had pointed to where he believed Trebird to be and then hurried away. That was all he knew.

Pebble thanked him and let him go. He could still be a suspect, she thought, but then, if he was guilty why would he admit to seeing Cloud at all. All he needed to have said was that he had left before she arrived. Perhaps he had been trying to deflect guilt onto Trebird? She supposed that it was possible, but it was a dangerous strategy on his part to appear to incriminate, however remotely, the High Priest. After all, the Sweeper was so lowly that normally no one even noticed him. A priest could easily destroy him. She tried another tack. Could Trebird have met the girl? He had denied seeing her. Why? If she had really intended to go to the Hypogeum, as she had told her father, Trebird could have simply admitted to seeing her and then sending her on her way. None of it made sense. She needed to speak again with Lamaxe but it was no good waiting for him. He would be stuck with Trebird all day sorting out the preparations. Pebble would have to try to work it out herself.

She settled down on a bench. Suppose Trebird had met the girl – why? Had it been arranged? That didn't seem likely as she had stormed out of her father's house in anger on the spur of the moment. Had she simply come to see a priest to seek advice? Any priest. And Trebird had been the only one around? That seemed more likely, but, if so, why had Trebird not admitted to seeing her there? A different thought struck her. Maybe she had been seeking Lamaxe? He was nearer her age and Lamaxe had said that she had been keen on him when they were younger. Yet the Sweeper had said that she had asked for Trebird. Why the old one? Mind you, she thought to herself, Trebird was not as old as he seemed, was he? He always acted as though he was ancient. He had a formality and crustiness about him that she supposed came with playing the role of High Priest. An awful image of a pompous Lamaxe as High Priest popped up in her head and made her laugh despite herself. She suppressed it.

What did she really know about Trebird? He was about thirty and had been High Priest for some years. Lamaxe remembered him being married but his wife had died in an epidemic a couple of years ago. He had apparently been a much more jovial figure before that but had turned in on himself after her death. It seemed as though he had suppressed all internal emotion and had become just a High Priest. The person had been subsumed into the role. She was rather pleased with that last thought. It sounded rather impressive to her. She thought that she would make sure to use the phrase when she discussed this with Lamaxe later.

Since she was in the kitchen and the cook was not around she looked for something to eat and drink. There was some bread which she dipped in the remains of a lentil stew. It was good, if cold. Then she found a skin of water and drank deep. It was thirsty work all this thinking. What can Cloud have wanted? And what effect might it have had on Trebird? If she had wanted advice he would surely either have taken her seriously or sent her away with a flea in her ear. Why else might she have come? Suppose she had come seeking a better husband than Chitah in order to thwart her father's plans? But surely she would then have come looking for Lamaxe? Not that she, Pebble, would have had any intention of letting Cloud get away with anything. He was her's – no question! No, but perhaps after all the High Priest was an attractive proposition. He was twice her age but still not too old. He had high status so her father could not publicly be too outraged. He could give her a good life: servants within the temple, a good standard of living and no need to undertake backbreaking work in the fields. As she reckoned this, Pebble couldn't help thinking of her own situation should she marry Lamaxe. Of course, she would want to keep working as a sculptor, but in other respects it did seem a good life if you didn't mind it impinging on your freedom. For Cloud, as important as all of these issues would be, the fact that he wasn't Chitah was perhaps his greatest asset. He didn't smell. And she would have been away from her odious father. Perhaps then she did offer herself to Trebird?

She took another piece of bread and dipped it. How might he have reacted if she had? Cloud was a good looking girl by all accounts. Would he accept? Would he be horrified at anyone trying to replace his wife? Well, she thought, he was a man, so perhaps he wanted a little on account there and then and she had resisted? But no, she didn't really believe that. Trebird was not like that. It just wasn't in character. Indeed, from what she had heard of Cloud, it was more likely to have been the other way around. She thought he was most likely to turn her down flat and throw her out. But if he had done that, why had she not then been seen since? It seemed too fanciful to think that after so many scrapes that day she had then been attacked by a stranger on the road to Hal Saflieni. But even if she and Trebird had quarrelled, what possible circumstances could lead to her death? Pebble could get no further in her explanation. The day was getting late so she decided to seek out the others and try to detach

Lamaxe from the High Priest. Ideas always worked better when they were shared.

She heard the noise even before she entered the third temple. As she approached, the Boy came rushing out looking stressed, though he smiled in his friendly way when he saw her.

'Hail!' he said. 'Excuse me, ma'am. I must go now to find a suitable ox for the sacrifice.'

She smiled back in sympathy so he was encouraged to show his feelings more clearly.

'No matter that it is late in the day and that I am weary. No matter that I must walk some way and will probably miss my meal. After all, I am only the Boy!'

He charged off shaking his head. Inside, Trebird was sounding off with further instructions. Springox glided from place to place with his usual imperturbable look. Even so, Pebble could see the stress in his eyes. Lamaxe looked at her helplessly and shrugged his shoulders.

'Ah! Pebble. You have come to help,' Trebird called.

'Actually,' Pebble replied quickly, 'I came to suggest that you should all have a good long rest before the strenuous rituals tomorrow. Think how terrible it would be if the voice of the High Priest was less than sonorous or if the Oracle was unable to speak.'

Trebird seemed to give this some serious consideration. He looked around at the preparations so far.

'Well, what do you think?' he asked.

'It all looks most impressive,' she replied. 'Is there really much more to do? Once the Boy has returned with an ox you should be ready.'

Trebird turned to Lamaxe.

'Do you think you need to practice your Oracle speech again?'

Lamaxe shook his head firmly.

'Truly, I think I have it by heart,' he said. 'If you will excuse me, I will practice again in the morning while you are busy in the third temple.

'Good idea! All eyes will be on me. I shall not need your presence. We will just run through the procession once more today and then rest. Is the cook here for our meal?'

'I believe she is just arriving,' Pebble told him. She had no idea if it was true but the cook was a reliable woman of habit and she was quite certain that the meal would be ready on time.

That evening she and Lamaxe left the temple compound and made their way to a quiet spot where they would not be overheard. It was a warm evening and so peaceful after the hustle and bustle of the temple. As they lay on the grass in the moonlight she outlined her theories to him. Could it be the Sweeper? Could it be Trebird? Was Trebird really as dry and unemotional as he so often appeared?

'It is,' she said pretentiously, 'as though the person has been subsumed into the role!'

Lamaxe was not quite as impressed by this as she had hoped.

'He was emotional enough today,' he said. 'Why he has to have this competition with ab Headland, I do not know. I am sure that ab Headland does not care.'

'Yes,' she tried again, 'but that was about the importance of his role. It says nothing of his inner emotions.'

Lamaxe appeared to give this some consideration.

However, when he replied it was with a rather different and more personal concern.

'You don't think that I could become as dull and unemotional as that, if one day I became High Priest, do you?' he asked.

'I'll make sure that you do not,' she answered. 'But maybe he would not be like this had his wife lived?'

Lamaxe nodded and they went back into the compound to sleep.

# 16

The day of the ceremony dawned. It began as normal with them all having their porridge in and around the kitchen. They also had warm spelt biscuits and fruit as it was a special occasion. Pebble made the most of the opportunity to take Springox aside and quiz him on the Sweeper. He laughed at her suggestion that the little man could have had any involvement in Cloud's disappearance.

'He is the shyest, mildest man I know,' he told her.

'Shy doesn't mean not dangerous,' she replied.

Even so, she could not quite believe it herself. But who else? Trebird? How could the High Priest be involved? Perhaps she had better test Trebird herself, she thought. But how? Still musing on what to do she bid farewell to Lamaxe who went off to the Oracle chamber to run through his speech one last time. She brushed the crumbs from his chin and kissed him lightly on his forehead as he left. Then she made her way to the meeting space in front of the third temple. The ceremony was not due to start until noon but people were already beginning to gather. Lamool ab Headland was there early, sitting in his place on the bench by the entrance way and most impressive in his best clothes. If Trebird's intention was to undermine his authority in favour of that of the temple, then the Chief seemed ready for the competition. Cliff sat quietly by his side. He gave Pebble a friendly nod as she passed. She looked around at the others. Ayya and Sky were of course absent but Chitah was there, almost hidden by the crowd and talking intently to another, slightly older man. As the Boy hurried past she stopped him to ask who the man was.

'A farmer by his dress. I cannot see clearly in the crowd but think it is ab Speltland,' the Boy replied. 'Does it matter? If so, he does have two very pretty daughters and one of them is just fourteen.'

As he said this he winked at her. He is growing up, she thought to herself. He is becoming almost as cheeky as the Boy at Ragusa. This led her to speculate on how her ex-patient was faring and a tear welled up in her eye. They had seen so much horror recently and she wondered when it would end. Still, she thought, returning to the matter in hand, it seems Chitah has moved on. Another daughter of another farmer! Perhaps he will yet get his heir after all?

She put her nose into the temple to see where the others were. Springox was carefully putting the sacrificial bowls in place and checking that the round stone moved easily from the front of the altar so that Trebird could remove the knife. As she watched Trebird bustled past.

'Never mind that,' he told the Superintendent. 'This is a special ceremony. No secret appearance of the knife. And I will keep on my fine new skirt throughout the ceremony for all to see. Look, I have my own knife ready for the sacrifice.' So saying, he brandished a rather larger obsidian knife with a finely carved handle of horn. She had never seen this one before but could not but admire the workmanship. Trebird noticed.

'Is it not a fine piece?' he asked.

She touched the handle lightly with her hand, stroking the carved horn and tracing the inlay with her finger.

'Fine indeed,' she answered.

'And sharp,' he added. 'It is the finest obsidian.'

She was suitably impressed but couldn't help wondering how he had acquired it. He turned to the Superintendant.

'All seems to be in order. Did the Boy return with the sacrificial animal?'

'He did, holiness,' Springox replied, 'late last night. He couldn't get a white one, though!'

'No matter.'

'Then, everything is ready.'

'Good. I will go and check on Lamaxe,' the High Priest concluded and swept down the temple aisle.

Pebble knew of the secret passageway so guessed where he had gone. She decided that this was her best opportunity to challenge him. If she left it until after the ceremony he would be far too full of his own importance. Also, since his mind was focused on the ceremony she thought he might just make a slip. However, she had to go the long way around, across the open space and down to the first temple.

Lamaxe was waiting in the Oracle room sitting on the cool bench and practicing his speech when Trebird arrived noisily in the apse of the first temple cutting him off in mid sentence.

'Is all ready?' he asked, speaking through the aperture in the wall.

'It is,' replied Lamaxe.

'And you? Are you ready?'

'Almost,' the assistant priest replied.

'I thought you could put greater emphasis on my saving the community. That is the point, you know.'

Lamaxe unseen nodded.

'Yes, all right but you interrupted me,' he answered. 'Anyway,' he added rather peevishly, 'it has to sound realistic, you know.'

Trebird harrumphed at this.

'I will be the greatest High Priest on the island,' he told his junior, 'and you will help make this happen. Don't worry. You will get your reward.'

Lamaxe couldn't think of anything that he wanted at the moment other than a quiet life with Pebble. He remained unhappy about the figurine and the way Trebird was using it. He liked ab Headland, who despite his awful sense of humour, was a decent Chief, and he hated the dissention that Trebird seemed intent on creating. Surely religion should be about integrating communities, he thought?

'Well! Get on with it,' his superior shouted when he made no response.

Lamaxe nodded and hurried outside. In the narrow passageway he took a deep breath of fresh air. Trebird also exited the temple and as Lamaxe passed he slapped him on the back in an apparently friendly way.

'Don't worry,' he said, 'It will all go well I am sure. It will be magnificent.'

With that Trebird began to make his way back to the third temple across the yard. As soon as the High Priest had turned his back, Lamaxe slipped back into the

Oracle room. At least he would have a few moments of peace there away from all the hustle and bustle.

Trebird had only gone a few yards when he met Pebble coming from the other direction.

'Trebird,' she called, 'may I speak with you?'

'Well!'

'In private?' she asked.

'I am very busy. Cannot it wait?'

She explained that it would not take long so rather irritably he ushered her back into the temple apse.

'Well?' he enquired. 'Make it quick.'

She had prepared herself for this moment and had even rehearsed what she was going to say as she had walked around the temples. Even so, she hesitated.

'Well?' he repeated, irritably.

'Cloud,' she said at last. 'I think I have worked out what happened.'

He looked at her slyly.

'You have?' was all he said.

'I know that she did come here that day. Two people saw her entering the compound. You were the only person here.'

The High Priest shrugged his shoulders.

'I have told you that I did not see her.'

'Ah, but you did,' she continued. 'It was you she was looking for. I have a witness. She found you.'

It was a bald statement of fact and he didn't immediately contradict it.

'Why would she be looking for me?' he asked.

'For comfort… and more. She had argued with her father who was insistent that she marry Chitah. Chitah is old and has body odour. Cloud told her mother that. You often appear ancient because of how you play your role, but you are still young enough to give her comfort.'

Trebird shook his head.

'Cloud was very determined. She flung herself upon you,' Pebble persisted.

He shook his head again.

'Trebird,' she continued in a restrained voice. 'It is two years since your wife died. We all know that you still miss her, but you are human and Cloud, I am sure, was very persuasive. Do you deny it?'

The High Priest shrugged his shoulders. His voice was little more than a whisper.

'She was very persuasive…'

He seemed to turn in on himself as though he was not speaking to her at all.

'It was in the third temple. We did it on the altar. She said it was a celebration of fertility for Our Lady. Nonsense, of course, but I couldn't resist.'

Pebble smiled.

'No great harm was done at this point,' she said.

Trebird sighed.

'But why, then, did you go on to kill her?' she asked after a pause.

The silence was impenetrable. Both held their breath. Lamaxe, next door, was drawn to the window in the dividing wall, desperate not to miss a word. Then Trebird turned to face her directly and she could see a solitary tear run down his cheek.

'Why?' she repeated.

The High Priest's shoulders slumped. He seemed very tired.

'We lay on the stone bench. Quite naked. I was about to dismiss her. Then she began to speak of marriage. At first I was not even listening but then it began to dawn on me that she was talking about marrying me; about replacing my wife.'

He was silent for a good few minutes. Pebble wanted to encourage him to talk but dare not break his mood. Eventually he continued.

'I tried to explain that no one could ever replace her but she laughed at me. She said that she would announce it to the congregation; that it would solve all her problems; that she in return would give me pleasure far greater than my own wife had done. I could not stand it.'

He pushed his face into hers and his jaw jutted out.

'I could not bear for her to speak about my wife like that. I ordered her to stop. She wouldn't. I placed my hand over her mouth but she pulled away. She stood there in front of me, naked, and she laughed at me.'

'What happened next?' Pebble whispered when he had gone silent.

'I sat on the bench and put on my clothes. I felt so guilty. Not about the sex. It is said in the old days that priests had sex in front of the altars for the good of the harvest. I felt guilty about my wife.'

'And,' Pebble continued, gently but relentlessly.

'She jumped onto the altar, still naked and still laughing at me. She began dancing on the altar. She kicked off one of the wooden bowls. Blasphemy! I could feel my sacrificial knife within my clothes. I waved it at her as a sort of threat. As I clasped it towards her she jumped down into my arms and it stuck into her. She made no noise.'

He hesitated again.

'No!' he said in the quietest of whispers, 'that isn't true. She made one grunt, just as the sacrificial animals do.'

He remained standing but his body slumped so that suddenly he looked very old and worn.

'It was then that it occurred to me that she was a sacrifice,' he continued. 'I lifted her body and placed it on the altar to allow her blood to flow upon it. And then she was dead.'

Lamaxe, in his Oracle hiding place heard all this. He was shocked. Pebble had worked out this scenario herself but he could hardly believe that it was possible. Trebird could be a tyrant but he had also on occasion been kind to him. It had been Trebird who had schooled him in the rituals; who had taught him the theology he knew. Without Trebird he would never have become a priest. He sat with his head in his hands.

Meanwhile, the tone of the conversation outside was beginning to change. Pebble had turned to leave but Trebird grabbed her arm and held her.

'The question now is what to do with you?' he said, his eyes glaring.

There was no apparent threat in his voice. He spoke as though discussing what he might have for lunch. It was also clear to Pebble that the question was not addressed to her but to himself.

'Dare I let you go?' he continued. 'You cannot prove any of this, but will I ever feel safe?'

He rubbed his chin as he continued muttering to himself.

'It would be a shame to deprive Lamaxe of his companion. He is a young fool but harmless enough and useful. But if I let you go how can I ever be secure?'

All this was said in such a quiet and matter-of-fact way that at first Lamaxe didn't recognise the enormity of the threat. Trebird had his large obsidian knife. It was designed to pass easily through an ox's hide. He could slice through Pebble in a moment. He felt for his own knife. It was pitifully small in comparison and although no more than inches away he would have to go down the passageway and around the temple to reach Trebird. Could he do that in time? He would have to run as fast as he could and then face him in hand to hand combat. He moved towards the door but as he did so another voice was heard.

'Trebird! Trebird!' the voice called. 'It is noon. The congregation awaits you. Come now.'

With that Springox glided through the temple door. The others stopped in their tracks.

'Ah, there you are, holiness,' the Superintentent continued. 'Come at once. Ab Headland is getting impatient.'

Trebird slipped his knife back into his clothes. Springox took his arm and gently but forcefully led him away. Trebird thought for a moment about killing the old man as well as the sculptor. It would be the work of a moment but it would also have complicated matters even more. Pebble could prove nothing. She could be dealt with later.

Pebble did not move from where she stood after the High Priest and the retainer had left but she began to shake uncontrollably. Lamaxe sprang into the temple and ran to the apse.

'I was about to rescue you,' he told her.

She sank into his arms still shaking.

'But this is better,' he continued.

He hugged her tightly.

'You must be brave, as you always are. You are in danger and we both need help. Let me think.'

Pebble remained as she was, clinging to him.

'You must go immediately to my brother Oyeh and tell him to arm himself and come here with as many people as he can muster. That way you will be safe – Trebird will be busy during the ceremony – and you will bring reliable help. In the meantime, I will devise a plan to resolve this.'

He kissed her firmly on the forehead.

'Go now,' he said.

She offered him a weak smile, let go of his arms and left, looking back as she went.

She ran as fast as her legs would take her, out of the temple compound and down the path to Lamaxe's family farm. She could feel herself still shaking when she arrived. Most of them were out working in the fields. Her first thought, despite the urgency, was to look in on the sick child, Ossay, so she headed for the house only to be met by Lamaxe's mother, who had been tending him. The old lady greeted her with open arms.

'Good news! Good news!' she cried. 'The child is much better. Lamaxe's strange prayer has worked. The Goddess is merciful.'

Pebble, still shaking, smiled. She tried to pull herself together.

'Good,' she said. 'And the reed removed?'

'Not yet, but he is much better,' the old lady told her.

'And your granddaughter, Seacloud?'

'She is still well.'

They stood there holding each other in their arms and it was only then that Starbright felt her trembling.

'What is it, child?'

Pebble explained as briefly as she could so the other woman poured her a drink of fresh water and went to fetch Oyeh. She reappeared with her son who, having embraced Pebble, then went straight to the hearth, picked up his spear and strapped on his axe.

'Is there no one who can come with us?' asked Pebble.

'No one,' he replied. 'Ayya's farm is nearest but he died this morning. Sky is little better and in mourning. I cannot delay.'

With that he prepared to leave.

'No, wait!' she said. 'I'm going with you.'

'First you must recover. Then you can go to your man,' Starbright wisely told her.

'Good advice,' she replied, 'but he needs me now.'

She and Oyeh left together.

The sun was directly above the temple as the High Priest led the procession through the semi-circular courtyard in front of the third temple. He bowed his head as he stepped over the huge threshold stone in the entrance way and led the congregation through the temple portal. The stone, as always, felt cold upon Trebird's feet after the warm sunshine outside. He blinked as he moved from the brightness of day to the dim interior. Once in the square court inside, he turned to face the huge statue of Our Lady and abased himself before it, muttering words of prayer. The Goddess stared as impassively as ever over his head. After some minutes, he rose, took a guttering torch from the Boy and proceeded magisterially into the main body of the temple. He stopped when he reached the archway and waited on the stone bench, raising the torch to light both the sacred area and the main body of the temple behind him. The Boy followed him but there was no sacrificial beast this time. It was for use after the pronouncements of the Oracle. Then they both waited for the congregation to follow. Ab Headland entered the temple next followed by the others in order of rank. Once they were all inside and had suitably arranged themselves, Trebird, moving forward through the arch into the most sacred area, raised his arms and began the ululation.

Lamaxe, back in his Oracle hiding place, could hear the strains of the first ritual going on in the third temple. He could hear the sound of Trebird's voice clearly above the chanting of the others. The ox was lowing outside where it was penned behind the Oracle chamber, away from sight. The young priest must quickly devise an alternative plan. He could challenge Trebird during the ceremony. If he timed it right Oyeh would arrive with help and he could tell all that he had heard from his hiding place. How could Trebird deny it? But, of course, he still had no real proof. True, he and Pebble had both heard the confession but would they be believed over Trebird? After all, he was High Priest. Also, it would require Pebble to be there as witness and he didn't want to expose her to that sort of danger. Not that Pebble herself would mind. Mind you, he thought, he had never seen her shake like that. She was normally steady as a rock. He chuckled somewhat hysterically despite himself – Pebble / rock! He shook his head. I must be losing my wits, he thought. There was not much time now. Already he could hear the faint sounds of feet making their way towards his temple and the Oracle. Trebird would be leading the procession with

Springox and the Boy by his side. They would all be there: the farmers and the traders, ab Headland and Cliff. What should he do for the best?

He heard the shuffle of feet as the party entered the first temple. Trebird began another ululation. The High Priest always thought that that got the congregation in the right mood. Then he called upon the Oracle in the usual way. However, as agreed, he carried on his speech in a rather different way from usual.

'Oh Oracle!' he called. 'Our community is in great danger. I – Trebird ab Tarxian – must save it from its fate. Blessed Oracle, tell us what I must do?'

Lamaxe was now to make his prepared speech.

'Indeed,' said the Oracle. 'Great evil has been done.'

This caused a murmur of concern to rumble through the audience.

'What evil is this, oh, Oracle?' the High Priest asked.

Then Lamaxe decided not to stick to the 'script'.

'An innocent young woman has been cruelly slain within the temple precincts and the altar has been defiled. Our Lady demands reparation for this abuse.'

Lamaxe said this on impulse. He hadn't really thought it through but he knew that people believed unquestioningly in the Oracle. Would they believe the Oracle over the word of the High Priest?

Trebird was so caught up in the moment that for a moment or two he did not recognise the diversion from the plan.

'I am High Priest' he extolled, making a grand gesture with his arms. 'What can I do to save my community from Your wrath?'

Only then did the meaning of the Oracle's words penetrate. Lamaxe made the most of it.

'The girl Cloud has been cruelly slain. Our Lady demands the sacrifice of the perpetrator in exchange.'

Once again, he hadn't fully thought it through. Indeed, his hand went to his mouth when he realised what he had said. The Goddess had never demanded human sacrifice. Was this the right thing to do?

There was a rustle of surprise and expectation in the crowd. Lamaxe could almost smell the fear arising from them. They knew that Cloud was missing. They knew that Lamaxe had been seeking her but without success. But who knew what had happened to her? Most had heard the rumour that she had been heading for the temple or the Hypogeum. Now they feared it must be true since the Oracle had said it. But, who was the perpetrator and how could they possibly bring him to justice? Would they all be punished? They were doomed…

Lamaxe lowered his voice still further to accentuate the echo.

'You know, priest!' he boomed. 'You know her fate!'

An absolute silence fell on the congregation as they digested this remark.

'Nnnnnnnnnooooooooooooo!' The cry arose slowly from Trebird like that of an animal howling in pain. It increased gradually to an earsplitting pitch. The High Priest looked distractedly from the Oracle wall to the crowd and back again.

'You killed her,' the Oracle continued. 'You slaughtered her on My altar. But she was already mine. This was sacrilege!'

Another gasp went around the crowd as ab Headland turned to his son and was heard to whisper, 'I didn't think the old man had it in him.' Cliff hushed him.

Trebird turned again to the congregation and foolishly tried to explain.

'She had not dedicated herself to Our Lady,' he pleaded. 'She just wanted me.'

He slapped his chest as he said this. The congregation were now completely confused but they knew that the Oracle never lied. How dare their beloved High Priest contradict the Oracle. That was blasphemy. They began almost imperceptibly to move forward in a vaguely threatening way. Trebird realised his mistake almost at once. Never contradict the Oracle. He drew his obsidian knife and spun round. The crowd retreated.

Lamaxe decided on one last push.

'Only the greatest sacrifice will suffice,' he said, quietly now.

Trebird looked around. There was no way out; in front of him, a confused but angry crowd, behind him, the accusing voice of the Oracle. He pulled himself up to his full height and stared at the crowd. Then he strode over to the altar, bowed, twirled himself around just once and flicked the knife to slice open his own throat. There was a gasp from the crowd but no sound came from Trebird. He stood rigid for a moment and as the main artery was severed, his blood pumped out and shot across the altar surface. Then his knees gradually buckled and he collapsed, falling in on his skirt so that it spread out around his body. As the blood continued to flow, the green skirt gradually turned to brown.

Springox and the Boy ran to him. The Boy pulled off his own skirt and tried to stem the flow of blood but it was hopeless. Trebird was skilled with the knife and he had completely severed the main artery. In the confusion Lamaxe slipped out from behind his hiding place and joined the back of the crowd. He called on the others to step aside and bent down beside the body. As he appeared to examine it he found the small hard object hidden in Trebird's clothes and slipped it into his own hand.

'He is quite dead,' he told the crowd who began wailing and tearing their clothes in fear.

Then a sudden inspiration struck Lamaxe.

'Trebird has sacrificed himself for the good of the community,' he called, being careful this time not to use his Oracle voice. 'You are all saved!'

Ab Headland gave Lamaxe a quizzical look. Then he took control. He turned to face the congregation.

'Let us leave the scene at once,' he said. 'Return to the third temple where Lamaxe will lead a prayer.'

As they turned to go he pulled Lamaxe aside.

'Do you really think they will fall for that?' he whispered. 'The Oracle was accusing Trebird of sacrilegious murder.'

'I hope they are too shocked to think about it,' Lamaxe replied, 'Let us concentrate on their being saved.'

Ab Headland chuckled quietly and dug Lamaxe in the ribs.

'Quite a sacrifice, though, wasn't it? If you don't mind I shan't stay for the sacrificial meats. I get the feeling they might be a bit tough.'

'Hush!' Cliff told his father again. 'Stay in role for once.'

They had just come out of the temple entrance when Oyeh and Pebble arrived. As they ran up, Oyeh was drawing his axe and Pebble held his spear.

'Brother,' Lamaxe called, raising his hand in greeting. 'It is all right. It is all over. Trebird is dead.'

Oyeh stopped his run but Pebble continued, flinging herself at Lamaxe so hard that he stumbled and nearly fell. She dropped the spear and he buried her head in his shoulder and smoothed her hair.

'It really is all over now,' he said tenderly, 'But I must go and pray for the congregation. I suppose I am their only priest now.'

# 17

Lamaxe made the service a long one. As usual he and the Boy had stripped down to their loin cloths and he had performed the trick with the hidden knife. He felt it was important to demonstrate to those assembled that he could do it as well as Trebird. He concentrated heavily in his prayers and his speech to the congregation on thanks for redemption. He told them that Trebird had sacrificed himself for the good of the whole community so that the sacrifice of the ox was really unnecessary. However, he added, conscious that sacrificial meats would ensure that the crowd left in a good mood, he would sacrifice the ox anyway as a further thank you to Our Lady and a plea for their future good fortune. That sacrifice went well. The animal's blood gushed all over the altar and the intestines were clean and healthy – a sure sign of a good future. He made every member of the congregation walk past the entrails and inspect them to demonstrate their purity. It all took a long time but eventually the service ended. Lamaxe bent low before the altar apparently in a final prayer. He took the copper figurine from under his skirt which had been lying on the floor and, removing the round stone from the front of the altar, hid it in the hole with the knife among the bones and horns.

Afterwards, he thanked Springox and the Boy for their help. The Boy was quite tearful though he had been cursing Trebird earlier. No matter how common death was in the community, a sudden death, especially a violent one, still had an impact. As the priest exited the temple he discovered ab Headland calling on everyone to attend an extraordinary community meeting outside. All the elders who were present arranged themselves around the curved stone seat along the front of the temple wall. They left the place vacant where Trebird should have sat. The women crouched opposite as they were supposed to do.

'Come,' said ab Headland, taking Lamaxe by the arm. 'Sit!'

'But that is the Trebird's place,' stuttered Lamaxe.

'No,' replied the Chief, raising his voice. 'That is the place of the High Priest.'

He turned to the congregation.

'I propose that Lamaxe ab Tarxian be declared our new High Priest,' he called.

Despite a few bewildered faces in the audience a cheer went up from the majority.

'Say something, lad,' he whispered to Lamaxe, pushing him forward.

Lamaxe surveyed the people. They were his people now. Among the women he could see Pebble grinning at him.

'Thank you, oh people!' he said, trying to sound particularly serious and holy. 'If you will have me, I accept.'

A roar of approval went up from the crowd this time. It had been quite a day.

For once the meeting didn't drag on and Lamaxe listened intently to every word. Many wanted to discuss Trebird's peculiar death in more detail but neither Lamaxe nor ab Headland were going to allow that to happen. Strangely, no one asked further questions about the relationship between Trebird and Cloud. It was as though they had chosen not to hear the actual accusation made by the Oracle. It made Lamaxe wonder if they had ever actually listened to any of his carefully prepared speeches. In this case, he decided that they were just grateful to have their fears resolved. The difficult part of the discussion was about Trebird's funeral arrangements. What did you do with the body of someone who had sacrificed himself to the Goddess? Ab Headland's joke about sacrificial meats came back to haunt them. Could Trebird be given a great funeral as a hero of the community or should his bones be distributed like a sacrificial victim? Chitah was keen on the latter. However, most were sufficiently in awe of the old High Priest that they were prepared to have him disposed of in a fitting way and the former was eventually decided upon. It was to be a great occasion and Lamaxe would officiate.

Once the meeting broke up ab Headland took his new High Priest aside.

'Right, lad. You're the temple boss now, sort of! High Priest! What do you intend to do?'

Lamaxe didn't even have to think about it.

'First, I'm going to marry Pebble,' he declared, 'if she'll have me.'

Ab Headland laughed uproariously.

'I meant how are we going to work together?'

Lamaxe grinned in embarrassment but didn't

immediately answer. Then ab Headland added, 'I can see that we're going to get along just fine.'

'I'd like us to get along,' Lamaxe answered truthfully. 'I've no interest in playing power games with you. Communities should work together.'

'Now, what about the figurine?' asked the chief.

'What about it?' asked Lamaxe.

'Cliff told me what you had brought back with you. It could be a source of trouble now thanks to Trebird. What wasn't obvious to me was what Trebird was intending to do with it. Stupid of him, really! Chiefs and High Priests need to get along. I hope you don't want a power struggle as well because I'll win you know.'

Lamaxe nodded.

'Good. So where's the copper figurine?'

Lamaxe shook his head. 'What copper figurine?' he replied.

There was a brief pause while ab Headland thought about that.

'Good lad,' he said eventually, smiling broadly. 'That's the right attitude. Let's meet tomorrow to discuss new working arrangements between us. In the meantime you go and find your sculptor.'

Pebble was already by his side when Springox and the Boy came to congratulate him and pledge their future support. He thanked them.

Then, he turned to the Boy.

'What was your real name?' he asked. 'Before you trained as a priest, I mean.'

The Boy hesitated.

'Why do you need my name, holiness?'

'Don't be silly,' the new High Priest replied. 'I will now require an assistant priest. One who can speak the Oracle and assist me with the rituals. If you are to be my priest you need a name.'

The Boy looked stunned. He hadn't thought about his own promotion.

'What is your name? Surely you know your own name?' Lamaxe asked again.

The Boy looked downcast.

'My family name is ab Sandcove,' he answered. 'However, I have no close family left. There was only my aunt and when she died I joined the temple.'

'And your given name?'

The Boy shook his head. Lamaxe was beginning to be irritated. I could become just like Trebird, he thought, smiling inwardly at himself.

'Your given name?' he repeated more forcefully.

'Holiness,' the Boy responded abjectedly.

Lamaxe waited looking stern. Eventually the Boy continued.

'I was born unexpectedly in the fields. My mother named me after the first things that she saw.'

'Well?'

'Ratnest,' he whispered. 'But, Ratnest is no name for a priest – I was known as Ratty all my childhood and I hated it.'

This brought laughter both from Lamaxe and Springox but Pebble put her arm around the Boy's shoulders in sympathy.

When the mirth had died down Lamaxe took the Boy by the shoulder and looked him firmly in the eye.

'Let us break with tradition,' he said. 'We don't need to use your original name once you become a priest. After all, your family are all dead so few will remember it. Let us adapt it. I shall call you…' He paused to think.

'I know,' interrupted Pebble. 'You have proved very useful. You could be known as Useful Helper, which you are.'

'That is too radical a departure from tradition,' said Lamaxe. 'We will adjust your name with an inversion. What about Nestra?'

'As you wish, holiness,' he replied, his head still bowed.

'From now on you will be Nestra ab Tarxian, for you are my assistant priest.'

The Boy bowed his head.

'Mind you,' continued Lamaxe, 'you're going to have to work on your voice for the Oracle.'

The Boy looked up and grinned.

'Thank you, holiness,' he said using the deepest tone he could muster.

'You can legitimately call me Lamaxe now, Nestra, at least in private. And others shall call you, holiness. Your first task as assistant priest is to find us a new Boy so that you no longer have to do so much of the menial work. You should do that immediately because we have a funeral and a wedding ritual to hold soon.'

'A wedding?' asked Pebble.

'If you'll have me?' replied the new High Priest with a grin.

'We'll discuss it,' she replied.

It was not until that evening that Lamaxe and Pebble had any time to themselves. Still not officially joined together they walked out of the temple compound and lay in the grass. The Southern Cross was glowing in the night sky and they both stared silently at it for a while. Lamaxe was the first to speak.

'Well?' he asked, not daring to put the question into words.

'Well,' she replied.

He hung his head and she smiled.

'I would be very happy to marry you,' she said, 'but I couldn't stop working. Sculpture is part of me.'

'Of course! There is more than enough work for you here.'

'Maybe,' she said. 'But if I'm offered something interesting elsewhere, I might want to go.'

He nodded.

'You wouldn't be away for too long, would you?'

And so it was settled.

As they walked on he began muttering quietly, as if to himself, of the other thing that was on his mind.

'The missing girl problem seems to be solved, I suppose?' he said loudly.

There was further silence.

'You know, I still can hardly believe that Trebird killed her,' he continued after a while.

She turned and planted a kiss on the end of his nose.

'Priests are only human,' she said. 'You should know that better than anyone.'

'I don't suppose he meant to kill her – just an accident as he said.'

'That is what he seemed to say but we will never know for sure,' she replied. 'Maybe it was blind rage? That would have been in character.'

They lay in silence again. He turned to embrace her but she shrugged him off, still deep in thought.

'What I don't understand is why he reacted as he did to your Oracle. He knew better than anyone that the voice of the Oracle was you.'

'Ah! You don't understand the theology,' the newly created High Priest replied.

'You are getting pompous already,' she giggled.

Lamaxe ignored her.

'The voice of the Oracle is me, but that doesn't mean that the Oracle isn't real. Nor does it mean that what it says is not true and doesn't come directly from Our Lady. We priests are merely the cipher through which the Goddess communicates.'

Pebble gave him a quizzical look but it was lost on him in the darkness.

'Anyway,' he continued, 'in this case, what the Oracle said was true. He did kill her. How could he deny it?'

Pebble thought about that.

'So despite his cynicism and his maneuverings for power, you think he really did believe in Our Lady?'

Lamaxe was shocked.

'Of course, he believed. He was a priest.'

Pebble could only smile at this. He turned to embrace her again and this time she did not resist.

*

The next day, Lamaxe was busy with the funeral arrangements for Trebird. Malta can be very hot so however many herbs are used, funerals need to be held quite soon after death. Pebble, left on her own, decided to visit Lamaxe's mother and the newly widowed Sky. It was a beautiful day for a walk so she strolled, enjoying the sunshine and the peacefulness of being on her own after the turmoil of the last few days. She and Starbright got on so well together and once Pebble told her the news she was welcomed heartily as a new member of the family. She found the older woman holding the ancestor stick that Lamaxe had given her.

'I was just telling my husband of the events of the last few days,' she told her.

Pebble nodded and waited until she had finished. While her prospective mother-in-law conducted the final offering to her late husband's memory, she played happily with Oyeh's two children, much better now thanks to the cleverness of Lamaxe. However, as they ate fruit and spelt biscuits she heard depressing news. Sky herself was now seriously ill with the same disease that had killed Ayya. She had been seen coughing up a great deal of blood. Pebble decided that she had better hurry along to see her. Someone should tell her the fate of her only daughter.

When she arrived the servants were creeping about their daily chores.

'How is she?' she asked.

'Very poorly,' came the answer, and she was shown inside.

Sky was lying propped up in her bed. Her face was horribly grey, which matched her bed coverings. Pebble knelt by her side.

'Sky,' she whispered. 'It is Pebble, the sculptor.'

The old woman stirred but did not speak.

'I come from Lamaxe, the priest.'

This time there was a more positive movement from the bed.

'Cloud? Is there news?'

The voice was hoarse and broken and ended in a coughing fit, as though it had not been used for some time. Pebble was shocked. She had seen her only a couple of days ago tending to her husband. The decline must have been quite rapid. Now the problem was what to tell her? Could she tell a dying woman that her only daughter had been murdered? It seemed cruel. Still, she would know soon enough in the afterlife when she joined the community of ancestors and found her daughter already there. That is, if the priests were right.

'We think we know what happened to her,' she answered, ambiguously.

'Where is she?' the sick woman asked.

'We have not found her yet,' came another ambiguous reply.

Sky put all her strength into lifting her head off the bed. She leaned forward, face to face with Pebble.

'Find her,' was all she said.

They were her last words. With a sigh, she fell back on the bed and expired.

*

Lamaxe had three funerals to conduct in quick succession. He insisted on conducting Trebird's first. When the day of the funeral arrived, the procession wound its way slowly to the Hypogeum. In the absence of family the body was carried by Cliff and Oyeh. It seemed right that the Chief's son and the new High Priest's brother should do the honours. The whole community attended. They were greeted at the entrance by Lamaxe, Nestra and the new Boy, all in full priestly garb and by ab Headland in his best robe. Both Lamaxe and Oyeh felt very strange playing major parts in another funeral so soon after their own father's death. Both wondered if he was watching them from the place of the ancestors. Lamaxe was particularly distressed when they descended to the burial area but managed not to show it and maintained a professional stance. As a priest you got used to the smell of corruption but it was different when it was your own family. He greatly appreciated the ergot potion which numbed his senses. Lamaxe was lucky because it could give violent dreams but his had always been benign. Overall the ceremony went well. He slaughtered the sheep in the prescribed manner, cutting it so that the head and lower limbs remained intact in the skin and placing it reverently in a basket to be laid upon the corpse. Nestra again did the drumming. They had not yet had time to train the new Boy.

After the funeral and the feast Lamaxe was weary. His head throbbed from the ergot and from the strain. Pebble joined him in the temple courtyard in the late afternoon and made him sit on the stone bench along the wall.

'I can hardly lift my head. I need to sleep,' he told her.

'Then you will be too tired to walk with me outside the temple compound?' she said teasingly.

'Truly, I am,' he replied. 'The sooner we are joined and you will enter my house the better.'

She smiled and kissed him lightly.

'Not long now,' she said.

They sat there peaceably side by side with their eyes closed. Indeed, Lamaxe was dosing when a noise disturbed them. It was a voice calling from the temple compound entrance.

'Hey! Anyone at home? I seek a priest.'

Nestra, very conscious of his new responsibilities and still in full ceremonial dress, rushed to help.

'I am a priest,' he told the newcomer with great pride in his voice.

'I seek Lamaxe ab Tarxian,' the newcomer replied. 'I have a message for him.'

Nestra blocked the way.

'Give your message to me,' he said.

'I was asked to deliver it in person. I am an honest trader and will fulfill my task. Go fetch him, Boy!'

Lamaxe stirred himself. He could see Nestra's face turn scarlet. He was not going to allow his new found status to be threatened in any way. The other man was dressed like a trader and was armed. A finely carved obsidian knife was clearly visible in his belt.

'Who seeks the High Priest?' Lamaxe called.

'Not I,' said the stranger. 'I seek Lamaxe, the assistant priest.'

'I am Lamaxe.'

'Is he?' the stranger asked Nestra.

The new assistant priest nodded in agreement.

'Then it is to you that I must deliver my message.'

Lamaxe reluctantly stirred himself and went to meet the newcomer. Pebble followed behind him.

'What is the message?' he asked.

The man quickly crossed the courtyard.

'I come from Ragusa,' he said. 'Mountsea, the priest, asked me to deliver the following message.'

'Yes?' asked Lamaxe, tiring of the man's ability to obfuscate.

The newcomer coughed pretentiously, clearing his throat.

'The Boy lives,' he said, declaiming the words.

Lamaxe waited expectantly for more, but that was all the stranger said.

'Is that it? Nothing more?'

'Nothing more.'

Pebble pushed between the two men.

'But how is he?' she asked. 'Is he recovered?'

'I know not,' the trader answered. 'That is the whole of the message.'

Lamaxe formally thanked the stranger and asked Nestra to arrange some refreshment for him.

Pebble was bitterly disappointed. It was good that the Boy lived but they knew nothing of his condition. Could he walk? Could he talk? Could he still be a priest?

'It was good of Mountsea to send the message as he promised by the first trader. It is just a pity that the first trader was one without any curiosity,' Lamaxe said bitterly.

Pebble sniffled.

'Perhaps one day we can return to Sicily and see for ourselves,' she said.

'Perhaps,' was Lamaxe's surprisingly wistful reply.

The wedding or 'joining ceremony' went well. Oyeh headed the family, looking very important in his best tunic.

Lamaxe's mother had brought his father's ancestor stick with her to be part of the spectacle. Springox and Nestra worked very hard and ab Headland provided the food for the feast afterwards. Even the Sweeper so overcame his shyness as to wish them well. The next few days were filled with joy as far as the two lovers were concerned but after the moon had turned Pebble noticed a shadow in Lamaxe's eyes.

'What troubles you?' she asked one evening.

'Unfinished business,' he replied.

She said nothing but looked quizzically at him.

'Two things,' he said. 'The copper figurine is still under the altar. I do not know what to do with it.'

She smiled but knew better than to interrupt his train of thought. After a few moments of silence he continued:

'I have promised ab Headland that it no longer exists but I can't just throw it away. It is an image of Our Lady. What can I do with it? It troubles me. Also, where it is, it could easily be discovered by Nestra or the new Boy. How would I explain it to them?'

Pebble kissed him lightly on the forehead.

'And the other thing?' she asked.

He shook his head.

'Cloud's body. Where is it?'

Pebble said nothing but thought long and deep.

'The figurine is but a trinket. Its value was to Trebird only,' she said, choosing her words carefully. 'And he wanted it for nefarious reasons. But you are correct. It is an image of Our Lady. As you say, you should dispose of it appropriately.'

Lamaxe nodded.

'As for Cloud's body,' she continued, 'she certainly deserves a proper funeral according to the rituals in order to unite her with her ancestors even if there are none of her family left to mourn but since we do not know where the body is there is nothing that we can do about it.'

It was Lamaxe's turn to stay silent. He was so long in replying that she began to think that he had gone to sleep. Then he spoke:

'I think I know where her body is.'

'What!' Pebble was astonished. 'Trebird told you?'

'Of course not! I worked it out.'

Pebble snuggled into his arm.

'Well,' she asked?

'After her disappearance, when I was first seeking her, I visited Chittah's place and on the way back I was caught in a sudden violent storm. In my hurry to avoid the rain I lost the path and fell into some mud. It was on the edge of Trebird's garden.'

'I vaguely remember you telling me to avoid the area,' Pebble replied.

'I thought at the time that mud was odd in summer. Even fierce rain normally only lays the dust. It was only recently, when I knew that Trebird had killed her in the temple that I thought of it again. In such a hard baked area, the earth must have been very loose to turn to mud. It must have been disturbed recently. So it could be where he buried her body. It is quite close to the temple compound and he did not have much time to do it unobserved. I am sure that that is where she lies.'

Pebble's face turned into a broad grin. However, before she could speak he squeezed her tightly.

'The trouble is, should we now disturb her by digging her up. Is it best to leave her where she is both for her own sake and for the temple's?'

They both sat silently for some time holding each other. Then Pebble's subtle mind went to work.

'I have a possible solution,' she said. 'If we can find Cloud's grave we could sanctify her resting place with the copper image of Our Lady. I know it would not be a proper ritual funeral at the Hypogeum but surely with that image she would be welcomed by Our Lady. Perhaps she could go directly to live with her in the Southern Cross?'

Lamaxe put his arm around her but did not speak at first. He wasn't at all sure about her theological interpretation. However, there would be a certain justice to it and it would solve both problems.

The following evening, just before dusk, Lamaxe slipped unnoticed into the third temple and loosened the round stone under the altar. His hand felt about inside among the bones and the horns until he found the tiny object. Secreting it in his clothes, he first collected a digging tool from near Springox's hut and then joined Pebble in the courtyard. Springox, on his way to his bed, wished them goodnight as he passed. Once the Superintendent had disappeared into a building, they took each other's hands and walked out of the entrance into the night. Night falls quickly in these latitudes but Lamaxe found the spot quite easily in the gloom. He took out the tool and began to dig. Pebble interrupted him and took over using her stone hammer and chisel to break up the surface earth. This was much quicker though they had to be careful not to make too much noise. Soon between them they had made a reasonable hole and she increased its depth using her flint scraper. Eventually, the hole was big enough for the figurine and deep enough for it not to be disturbed. Pebble thought that the texture of the soil had changed into something more spongy as she dug down but chose not to investigate further, fearing that they had struck the body. An unpleasant odour drifted upwards. She didn't mention this to Lamaxe in case he wanted to investigate further and see if it really was Cloud's body. Better, she thought, to leave her in peace.

'That is enough, I think,' she said.

Lamaxe nodded and took the object out from under his clothes. It glittered in the moonlight.

'See,' whispered Lamaxe. 'It reflects the Southern Cross. Our Lady approves.'

He wrapped the figurine tightly in a piece of cloth and passed it to Pebble who dropped it into the hole. Lamaxe muttered a few words of prayer at the same time. Then they both filled in the hole, patting the earth firmly in place with Pebble's hand hammer. The Southern Cross looked down upon them as they wandered silently back into the temple compound and went to bed.

# EPILOGUE

## MALTA

*The Present Day*

The rather scruffy, middle-aged academic stood up at the front of the room and clapped his hands to gain their attention. As the noise settled down he stroked his beard – a habit of his.

'Hello. I'm Tim Fellows and I'd first like to welcome you all to this annual departmental dig. As you will know, every year the Archaeology department organises such a dig for its post-grad students and really it has two main purposes. Firstly, it allows us staff to continue our research activities with a little help. Secondly, it gives you, our students, genuine practical experience in using the tools of the trade. I suppose it also has a third purpose which is to allow us, the staff, to get to know you, the students. This year's dig, though, is very special. Because of my own research interests in the Copper Age in the Mediterranean and some work I did previously in Malta, quite exceptionally, we have been invited by the Maltese Archaeological Society to conduct a dig here. Now this presents you students with a wonderful opportunity to do some real archaeology in a fascinating place.'

He paused.

'And get a sun tan into the bargain.'

As he hoped there was a small ripple of laughter at this point.

'However,' he continued, 'it also represents an enormous responsibility. Malta's archaeological sites are some of the most fabulous in the world and are not to be touched by mere students so our actual digging will be severely restricted to a few very clearly defined areas. The main sites have mostly already been thoroughly investigated and many are of World Heritage status so we will only be working in those areas in which we are allowed and in which geophysics results suggest interesting anomalies. Is that understood? Nevertheless, the archaeology is so rich that… well you never know.'

Another ripple went around the audience; this time of anticipation.

He took the opportunity to sip some water and unobtrusively to inspect this year's student group. The usual suspects, he thought, but no doubt some would prove interesting in one way or another. There was the inevitable crowd of spotty youth – young men with straggly beards and thick spectacles who almost certainly enjoyed folk music. Mind you, it was the girls that he was mainly interested in. Perhaps the greatest advantage of having a wife who was an anthropologist was that she disappeared every summer to study her South American tribe and was effectively uncontactable for two or three months. This ensured that she lacked curiosity about his own field trips and what he got up to while abroad. There were three women of interest this year. One was an absolutely stunning blonde. He must get her name. Then there was a less stunning but very attractive brunette. He had seen her around the university and knew her to be an outstanding student, not that he was primarily interested in their intellectual abilities. Mind you, since he also wanted them to help him dig, they had to be archeologically competent. The third one he knew. She was a very competent mature student whom he had taught. He liked her enormously as a person but then so did his wife. There were ten PhD students in all with three academic staff who would take one team each of three or four. He had chosen the most promising geophysical survey results for his own team to study. There were some advantages to being the professor.

He continued his talk.

'Malta's history is long and complex. There have been people on Malta since Neanderthal times. Its greatest assets though, from our point of view, are its temples. The earliest of these pre-date the Egyptian pyramids by 1000 years and are the some of the oldest freestanding stone buildings in the world, which is why they are World Heritage sites. Only Göbekli Tepe in Anatolia has older free standing stone buildings. The very earliest temples belong to the period from 4500 to 2500BC so the culture lasted right into the Copper Age. They are all Neolithic and so…?'

He paused awaiting a response from the class. Several hands rose in the air. He pointed at a rather spotty youth.

'I'm Jimmy, sir,' the lad replied in an estuary accent. 'So… they must have been built only using stone tools.'

'That's right. The more sophisticated ones date from

later, from around 3500 to 2500 BC – still incredibly early for such buildings. That is what is referred to as the Copper Age.'

The blonde raised her hand.

'If it is Neolithic, why are they called Copper Age?' she asked. 'Surely that implies use of metal?'

She had a cool, aloof voice to suit her manner.

'Good question,' he replied. 'What's your name?'

'Rebecca,' came the reply.

'Does anyone know the answer to Rebecca's question?' he continued.

The brunette raised her hand this time.

'I'm Jane,' she said, 'It refers to a culture that spread from the East and gradually included most of the Mediterranean. It was they who learned to use copper for the first time.'

She spoke with a gentle voice and with a slight smile. So, he thought, intelligent and approachable. Can't be bad!

'That's right,' he continued aloud. 'But although some copper artifacts have been found in Malta in this period no metal tools have ever been found so we can safely assume that all of the temples were crafted by hand with only stone tools. Quite a remarkable feat, don't you think? And then the whole temple culture appeared to collapse some time after 2500 BC. We don't know why but by the time of the Phoenician invasion, it had all gone.'

There were nods from the audience.

'OK, organisational matters,' he continued. 'We will split into three groups to concentrate on three areas that geophysics says look interesting. Obviously none of these are on any of the World Heritage sites but we have been allowed, because of my academic reputation' – at this point he preened himself – 'to dig not far from the walls of the Tarxian temple compound. We are going to try to trace an ancient pathway. My group will be in charge of that part of the dig so that I can be seen to be supervising it. OK?'

There were several nods from the crowd and his two university colleagues exchanged a knowing glance.

'Right!' he continued. 'After this meeting we will all go to have a meal and a drink together to get to know each other better and then we academics will pick our teams. OK? Any other questions?'

Jane raised her hand again. She really was a rather attractive girl now he thought about it and not at all standoffish. He was beginning to think that she would do fine.

'Yes?' he said, smiling encouragingly.

'I always like to wonder about the people themselves not just the artifacts. Do you know where these people originated, Professor?'

'Well, Jane,' he replied, his smile broadening. 'We don't know for certain. They might have come from Spain but it's possible that they came from somewhere around Anatolia – that's modern day Turkey – and gradually spread along the Med. What is pretty certain is that they arrived in Malta from Sicily. There is lots of evidence of trading between the two.'

'Why are their origins so uncertain?' she asked.

'Well, long after their culture collapsed the island was taken over by the Phoenicians, who also came via Sicily. We know a good bit more about them because they had a written Semitic language. We don't know anything about the earlier people's language, though if they did come from Anatolia they might have used an *agglutinative language*.'

'A what?' she laughed.

'Sorry,' he replied, pleased that she seemed impressed with his technical knowledge and wanting to show it off. 'We're getting a bit technical here. It just means that the words are made up of a linear sequence of morphemes. A morpheme is a basic unit of sound from which you build up into a word or phrase and each component of meaning is represented by its own morpheme.'

'So what might it have sounded like?' she persisted. She smiled sweetly at him as she spoke.

'No idea,' he said, shrugging his shoulders. 'With archaeology you find the monuments and the detritus. All you know about the people is what you can infer from that.'

At dinner he managed to wangle it so that he was sitting next to Jane. He had pretty much decided to home in on that one. Unfortunately, it meant that he was also stuck with young Jimmy but you had to take the rough with the smooth. He noticed that Rebecca sat on her own and kept herself very much to herself. Yes, he thought, I've made the right decision. At the end of the meal he consulted with his colleagues. They knew his game perfectly well, but so as not to make it too obvious he told them that he had been impressed with both the students he had been sitting with and proposed to have the two of them as his team. Since no one else really wanted Jimmy and they knew that they had no chance of getting Jane, they agreed. They were allowed to decide on his third student. he didn't really care. He broke the news to the three students. Jimmy said, 'Bugger me!' very loudly. Jane accepted demurely but then gave him a wicked smile of triumph. He found this encouraging and exciting as well though all she actually wanted was to work with the most famous of the academics available.

*

'Professor, can you come over, please?' Jane called.

The middle-aged academic moved slowly under the hot Maltese sun. As he approached her he pushed his wide-brimmed straw hat back from his face. His colleagues referred to it behind his back as his 'Indiana' hat. Even with it raised, against the sunlight she could see little of the features of his face. Only his straggly beard showed within a halo of sun.

'I've told you before, call me Tim,' he oozed. 'We can't work this closely together and maintain status distinctions like that. Now, what is it, Jane?'

'Where I've been digging, it looks interesting. It seems to be a burial, but a peculiar one. Do you agree?'

'It is certainly an odd place for a burial. Let me have a look,' he replied, bending over her. He steadied himself by placing his hand on her shoulder.

'Um!' he agreed, 'it does look like bone.'

'It couldn't be Copper Age, could it?'

He cogitated for a while, pulling his beard as he did so. One of his more irritating habits, Jane thought.

'Well,' he eventually answered, 'we know that there are later funerary remains found within the temples, and there is a medieval 'bone pit' over there but we'd expect Neolithic bones to be found in the Hypogeum. It must be later.'

'Ok, boss.'

'Oh,' he added, 'unless they had a clear out!'.

He leaned lower so that his face was next to hers.

'Just keep carefully digging and look to see if there is any evidence of articulation,' he said.

By the end of the day she had cleared an area around the body. The professor came across to see how she was doing.

'It is interesting,' he said.

'Can I show you what I think I've discovered?' she asked.

He nodded approval and touched her arm gently.

'Go ahead,' he said.

'Well,' she began, 'as you can see the body is placed very strangely in the grave. It isn't in any of the normal positions. It's almost as though it has been just dropped in.'

'Umm!' he said.

He must be thinking, she concluded.

'The only place where I have seen this is in medieval plague pits,' he said eventually. 'Oh, and in Bosnia after the war. I was drafted in one summer to help. I think you might be right. The body looks as though it has been tipped in.'

He scrabbled down into the grave.

'Let me give you a hand,' he said.

He contrived to get into the grave pit with her so that their knees just touched. She found this a bit irritating as it interfered with her work but didn't like to say anything. She just moved away slightly.

'Let's see if we can get a clearly defined edge to the grave cut, shall we?'

He worked away at it. As he became more involved in what he was doing he casually elbowed her aside.

'Look,' he said eventually, 'there is no clearly defined edge. It isn't so much a grave as a hole in the ground.'

'But how could that be? Surely it is too close to the temple to be a slave burial of some kind?'

He laughed.

'They might have disposed of a slave like this, I suppose, but you are right. It is too damn close to the temple to make any sense.'

Then he put his arm around her and hugged her tightly.

'Well done, anyway. Come on, let's stop for today and go and get a meal. We can continue tomorrow.'

Over the next couple of days they carefully cleaned the body in the daytime and Tim made his pitch to her in the evenings. It was only towards the end of this time that Jane found another anomaly in the grave. There was something in the chest cavity.

'Tim!' she called. He had been taking a short break to down some water. 'Quickly, come and look at this.'

'What is it?'

She carefully lifted a clump of soil.

'I don't know. It was in the chest cavity. It looks as though it has fallen through as the body decomposed.'

She handed it to him and he took it over to where he had left the water bottle. He gently poured the water over the lump. As the outer earth fell away, they both saw a glint.

'So, it is Copper Age,' she said.

'My God!' he exploded. 'It's a copper image of the Fat Lady. Where the hell did that come from?'

*

He woke early. He never could sleep for long when it was so hot. He turned and looked across the bed. Jane's eyes were fast shut and her hair fell rather charmingly across her face. He gently turned the bedclothes down a little so that he could see the curve of her breasts. It had been a good summer, he thought. Jane had proved to be a good choice. Not just for the sex either. Her finds were really very interesting and he had agreed that her name should be included on the article he intended to write. 'A Copper Age anomaly' he was going to call it, though Jane insisted on seeing it as something more romantic. She desperately wanted to think of the body as 'the missing Copper Age princess' – they had definitely identified the body as that of a girl. A young girl at that! Her wisdom teeth had not yet broken through. Jane in her imagination had woven a complicated story about a love triangle that had gone wrong. She had convinced herself that the poor girl had committed suicide and that some kindly relative had buried her as near to the temple and to her goddess as they could manage and had left her favourite copper piece in her grave. But he knew that all that could be said was that it was an anomaly. Poor Jane! A promising archaeologist but a terrible romantic, he thought.

It was the latter that worried him somewhat. The dig was almost over. His wife would be back from the South American jungle soon and they would pack up and go home. Jane would go back to complete her PhD and then move on to take up an academic job. He had already been thinking of who owed him a favour. She shouldn't have too much trouble getting a reasonable post once the article was published and her doctorate finished but he wanted to make sure, for his own marital peace of mind that she went to another university distant from his own. He wondered how she would take the rejection. He didn't want a scene. He opened the French windows and went out on to the balcony. It was another cloudless day. He stood there marveling at the blue sky for a while. Then, he went back into the little kitchen and started to make coffee. He heard rather than saw Jane stretch as she awoke. He made a second cup for her and brought it through. Putting it down beside the bed he leaned over her but she brushed him aside.

'I do wish we knew something more about their language, you know, and more about their social customs.'

'I've told you before,' he chuckled, 'all archaeologists deal with is the detritus that is left and what we can infer from it. That is all we can know.'

'Still,' she said, 'That poor girl! It would be nice to give her a name.'

He chuckled.

'Grow up, Jane,' he said. 'If you want to be a professional archaeologist, you've got to stop romanticising about these people. They weren't like us.'

'I know,' she said. 'But even in the Bible the characters have names, and some of that is Bronze Age'.

This time he laughed loudly.

'All right,' he said, 'Let's pander to your imagination. Look out of the window. What do you see?'

She got up from the bed draping the cover around her body and went to the window.

'Nothing but a clear blue sky,' she answered.

'OK,' he said. 'How about we call her 'Bluesky'? That's as good a name as any.'

She was silent for a few moments but then gave a little cry.

'Look!' she said. 'Up there – can you see it? A tiny cloud.'

She pointed at a faint whisp in a sea of blue.

'Why you can hardly see it?' he answered. 'But, yes, it is there.'

'I shall call her 'Cloud,' she said. 'That is more like her. Tiny and lost in a huge open sky. But, if you look closely enough, you will find her.'

# PRE-HISTORICAL NOTE

The temple period in Malta began about 4100BC and lasted until some time after 2500 BC. The island was overtaken by the Phoenicians but this was a few hundred years after the Temple culture had disappeared. It appears to have collapsed internally. One likely theory is that movements of population from Italy into Sicily resulted in major change which disrupted trade routes, especially for wool, and that this caused its downfall. The other popular theory is that climate change affected agricultural production and made it unviable.

One of the difficulties with trying to bring to life a preliterate society is that knowledge is mainly limited to the physical remains and archaeological interpretation of them. In the case of Malta and Gozo the physical remains are impressive. The temples and Hypogeums are remarkable. They were built and decorated using only stone tools and must have required remarkable organisation since the island population has been estimated at only about 10,000 at the time. With the exception of Göbekli Tepe in Anatolia, the early Maltese temples were the first ever freestanding stone buildings in the world – centuries earlier than Stonehenge.

Archaeologists believe that Malta became a sort of 'sacred isle' with a highly developed religious culture. However, it does not appear to have been ruled by a theocracy but was sub-divided into a number of chiefdoms. I have assumed that power in each region was shared between the chief, the elders and a handful of part-time priests.

This was an agrarian society. The Neolithic period saw the first stable farmsteads develop. Several crops are known to have been grown including barley, emmer wheat, lentils, and club wheat. They also hunted wild birds, hedgehogs, rabbits and even the land tortoise. However, the main source of wealth on the island appears to have been the wool trade. Textiles were dyed and made on the island and exchanged for raw wool and other goods. There is archaeological evidence of dyeing vats like those of ab Headland. There is also evidence of other trade. An analysis of the amount of vines grown on Gozo argues for wine production far in excess of the island's ability to consume it and at least one sunken ship has been found with evidence suggesting that it was exporting wine. There were many links with Sicily which is believed to have been the main trading partner. The best flints came from Lipari. Remember that without any currency all trade would have been by some form of barter.

This novel is set towards the end of the temple culture in a period referred to as 'the Copper Age'. This term is used across the Mediterranean area but it is something of a misnomer in the case of Malta. Copper figurines have been found on the island during this period but not a single metal tool has been discovered. Everything was made by hand using stone or wooden tools. There is evidence of copper working in Sicily, but even this appears to have been re-smelting of existing copper items, as in this story, rather than ore extraction. Our priests are those of the Tarxian ('x' is pronounced 'sh') temple complex. This is a complex of three temples built over a substantial period of time, but archaeologists believe that rather than each temple replacing the one before it, they were additions and all in use at the same time, presumably serving slightly different functions. This is how I have used them in the story. The Tarxian temple complex is described in the Maltese museum catalogue as 'one of the finest megalithic sites that has been excavated to date.' It is located just to the east of another prominent Neolithic site, the Hypogeum at Hal Saflieni. This appears to be associated with the temples.

We cannot know for certain the precise link between the temples and the Hypogeum but there do seem to be some parallels with other Neolithic cultures. Stonehenge in England is now thought to be associated with Woodhenge, just down the river; one associated with death and the other with life. There seems to be a similar relationship in Malta/Gozo between the temples (life) and the Hypogeum (death). Recent brilliant work at Xagra has given much clearer evidence of how death was organised and my account of the funeral is heavily reliant on Malone et al's interpretation of their archaeological findings.

I have tried to reproduce the physical features of the Tarxian temples accurately based on Zammit's work. Remains of the Oracle room still exist with its stone bench, as does the hidden passageway between the temples which appears to have arisen from the overlapping of temple structures. Archaeological experiments have shown that a deep bass voice in the Oracle room produces excellent resonance within the temple chamber. The layout of the apses and altars can still be seen though all that remains of the living quarters are the torba floors. A reproduction of the statue of the 'Fat Lady' Goddess still stands at the entrance to one of the temples, though the statue is broken now and only the lower part remains. The original is in the national museum. The Fat Lady image is very common across Europe in Neolithic times. You can still see the hole in the hollow pedestal under the altar covered by the round stone. It still has animal horns and bones inside. Round stone balls and stone dishes are strewn everywhere outside the temples. Archaeologists cannot decide if they were designed simply for a game of chance or if they were part of a religious ritual. In all probability, they were used for a mixture of the two. They may even have been used to help move the stones in place when the temples were built. One set of what are thought to be ancestor or Shaman sticks has been discovered recently. There is evidence from the orientation of religious sites that the Southern Cross was important to the religion. It was the most outstanding feature of the night sky at that time. I have assumed that, as in many other religions, the Goddess is thought to reside in a heavenly body. In this case, the Southern Cross.

Being preliterate, we have no knowledge of the language that they spoke. There are also no records of other, literate people visiting the islands at this time. Some think that its people may originally have arrived from Africa, others, via Sicily, either from the Iberian Peninsula or from somewhere like Anatolia. If the latter then, as the odious Tim Fellows tells his students in the epilogue, they may have used a form of *agglutinative language* since the Hittites made reference to the people they drove out of Anatolia speaking in this manner. However, since we have no idea what the morphemes might have sounded like this doesn't help much. Anyway, I dislike stories where the authors attempt to create odd speech patterns for the sake of authenticity so I haven't tried. All I have done is to give the 'pirates' cod Italian accents to distinguish them as foreigners.

Where language does come into it is in the names. I decided that names would reflect familiar things in the landscape and that the characters would have personal and family names. I also tried to combine words for other, mostly physical, things as names. Thus 'Lamb-Axe' comes to be Lamaxe. Family names were not introduced into Europe until very late in history so it is perhaps a bit of a cheek to invent family names in pre-history, although other ancient societies, like the Classical Romans for example, thought them important. The Maltese were farmers so land and land ownership must have been important and since land tends to be worked by families it seems reasonable to think that family was also a significant institution. The ancestor sticks further suggest they either revered or worshipped ancestors. Anthropological studies of existing societies suggest that most non-literate societies tend to count their remembered history in terms of about ten hypothetical preceding generations. Without writing, people don't seem to be able to manage to hold much more information than that although the Bible suggests that the Bronze Age Jewish ancestral trees went farther back than that. This doesn't mean that they forget or ignore earlier history but merely that historical events get compressed into roughly that many generations.

To emphasise the importance of land I have used a form of family name that emphasises place so 'ab' should be seen as 'from' rather than the Welsh 'ap' which is 'son of'. For the most part I have not used place names but some of the locations are so well known that I have felt obliged to use the modern names. So 'Tarxian' and 'Hal Saflieni' are the Maltese names of actual existing places. The modern Maltese language derives from ancient Phoenician so our characters certainly wouldn't have known them by those names. Similarly, with Ragusa in Sicily; which is a much later Greek settlement. Nevertheless, it does have a complex of Copper Age rock tombs that arguably bear some slight resemblance, though much smaller in scale, to the Maltese Hypogeum.

What I have also made up are the theology and the social conventions of Copper Age Malta. It is generally accepted by archaeologists that the 'Fat Lady' is a fertility goddess. This seems reasonable since the shape of the Goddess is similar to the huge numbers of stone fertility goddess figurines which appeared all over Europe with the arrival of Neolithic culture and continued in the many Bronze Age variations of the goddess known in Greek as Astarte. There is an alternative Feminist explanation which claims that she represents a female-dominated society but this seems to me less likely. However, I have tried to portray a society in which some women, like Pebble the sculptor, could live independent lives. For balance, I have also included one case of a domineering male who beats his wife and bullies his daughter.

We have no basis for knowing what were the values, customs and folkways of this society. Without any written texts either locally or from visiting literate travellers we cannot know how they thought and acted. I have tried to invent social mores and customs which seem to make sense for that type of society based on knowledge of others. For example, I have required trainee priests to undergo a rites de passage in which they lose their personal and family names in order to be integrated into the 'new family' of the temple. Rites de passage are common to most societies. I have envisaged a priesthood that has a complex theology and system of rituals. This seems reasonable – just look at the theology of Ancient Egypt. I have assumed that the Chief in a preliterate society is the holder of their history and so must play the role of great storyteller. I have also invented a moral code for a society that believes in a fertility Goddess as well as the importance of the family. Thus, sex before marriage is fine but never under a roof. A roof represents 'home' and thus family. If you think this is daft, then just read anthropological accounts of the moralities of real societies or look at some of our own beliefs.

We do know how people in this society made their living – farming augmented by hunting and fishing and trade. We know what they ate – from an analysis of seeds and bones etc. As well as cereals, they farmed goat, sheep, cattle and pigs. There is also evidence of dogs but whether as helper or food source is not clear. They also appear to have eaten rabbits and land tortoises. I have tried to create a believable account of the lives of people who worked hard, had a high infant mortality rate – the average life expectancy was about thirty – yet were pretty healthy and who believed in a fertility Goddess. What is certain is that they did not think like us. They were not modern people in funny clothes. However, just because they did not have a written language doesn't mean that they did not have highly sophisticated beliefs, contemplated deep thoughts, felt emotions deeply and had a sense of humour. One of ab Headland's dreadful jokes and stories is actually the first ever joke known to have been written down anywhere in history. It is contained in a Sumarian document so ab Headland's remark that the joke would still be circulating in hundreds of years' time is not far short of the mark. I've been unable to resist adding a bit of my own sense of fun in places and I hope readers will excuse the incident when Lamaxe and Pebble fail to invent writing.

# FURTHER READING

The best way to experience the majesty and scale of the temple buildings and to get some feel for the kind of society that might have built them is to visit Malta and Gozo, which anyway are fabulous places.

However, if you want to read more about the Tarxian temples I can't think of anything better than the original archaeological reports of Thermistocles Zammit. He writes with great clarity and they are well illustrated with drawings and photographs.

Sir T. Zammit, *The Copper Age Temples of Hal-Tarxian, Malta. A short description of the monuments*, 1965.

Sir T. Zammit, *Prehistoric Malta: The Tarxian temple*, 1930.

There is a vivid reconstruction of a funeral in:

C. Malone, S. Stoddart, A. Bananno and D. Trump (eds), *Mortuary Customs in Prehistoric Malta: excavations at Xagra (1987-94)*, McDonald Institute Monographs, University of Cambridge, 2009.

There is a brief description of Ragusa and other rock tombs in:

R. Leighton, *Sicily before History: an archaeological survey from Paleolithic to the Iron Age*, Duckworth 1999.

If you want to learn more about Maltese Neolithic farming you might try:

C. Savona-Ventura and A. Mifsud, *The Maltese Neolithic Domesticated Mammals*, 1997. This also makes references to domestication of dogs.

They were a pretty healthy lot by all accounts, living long enough to suffer tooth decay. There is a good account of the identifiable illnesses in:

C. Savona-Ventura and A. Mifsud, *Prehistorical Medicine in Malta*, Mosta 1999.

They find some evidence for successful trepanning of live individuals (the Boy), of TB (Ayay) but not of diphtheria (Ossay) though they do find evidence of similar infectious diseases.

Sea trade routes are discussed in:

L.B. Brea, *Sicily before the Greeks*, London, 1957.

The wool trade is specifically mentioned in:

R.R. Holloway, *The archaeology of Ancient Sicily*, London, 1991.

Or in more detail in:

C. Sagona, '*Silo or VAT? Observations on the ancient textile industry.' Oxford Journal of Archaeology*, Vol 18, Issue 1, Dec 2002.

However, whilst I have tried to base my version of Copper Age Malta on the available literature, please don't assume that my version is accurate. It all happened (if it did) a long time ago.

David M. Smith

BOOK ONE OF THE HIDDEN TRILOGY
HIDDEN
BY THE LEAVES
S D L CURRY